Starving for Love

Starving for Love

T.C. Littles

www.urbanbooks.net

Urban Books, LLC
300 Farmingdale Road, N.Y.-Route 109
Farmingdale, NY 11735

ISBN 13: 978-1-64556-431-7
ISBN 10: 1-64556-431-2

First Trade Paperback Printing January 2023
Printed in the United States of America

10 9 8 7 6 5 4 3 2 1

*This is a work of fiction. Any references or similarities
to actual events, real people, living or dead, or to real
locales are intended to give the novel a sense of reality.
Any similarity in other names, characters, places, and
incidents is entirely coincidental.*

Distributed by Kensington Publishing Corp.
Submit Orders to:
Customer Service
400 Hahn Road
Westminster, MD 21157-4627
Phone: 1-800-733-3000
Fax: 1-800-659-2436

Starving for Love

by

T.C. Littles

Prologue

Bird

"Ain't shit sweet, ho! You think I'm playing about snapping your fuckin' neck?" I was leaning into the passenger-side window of my former best friend's car as I popped off on her in the worst way. I was in my feelings like a muthafucka. I'd been pulling this ole nothing-ass bitch out of the mud our whole lives, so for her to have stabbed me in the back the first chance she got was infuriating.

Shayla sighed that type of heavy sigh bitches push out when they're highly annoyed with a situation. "Come on now, Bird. You know we weren't ever that cool. Not as cool as you played it anyway. You've always got off on belittling me and Yoshi, if we're keeping it all the way honest. You're just salty 'cause the tables have turned and a bitch ain't begging for your hand-me-downs." She casually shrugged me off with a funny-looking smirk on her face. Her fresh-off-the-struggle ass did not even know how to carry herself like the bad bitch she was trying to portray.

"Bitch bye! You can stop boosting like you're self-made. I put you together piece by piece. You would not even know how to be Dora the Explorer of the hood if it

weren't for me teaching you how to hold your head up."
I did not care if Shayla had gotten power washed and no
longer seemed like the dusty piece of nothing she'd been
all her life, or that she was pushing a brand-new truck,
which I knew Murk had copped for her. She was still
the dope fiend's daughter who used to beg to be in my
shadows. She could front all she wanted, but I knew her
backstory, and I wasn't going to let her forget it.

"Welp! All righty, then." Shayla gulped. "Now that
you've finished reminding a bitch where she's come from,
let me go. Would you like me to tell Jay you said what
up when I meet up with him at Andiamo's? We were just
about to meet him there." She ran her manicured fingers
through her long-bone, straight weave, then turned
slightly toward the passenger-side window and placed
that very same hand on her pudgy stomach.

*You've gotta be muthafuckin' playing with my emo-
tions, God*, I said to myself. I was praying my mink
eyelashes were clouding my vision. It had been a year
since I'd laid eyes on Shayla, but it was obvious shorty
wasn't a virgin anymore. Her slimeball ass was very much
pregnant, and she was throwing it in my face in order to
get a reaction from me. What she did not know was that
I was refusing to take any more bullshit or bad news. I'd
been going through hell since me, her, and Yoshi fell out.
But it was clear them hoes had moved on with their life
and didn't give a fuck about me or reconciling. As cocky
as I was kicking it to Shayla, my feelings were all types of
fucked up, so all I knew how to do was act out.

"Naw, you ain't gotta tell that ho-ass nigga you seen
me. He'll know," I assured her. Then I flicked my trusty
blade from underneath my tongue and leaped through
the window like a lizard.

I stayed on slimeball shit. Hood princesses did not wear crowns.

Three years ago . . .

"Can you bring me a warm rag when you come back out, Shay?"

I rolled my eyes out of irritation when I heard my best friend's voice, and then I slammed the bathroom door behind me.

We were in the basement of his mother's house, which was set up like a studio apartment and was just for him. He had bragged so much about having privacy and about how we would not get interrupted that I had been itching to get over here. But after two minutes of him popping my cherry, I had wished that his mother would pop in and catch him in the act so he could get off me. As fine as Khaleef was, his sex game was terrible. I had been hyped up to lose my virginity, but I could've done better with my imagination. I now understood what my homegirl meant when she said guys with big packages who did not know how to use them were basically a waste.

As far as I was concerned, Khaleef was a scam. All that package, but with a weak-ass stroke game. He had been pumping, humping, and howling like he was ripping my guts out. I had been mad as hell when I started feeling droplets of his stank-ass sweat hitting my face. I was over sex if that was how it was going to be. I'd already decided that this time did not count as losing my virginity and that I was granting myself a do-over. The only reason I hadn't bounced already was that I needed the money he had promised me out of his check, and his direct deposit was set to hit at midnight. I was strategically planning on getting hungry for some snacks right after the clock struck twelve, and then I would walk him to the ATM at the gas station before having him walk me home.

I was already praying Thomas was out doing dumb shit with his homeboys and was not clocking that I wasn't home. The last thing I needed was for him to find out I had slept with Khaleef, who had been my best friend for years. I did not want my brother thinking I was out here tricking on a regular—especially when we needed to get our water back on at home. My cycle was set to come within a few days, and I wasn't trying to get caught with a messy coochie and no soap and water. It was already bad enough the kids at my school stayed talking about me because I did not have the finer things in life that they had access to. My parents did not have a job, I wasn't a hustler, and I did not really know how to get it out of the mud. All I really knew how to do was dwell in that shit. That was why me being over here with Khaleef had me feeling out of my element. I did not do stuff like this. And since the sex was so whack, I was sure our friendship was about to take a major hit.

After turning on the water, I soaped up a washcloth and got my hygiene together. The soap instantly stung on my freshly attacked cooch. I tried as hard as I could not to look in the mirror, 'cause I would've broken down and cried. I could not believe I'd cashed in my V card. After getting my hygiene together, I wet a washrag with warm water for Khaleef, as he had requested, but by the time I got back to the bed, he was fast asleep and snoring. He even had the nerve to be drooling. After moving his bigheaded ass over a bit, I slid in the bed beside him.

"Ain't this some shit. I should be the one knocked out, with my thumb in my mouth," I mumbled and tossed the washrag onto the nightstand by his side of the bed.

Part of me wanted to slide my clothes on and bounce, but I kept thinking about that direct deposit. Anyway, to pass the time until Cartier woke up, I grabbed my phone and headphones from my purse, then plugged up so I could write. Writing poetry, books—anything creative—was the only light I had in my life. It was like my soul thrived off creating, and it had been that way since I found my voice through writing as a kid.

Hey, boo. Are you good? Yoshi's text message popped up on my cell phone's screen. Although I was on a creep mission and wanted to keep every single second of this shit private, I needed Yoshi's advice. She had enough crazy drama spiraling around in her world that I knew she wouldn't look at me funny, judge the move I was making, or kick the shit back in my face at a later date.

I texted back. Yeah, as good as I'm gonna be. I'll hit you up as soon as I get home.

Ten minutes later, my hands were aching from how many words I'd typed. I was in the zone as I wrote a short story about a girl (me) and what I'd just done. It was easy for me to push my feelings out since the situation was real and not made up. I did have a vivid imagination, so it was easy for me to tell tales, but this one had a lot of truth to it. Khaleef's feelings would've been hurt if he read my short story, so I kept watching him to make sure he did not wake up and start peeking over my shoulder. With us being cool for so long, he knew I loved writing, and he had always supported my craft. That was the main thing I'd miss if we stopped being friends.

I had tales for days, stories for every second that I'd lived, and a creative way to mix all that shit together, a skill that no one else could master like me. Every artist had to have an ego to stay thriving in the game, and I was no different. One day, I was hoping to write a book. It was a dream of mine to get published.

Just then Khaleef woke up. "Damn, baby. My bad on dozing off. They worked me like a slave at the grocery store today." He turned toward me and started rubbing my back, and right on time, I hurried up and went to a different story on my phone. From the way he was rubbing my back, I could tell he was about to try to come on me for round two. "Put your phone up and cuddle with me for a minute."

"You see me in the zone, Kha. Let me finish what I'm doing." I pushed his hand back, because I did not want his vibes. I wasn't trying to be rude or to ruin my game plan, but my skin was crawling at his touch.

"Fuck them nursery you be on and come fuck yo' nigga." He surprised me when he tripped, and when he suddenly pulled his dick from underneath the covers.

"Aw, hell naw! What tip are you on? Nursery rhymes? Wow! That is disrespectful as hell," I yelled as I jumped out of the bed. "I see you've been fronting all this time for some ass. Acting like you liked my work." I felt stupid.

"Naw, I wasn't fronting . . . but I am chasing a nut."

"You just oughta pay me to fuck your 'cum quick, one-nut wonder' ass." I flipped up my middle finger and then started putting on my clothes with the quickness.

I knew me, and I knew I'd start flipping over shit and tearing up his mom's crib, and then we'd be boxing. And I wasn't scared of no boy. My brother had taught me how to wrestle when I was straight out of diapers, and most definitely how to defend myself once our family fell apart. Khaleef knew that he'd just gotten a piece of pussy from a tomboy, and that I'd wear his ass into the floor with these hands. Him calling my stories some muthafuckin' nursery rhymes was beyond disrespectful and had me livid, ready to spit on his hating ass. There wasn't no coming back from this beef. Which was why I slid some cash out of his pants pocket while I was getting my clothes off the floor. I had to do what I had to do, and I wasn't leaving out of here empty handed.

Chapter One

Shayla Stewart

Me and my family had been on struggle mode for years.
After forking the last few chicken-flavored ramen noodles into my mouth, I tilted the bowl up and drank the leftover salty juice that was swimming around in the bottom. I was chowing down as I sat on the front steps because I was hungry as hell and had been all day. I'd even nibbled on the moldy-looking corn dogs they served at school. It was the end of the month, and shit was on "every man for themselves status" at my house.

My dad came out of the house. "Hey, Shayla, you got some more of them noodles in your backpack?" he asked me, begging as usual.

I took one look at the man I was supposed to love and look up to and wanted to throw my noodles back up. His face was sunken in, his lips were chapped and cracked, his dark brown skin was dry and ashy, and his hair was so long and unkept that it was matted to his scalp and looked like it stunk.

Ricardo "Spiderman" Stewart had once been looked up to and respected by everyone in our neighborhood because he had been crushing life and living big. He had had a job at the factory, had been making good money there, with a 401(k) and full-coverage insurance, had kept a new car in the garage, and had had the nicest house in

the hood. Me and Tom-Tom had been the only ones out
of our friends to have fresh kicks, new clothes, and all
the newest toys. That had all been before Ricardo's crack
cocaine addiction surfaced and took over. My pops had
gone from passing out spare change to begging for spare
change. He chased his high whenever he wasn't high, and
he ain't give a fuck if he had to lie and say he was trying to
put food in me and Tom-Tom's mouth.

"Naw, Pops. I do not. But I would not give you any if
I did." I rolled my eyes, stood up, and pushed past him
to go change out of my school uniform. "And try taking
a shower and changing your clothes. You smell like a
porta-potty." I gagged involuntarily.

"One day you and your brother are going to regret the
way y'all treat me." He puffed out his tiny chest, then
scurried down the porch steps.

"I doubt it." I watched in embarrassment and sadness
as he rushed up the block in his worn-down dress shoes,
more than likely on his way to the corner store to beg for
some credit to get a beer. Then I opened the screen door,
stepped inside, and headed up to my bedroom.

Food was never on his mind unless me or my brother
brought it into the house. My dad got four hundred
dollars a month in food stamps for both of us, but he
sold two hundred of it every month so he could feed his
addiction, which left only two hundred to feed me, him,
and even twenty-two-year-old Thomas.

My brother used to have his own welfare case, but he
had got flagged for getting over on the system. He had
been getting food stamps, cash assistance, and even
Medicaid, all after claiming that he was mentally chal-
lenged and that this was why he was not able to get a job.
The scam had worked out sweet for a few months; then
the state had sent Thomas for a mandatory psychologi-
cal evaluation with one of their doctors. Not only was he

deemed mentally stable before the assessment was over, but he was also labeled a con artist. Thomas was lucky, but I was blessed, because all they gave him was community service, five years of ineligibility, and a restitution bill as punishment. I'd probably be getting high alongside my father if Tom-Tom wasn't around to hold me down.

Thomas had taken care of me since I was eight years old, which was when our mother abandoned us. He was thirteen at the time. We had been walking home from school when she rode past us in the passenger seat of a dark green Checker cab. We had just gotten out of school and had detoured to the penny-candy store for some fifty-cent bags of assorted Frooties. I remembered that day like it was yesterday.

"Hurry up and come on before Mama be talking shit," he urged me. He was always cursing behind our parents' backs.

"Leave me alone, Tom-Tom. I'm walking as fast as I can." I was more concerned with unwrapping one of the green-apple candies I'd just gotten from the store than keeping up with him. "And here comes Mama to pick us up anyway." I stuck out my tongue at him, then started walking to the curb, so I could get in the back seat of the cab she was in.

Thomas had his back turned as he was fussing at me, so he did not see the cab that was approaching us, with our mother in the front seat, waving. He did not see her until the cab zoomed right past us.

"Mommy! Mommy! Where are you going? I want to go!" I yelled after the cab, waving my hands in the air, sad because I loved going places with my mom. She always got me toys, snacks, and special surprises whenever I went along with her on grocery trips and errands, especially when she went to the mall. She even

took me to get my nails and toes polished on Fridays, when Daddy got a paycheck. I turned and faced my brother. "Why did Mommy leave and not take me?"

"Are you sure that was even her?" he questioned, watching the cab move even farther up the street. "Man, that wasn't her, dummy. We have a car, so she would not be in no damn cab. Plus, she would not have rode past us," he told me.

"That was her, Tom-Tom! Do not call me no dummy," I yelled. I hit him with my little fists and all my might, but, of course, he did not budge.

"Quit being a brat and come on." Tom-Tom did not care about my tears, because I always cried and threw tantrums when I couldn't go with her.

I stumbled the rest of the way home, eating my straw-berry candy, then did all the chores my mom would've had me do had she been home. I cleaned my room, emp-tied all the garbage cans into one big bag so Thomas could take it to the dumpster, vacuumed the living room, and even set the table for a dinner that wasn't cooking. I remember being restless as I waited for my mommy to walk through the door, be surprised that I was such a responsible big girl, and spoil me with some extra dessert.

"Tom-Tom, where's Mommy?" My stomach was start-ing to hurt because I hadn't eaten anything but junk food since lunchtime at school.

"I do not know. You saw her in the cab the same time I did. Maybe she has gone to the grocery store or something. I'm about to play basketball with my friends, so stay out the way."

Worried and afraid, I sat on the porch, waiting for Rose, as my mom was called, to arrive back home . . . until the mosquitos chased me in the house. I even tried calling the taxi company and asking where the driver *had dropped my mom off, but my description "the ugly man" was too vague for them to pinpoint the specific driver, and I did not have a number to identify the vehicle by. Of course, I did not think I had to have a number. I was only eight years old. All I cared about was my mommy. Tom-Tom, though, he wasn't thinking about Rose's disappearance. It seemed he was taking advantage of it. With our dad at work and her gone, he did not have a curfew or anyone checking when he got home. He ran wild with his friends all through the neighborhood from the time we got out of school until right before Pops got home from work. That was when shit hit the fan.*

The sound of a car alarm blaring in the distance snapped me out of my reverie. Life had been kinda spinning for me ever since that day my mom disappeared, I thought as I unlocked my bedroom door. I pushed it open and was smacked in the face by the hundred-degree heat. I hated having to keep my room closed up, because it always ended up being hot, stuffy, and stale smelling, but that was better than coming home to an empty room. I did not have much, but what I did have, I valued, and I wasn't trying to see it for sale at the corner liquor store. The corner store had an entire section of electronics, including TVs, phones, and video game systems, and it also had a section with jewelry. Basically, it was a pawnshop for poor folks, drunks, and prostitutes. And a lot of people that hit licks and needed to get rid of the hot merchandise hawked the items at the store. Even shadier behavior went on in the back rooms.

After taking off my school clothes, I hung them in the closet, then rifled through my dresser drawers for something I could wear. I had barely had a selection of summer clothes last year, so I was super struggling now, especially since I'd gained weight and gotten taller. It was obvious I'd gotten my height gene from Ricardo, because I was already pushing five feet six, and that was where I hoped the heredity started and stopped.

After trying on the seven pairs of shorts I had in total and not fitting into a single pair, I decided to turn a pair of denim jeans I'd worn throughout the winter into shorts. It was the best plan, especially since the jeans were worn at the knees anyway. It was easier and cheaper for me to grab a new fitted cotton T-shirt from the dollar store or Walmart than it was for me to cop some shorts. I'd been thinking of ways to cut corners for so long that I probably would not know what to do if I had money.

Since I was extra sweaty and hot from the walk home, I took a quick shower before changing. It did not matter how poor I looked; I never smelled that way. I had done lost count of how many bars of soap I'd swiped off store shelves when I could not afford this basic necessity. Rose might not have been around to teach me how to put on a training bra or insert a tampon, or to warn about how important it was for me to wipe from front to back, but I did remember her taking tons of showers and baths. She used to have the entire house humming with her mango-scented bath and shower gels. Anyway, after I got my hygiene together, I let my body air-dry since it was so hot. The box fan in my bedroom window wasn't doing shit but circulating the humidity, but it felt good against my damp skin for all of five minutes.

Bzz-bzz-bzz! My cell phone vibrated on the desk.

It was Bird messaging me on our favorite app since my mobile service was temporarily off. I was thankful as ever that we had Wi-Fi and that our internet bill was subsidized. Bird was one of my two best friends.

Bird: R U Home Yet?

Me: Yup, no thanks to you. :(

Bird: Aw, trick, shut up. Walking will lift that flat ass up. I'm OMW around there. "OMW" was text talk for "on my way."

Me: Fuck you. Okay. I'll be on the porch.

I slipped on my clothes and headed downstairs. As I walked through the living room, I heard my brother and his homeboys out on the porch. I wanted to see if Tom-Tom had come up with the few dollars I needed to get my cell phone back on. The bill was twenty-five bucks, and I was short twenty-five bucks. I opened the screen door and stepped onto the porch.

Tom-Tom looked over his shoulder when he heard our rickety screen door opening. "Sis, what's good? How was school?"

"Lame, as always." I sat down on a chair across from where he and his friends were sitting. I despised Tom-Tom's bum-ass crew with a passion.

"Well, that shit will be over in a few weeks. So, lame or not, tough it out like a champ," my brother told me. Tom-Tom might've been a middle school dropout, but he stayed on my head about school. I did not have to be a 4.0 student, but I did have to get my lazy behind out of the bed every day and apply myself enough to go on to the next grade. Most days Tom-Tom got up and walked me to school if I wasn't catching a way there with my girls.

He humbly preached to me all the time, but he had never followed his own advice by heading to a GED center. He was too busy getting dead-end jobs, getting fired from them, and then trying his luck at pulling off hood scams. I never gave Tom-Tom any pushback, because he had stepped up and raised me after Rose ran away and Ricardo checked out.

Ten minutes later, I saw Bird coming up the block, and I wanted to go back in the house to find some other scraps of clothing to put together. As always, she was looking cute as ever. She was wearing a hot pink maxi dress and a pair of pink sandals with Swarovski stones all over them, and her hair was wet and wavy like a mermaid's. Bird had what they called good hair, so she was always able to get away with quick hairstyles that required little to no maintenance. There was no way I could achieve a wet and wavy look without putting a full weave in my head. But, anyway, she was rocking the look perfectly, while I slouched in my seat like the dud I was.

"Hey, boo," she called as she walked up on the porch, popping her gum and switching her booty as hard as she could for Tom-Tom and his friends. Although she had a boyfriend, Bird was a huge flirt.

"Do not 'hey' me, trick. What happened to you coming to school today? They gave out some extra credit just for us being there." I was happy I had not ditched, because I needed all the extra boosts I could get out of math. All my classes, really, but that one in particular. I'd tried telling the counselor I struggled with numbers because I had been broke all my life and did not have a reason to count, but she had given me a peer tutor and had told me to buckle down harder to break the generational curse. I knew the counselor had told Bird the same thing, but she clearly wasn't taking heed of the advice.

"Girl, I ain't worried about no damn school," she said as she sat down on a lawn chair on the porch. "It's the end of May, and we are about to graduate. It's not like we are in the eleventh grade, and they can mess us up for next year. We're about to be done-done. I swear, I can't wait. You might not see me back in those hallways until the last week." Bird had always been nonchalant about school. It did not matter if it was the beginning of a semester or end of the year, she had always been like that. I never judged her or tried to coach her like Tom-Tom did me, though. Hell, I was barely earning Cs.

"Well, are you at least excited about prom?" I questioned, wishing I were going to prom, but none of the boys at school were checking for me. And even if they were, it wasn't like I could afford a dress, shoes, or the glam fee.

"Nope, not really. I would skip that, too, if it would not break Jayson's heart. He seems hella immature to me now that I've been kicking it with your neighbor. I'm kinda ready to throw my entire relationship with Jayson in the trash for Murk, but I'm going to try to wait till he leaves for college to spare his feelings."

"Whoa. This is new news. The last time we talked, you were going to get an apartment near Jayson's campus." I could not believe Bird was having a change of heart over her high school sweetheart and life plan.

Jayson was a beast on the basketball court, and he had kept college scouts in the bleachers at every game since his freshman year. They had watched his growth, his wins, and how he took the losses, and as a result, this year he had a handful of full-ride offers to Michigan colleges. All Bird had talked about after he signed his four-year contract with Michigan State University was getting out of Detroit on his back. She had even gone on the school visit with Jayson so she could go pre-apartment hunting. Murk was stroking more than the soft spot between her legs. He was messing with the sense in her head as well. She'd been creeping around with Murk for only a few weeks, and already her entire game plan was canceled.

"What can I say? Plans change, and shit happens," she said nonchalantly and shrugged. "But do me a favor and please do not tell Yoshi. I do not want her telling Duncan, because he'll definitely tell his boy." Our other homegirl was friends with Bird's soon-to-be ex-bae.

"Your secret is safe with me. But are you sure you want to break up with Jayson for Murk?" I wasn't trying to be a hater, but I also did not want to see Bird hurt and regretting her decision.

Murk was fine as hell and new to the neighborhood. All the dudes from the hood wanted to be him, and the broads wanted to bang him—not just Bird. Murk had money. He was the only dude whipping a Cadillac Escalade on rims, and the only dude flossing expensive name brands day in and day out. Plus, he always accessorized with a cold-ass chain, which I could tell wasn't fake.

Some white-owned real estate company had bought up all the abandoned houses that were salvageable and had completely renovated them. They were basically brand-new homes now, but they were still surrounded by the run-down houses me and my friends lived in. Anyway, Murk had moved into one of the houses about a year ago and had been running different females in and out of his front door every other day. My bedroom faced the front of the house, so it was easy to back up my truth with descriptions of the women, if Bird wanted to know.

"Hell, yeah, I'm sure," Bird insisted. "He had me talking in tongues, and you know I'm not saved. Jayson ain't no li'l boy, but Murk is hung like a horse. That might be too much information, I know, but I soaked in the bath for an hour after we had sex and my hookup is still sore." She started giggling in the lawn chair, with a grin on her face, then imitated how she was riding him when they were having sex.

"You're crazy as hell." I shook my head, laughing. Used to Bird sharing all her business and too much information, I did not even blink, not even when she was basically saying her cootie cat was blown out. She was outspoken, blunt, and unapologetic about everything she said and did. I was the complete opposite from Bird, because I was an introvert and I hated being seen.

"Do you want to hit the mall? He gave me a few hundred to get something cute to rock to the party."

"I guess," I said. I really wasn't in the mood for window shopping, but I hadn't been anywhere but the neighborhood and school in a while. "Let me pee really quick. I'll be right back." I got up, darted into the house, and visited the bathroom. Then I raced to my room to grab my big purse. I did not have any money, but I did have a lot of courage, and I wanted to be prepared if I saw something I needed. I wasn't a kleptomaniac; I was a survival stealer. I was running low on the bare necessities and needed to stock up.

When I got back on the porch, Bird was taking selfies and posting them on her social media page. She was a junkie when it came to being on the internet, and even more of a junkie when it came to get likes, comments, and followers. My pages, however, were bland, and I barely uploaded pictures of myself. If I did post a picture, it was only a headshot, because my clothes were not internet worthy. I wasn't trying to get caught up as a meme and go viral in some raggedy wear, or to be called out online by a classmate who knew my outfit was one of Bird's hand-me-downs.

"I'm ready," I announced to Bird, which made Tom-Tom look up from the dice game he'd been having with his homeboy Jabari. They weren't playing for nothing but a dollar out of three, but both of their broke behinds had been focused until Tom heard me address Bird.

"Where are y'all about to go?" he asked.

"None of your business. Damn." Bird rolled her eyes and pushed past him to go down the stairs. "Shayla is damn near grown, if you haven't noticed. Get your foot up off my girl's neck."

"You know I do not like your duck-acting ass, Bird. Please back the hell up and stop talking to me." Tom-

Tom shrugged his shoulders and threw his arms back so Bird would clear his space.

Bird started chewing on her bottom lip, I could tell she was itching to start talking shit and working on his nerves, like she usually did. But then she quietly walked down the stairs, opting to comply gracefully, because she knew Tom did not play when it came to me. Everybody from the hood knew Tom-Tom did not play about me, and in spite of him being mentally sane, he would knuckle up and stomp a nigga out without effort if he needed to.

"Bro, chill. I'm about to go to the mall," I told Tom-Tom as I followed Bird down the stairs.

"Why, if you do not have any money to spend?" he asked me.

"The same reason your broke ass be out with your boys without any money. Ugh. Bye," I snapped. I was pissed at him for putting me on blast. I ignored every word he said after that.

Even when Bird and I were completely out of range and could no longer hear him, I felt his eyes burning a hole through my back the whole way up the block. Tom-Tom hated me hanging with Bird because of the reputation she had, one that I wanted. On some petty shit, he always complained about her acting uppity, but he wasn't necessarily friendly to her either. He would barely speak to her and was rude when he did, and he would talk bad about her when she left. Either way, he could save the "Captain Save-a-Sister" speech when it came to loving the hood, 'cause for eight years he'd been mad deep in it. My brother had gone from shooting dice for change on the corner to breaking into cars for radios, which he would then exchange for cash with older guys in order to make up for where Dad fell short.

It was hot as hell as Bird and I walked up the block now. I kept wiping the sweat off my forehead and the sides of my head so that the edge control I tried to maintain my hair with would not melt and look all crusty against my hairline. I couldn't wait to get a summer job so I could afford some knotless braids.

"Here. You want to take a puff of this?" Bird offered me the cigarette she'd lit.

"Ugh, naw. I do not see how you smoke them nasty things," I told her as I turned my nose up and pushed her hand away. I hated the smell of cigarette smoke.

She shrugged and took a pull. "I used to feel the same way whenever my mother smoked around me when I was younger, until she gave me one." Bird rarely spoke about her childhood, because it was darker than mine was.

While I'd spent most of my life trying to cope with my mother abandoning me, Bird had spent most of hers trying not to mentally or physically succumb to her memories. She used to wake up screaming and crying, with tears rolling down her cheeks, every time me and Yoshi slept over at her place when we were kids, so much so that we stopped spending the night 'cause we thought her house was haunted. It wasn't until the Detroit Police Force surrounded her house one day and the coroner carried her father out in a body bag that we realized *he* was the muthafucka who had traumatized Bird.

At the innocent age of ten, she'd been the one responsible for taking her father up out of the game, and it had happened only moments after he had popped her cherry. Her mother was the one who had handed her the gun, knowing no judge with a sound mind and a God-fearing soul would lock up a child for an act of self-defense. After the police assembled a thorough rape kit, having retrieved bodily fluids, pubic hair, and her father's fingerprints from all over her tiny body and her Hello Kitty bedding set, the investigation ended and her father's murder case was closed without hesitation.

"Have you talked to Yoshi today?" Bird asked, changing the subject, which was cool for me.

"Nope. She was supposed to call me back last night but never did. But I heard Yani and Ms. Crawford in the background, so you know how that goes," I replied. All three of us had different types and levels of family drama.

"Well, come on. Let's pull up over there and see if we can get that grinch to watch her grandbaby so Yoshi can hit the mall with us. I know she's got to be going crazy in that house with her petty-betty mama and a newborn." Bird pulled the keys to her metallic red Malibu from her pocket and clicked the alarm off.

She was the only one of us who had a car. It was compliments of her dad's grandmother, who felt more than guilty about her son's behavior and chose to grieve him by showering Bird with whatever gifts she could afford. Usually it was clothes, shoes, purses, and electronics, but Bird had said one of her granny's lottery numbers finally popped, and she had hustled her out the whip before Granny could dip to a retirement resort with the winnings.

"If you break up with Jayson before prom, I'll gladly be your date," I announced as I slid in the Malibu's front passenger seat and melted into the bucket seat. As Bird slipped behind the wheel, I started checking out all the car's features.

"Ah, ah, be careful, before you fuck some shit up that you can't afford to fix." She smacked my hand back and turned the music up, completely oblivious to how I was cutting my eyes at her for that slick, backhanded-ass comment she'd made.

I was shocked she had slipped up and said that shit and hadn't even hiccupped behind it. Broke I was. But a fool I was not. If a person could casually disrespect you to your face, they had been boldly disrespecting you behind your back. As she started the engine and pulled away from the curb, Bird had me wondering what she had said about me when I wasn't around. My seething ended when we arrived at Yoshi's about ten minutes later.

"Hey, Yo-Yo!" Bird shouted out the car window as we pulled up into Yoshi's driveway. She was the third and final homegirl and completed our clique. Cool since we'd been kids, we had formed a pact not to let outsiders infiltrate our friendship, and we had been sticking to that shit like we'd hid a dead body together.

Yoshi looked over at us but did not comment or welcome us as we got out of the Malibu and headed her way. She was sitting on the porch, with her li'l mama cradled in her arms. Yoshi's daughter, Yani, was three months old and was the most adorable little girl on the planet. She had a head full of curly hair, chunky thighs, dimples in her cheeks, and funny-colored hazel-brown eyes that were gorgeous, like her daddy's. Yani was a spitting image of Duncan, as a matter of fact. He couldn't deny that little girl, even though his mother wished he could. But that was for Yoshi to tell her business.

"Aww! Look at my niecy pooh looking all cute in her banana pajamas," Bird cooed as we walked up onto the porch. She tried to kiss Yani on the forehead, but Yoshi moved Yani fast as hell.

"Do not come up here giving my baby fake vibes. You're a terrible auntie. She do not know you," Yoshi muttered as she mugged Bird.

"Whoa! Are you going through postpartum depression or whatever they call that shit? I've got some pills at the crib I can go grab that'll knock all that pissy-ass attitude you're serving me out your system. You're snapping on me, and I ain't did nothing but use condoms so I could stay living my life. Do not blame me that you're stuck in the house, bored." Bird was on a roll today with her insensitive, gut-punch comments.

"I'm not blaming you." Yoshi got up and laid Yani in the bassinette she'd dragged out onto the porch, then continued. "But I am calling you out for being fake as hell. All while I was pregnant, it was "I'm her godmom' this and 'I can't wait to spoil my niecy pooh' that. You even went as far as to fill my head up with that 'We're in this together' bullshit, which made me actually feel like I was going to have some help with Yani." Yoshi was trying to have a breakthrough moment with Bird, but Bird must not have taken those happy pills she'd been advertising.

Flicking dirt from underneath her nails, Bird did not seem fazed or amused. In fact, she gave little indication that she was even paying 100 percent attention to Yoshi's argument. I knew Yoshi was madder than a muthafucka at Bird's blatant disregard for her feelings, because Yoshi had touched on the topic last night, when we were on the phone. Once upon a time, Bird and Yoshi had been best friends, so this episode was looking real foreign to me.

"Do you be reminding Duncan of all those promises he was feeding you when you were pregnant? Or even what got you pregnant?" Bird knew her questions were rude and uncalled for, and a way to piss Yoshi all the way off.

"Damn, Bird. That was kinda raw, do ya not think?" I said, finally stepping out the shadows of the conversation to try to cool it down. "And, Yoshi, we're sorry for not showing up for you as your friends, and we're going to do better," I added as I stepped between them, trying to serve as the referee.

"Quit kissing her ass, Shayla," Bird said, turning on me, refusing to drop her bad mood. "We came over here to see if she wanted to get some air and go to the mall with us, and we got shit on instead. We did not deserve how she came at us."

"All right, all right, all right! I've heard enough garbage for one day. Yoshi, get rid of your so-called friends," Ms.

Crawford declared as she came out of the house like she had a cape on. She hated me and Bird. Hell, she sometimes acted like she couldn't stand Yoshi as well.

"Aw, shit. Here she goes," Bird mumbled, knowing good and damn well Ms. Crawford had supersonic ears. "This is why we do not come over here to see Yani, Yoshi." Bird rolled her eyes in Ms. Crawford's direction.

Ms. Crawford lifted Yani out of the bassinette and went back inside the house.

"Oh . . . you ain't gotta worry about being welcomed over here no more," Yoshi snapped. "As a matter of fact, I'm going to skull drag your funny-built ass off this block if you pull up over again."

Bird burst out laughing. "Girl, stop it! You do not own this block. Hell, your mom do not even own this run-down-ass house she's still fucking every thirty days to stay in," Bird viciously spat, with a devilish smirk painted on her face.

"Girl, I will skull drag your funny-built ass all up and down this block if you keep trying to punk me," Yoshi growled as she tried to push me aside so she could get to Bird.

"Whoa, Yo-Yo! Friend! You're out yo' shit! You know you can't scrap out here." I did not want her fighting, not with her baby only a few feet away.

But it was Bird who reached over my shoulder and threw the first punch! Still trying to play the mediator, I grabbed Yoshi by the shirt and pulled her back so she wouldn't hit Bird. Bird did not swing again, but she kept taunting Yo-Yo by laughing.

"Y'all ain't about to scrap out here!" I said sternly.

"If you do not get your motherfucking hands up off my child!" Running out the door full speed, with the infant in her arms, Ms. Crawford was two seconds from slapping piss from Bird.

Yoshi caught her hand in midair. "Naw, Ma. Fuck catching a case over this wannabe. Take Yani back into the house," she said, speaking calmly so her mother would feed off the same vibe. Yoshi knew the consequences of her mother being geared up to go hard. She was a monster—and that was an understatement—and the turn up would get more than real!

"I ain't going inside no damn house till these li'l heffas leave! You already know I do not play when it comes to me and mine!" Ms. Crawford must've been putting on a show for the folks that did not know her. 'Cause it was never a secret to us commoners that she wasn't a true fan of Yoshi's.

"This can be a dual beatdown if you want it to be," Bird snarled. She kept speaking out of turn to Ms. Crawford. You could tell the middle-aged woman was getting more than fed up as she attempted to tolerate Bird's smart mouth.

"I will beat your ass without ever putting my grandbaby down," Ms. Crawford spat back, taking two steps toward Bird.

"Shayla, get your fucking friend and go! I can't have my baby out here twisted up in all this drama. All of y'all are doing too much," Yoshi yelled. She was trying to do the right thing, which was to take her daughter from her mother's arms. It was clear that Yoshi was the only rational, thinking person on this porch, probably 'cause she had the most to lose.

Before I could move or try to pull Bird back to the car, the loud sound of music and screeching tires filled the air, catching me off guard. "I think that is our cue, B. Let's bounce!"

Yoshi's baby daddy had turned the corner on two wheels and swerved up onto the grass right in front of the house. Then he jumped out from behind the wheel and stalked across the lawn. Duncan Nobles was the popular guy everyone around here wanted to bang, but he was known to have an explosive temper, which matched his huge ego. He wasn't the type of guy you negotiated or compromised with. Yo-Yo knew that firsthand.

"I know yo' rat ass ain't got my li'l one out here in no ghetto drama!" Duncan might've been a young nigga, but by no means was he soft. There had been many times when we'd heard him going hard on Yo-Yo, and he'd even gone as far as to smack her up when she was carrying Yani. With all this showboating Ms. Crawford had been doing out here on us, you would've thought she had made him too afraid to bust bows or chin check her daughter, but that wasn't even close to the case.

"Tell her ass, Duncan. It's like the older she gets, the dumber she gets. I keep telling her about these two skeezers, but she won't listen." Diverting her attention from Bird, she walked right past Yoshi, giving her the side eye, and up to Duncan as he mounted the porch steps. "Here's your daddy, Yani pooh," she said, handing the little girl off. Ms. Crawford had done a complete one-eighty by putting her alleged precious daughter on blast. Just a few seconds ago she had been all about Yoshi.

"Call me if you need to talk," I told Yo-Yo, giving her a "Damn, that is fucked up" look.

Then I grabbed Bird's arm and walked her back to the car. She'd done enough damage. Plus, Duncan was prepped to give Yoshi even more. Bird's door was still open, so I pushed her inside the car. "Do not get your hardheaded ass out of this car," I muttered, then slammed the door shut. As I walked around the hood, I decided it was about time I took charge. Taking my place on the front passenger seat, I gave a deep sigh, glad the focus on us had died down, allowing us an easy escape. The family quarrel that was now going down was nothing

I wanted to be in the middle of. I endured enough stress from trying to carry my own burdens, so there wasn't enough energy left to pick up someone else's. Hell naw to that! When Bird started the Malibu's engine and finally pulled off, I felt nothing but relief to be out of the mess she had essentially created.

As Bird slowly steered the Malibu down the street, I looked in the side mirror to see what was going on behind me. My heart sank when I saw Duncan smack Yoshi to the ground. Yoshi lay still.

"Oh shit, B! That nigga just knocked Yo-Yo out." I sat up straight, then turned all the way around in my seat. "She's laid out in the middle of the street!" Shocked, feeling my stomach drop, I couldn't believe Ms. Crawford wasn't going to Yoshi's rescue. I guessed having a mom around did not mean she'd really protect you.

"That is what her ass gets for thinking money make it right for that nigga to dog her ass out. If she like it, I love it. Wanna hit the mall?" Bird was emotionless, but to some degree, I felt her.

"Yeah, I guess, but you did not have to pop off back there." Bird's issue might not have been directed toward me, but the truth had to be brought up regardless. Right was right, and wrong was wrong. "It's like you popped up over there just to gun for her head. What was up with that?"

"Girl bye, I'm not about to take the blame for how that all went down. Yoshi got caught up in her feelings because she feels dumb. That is not my fault." She whipped her long weave around just then and almost slapped me in the face with it. Bird knew that she was on some bullshit, and that this was the real problem of the day.

I'd watched how everything unraveled between her and Yo-Yo, so I knew Bird was the true aggressor in the whole situation. "You ain't gotta front with me, bitch.

You went for her, not expecting her to come back. Ole Duncan done got her tough!" I was joking at Yoshi's expense, but there was nothing really funny about her situation. She was nineteen, she was a high school dropout with an infant, and she was getting slapped up, with a mother publicly supporting it. Everything about her life screamed, "Fucked up."

"Ooh, now, that was crafty!" Turning onto the freeway and heading toward the shopping mall, Bird floored the gas pedal. "You're picking up some bad little habits hanging around me," she laughed.

Yoshi Crawford, aka Yo-Yo

Damn! Why can't this nigga keep his hands off me? This shit is embarrassing as hell.

I blinked my eyes a few times until I was able to focus, then released a glob of salty spit that had gathered in my mouth. My face was burning like hell, and from all the throbbing my mouth was doing, I could tell he'd split my lip and probably my chin. This shit was crazy as hell to be going through, but I'd become a pro at taking ass whippings from Duncan. The shock was that he was disrespecting me in front of an audience. Both his physical and mental abuse usually took place behind closed doors, where his all-American basketball player reputation could stay unblemished. If his coach, the teachers at school, or the recruiters at all the colleges that were throwing scholarships at him knew he was a woman beater, he could never take me and Yani out of this hood. That was the real reason I took his painful love.

"Yo, you know I do not like your nosy, nothing-ass neighbors being in my business. Get yo' ass up and in the house before I take Yani and bounce," he yelled. He was seething, like he wasn't the reason I was on the ground in the first place—and the cause of all my neighbors eye hustling us. He was lucky nobody was recording our drama-filled relationship on their phone.

Instead of me bringing any of that to his attention, I quietly peeled myself off the ground and sat there, catching my breath. Duncan had been putting his hands on me ever since I was three months pregnant. For me to be only five feet even and petite, I could take an ass whupping with the best of 'em. This was the first time he'd done it in front of anyone besides my traitor-ass, snake-ass mama, though. She'd been a witness and sometimes an accomplice to our throw-down sessions. Not trying to play the victim, but it had always been me against the world.

"Get your ass up, Yoshi, before I give you more reasons to stay down there!" Duncan shouted as he walked back and forth with Yani in his arms. I wished upon a star he would be as gentle with me as he was with her. Ever since I had birthed our baby girl, he'd been stuck to her like glue.

Any young mother would've been overjoyed to have the father of her child be as attentive to that child as Duncan was to Yani. I was so upset that my and Duncan's dynamic had changed since we'd become parents. Matter of fact, shit had been sweet until I showed him the pee-stick pregnancy test that indicated we were expecting. I was shocked I had not miscarried from how wild he acted behind the news—like no one had ever told him raw doggin' and nutting in pussy created a baby. I mean, it was true that having a kid before graduating from high school wasn't necessarily a fairy tale or no shit like that, but he'd been talking about putting a baby in me and having a family even before I spread my legs to give it up. Duncan's talk game was as good as his layup.

Anyway, he'd adapted to being Yani's dad now that she was here in the flesh, but he hadn't bounced back to being my high school sweetheart, my bae, and the love of my young life. I had been taking the brute force of his anger and getting abused more and more each day. But at this point, I was in too far, and I did not want to end up raising Yani all alone. Duncan had been getting scouted by colleges since he was in the tenth grade, and now the time was finally coming for him to leave for college. We'd always talked about this moment and how he would then take off to the pros. My baby was that damn good. And I wanted to be by his side for all of it.

My mother stormed over to me. "Yoshi Crawford! If you do not get your weak ass up, you better! First, that skinny bitch Bird punks you, and now Duncan. I thought I raised you better than this."

"Leave me alone, Mama. Damn!"

A moment later Duncan grabbed my hair and pulled up on it. Feeling my scalp start to burn as Duncan yanked me up from wallowing in my pit, I jumped to my feet. Duncan pulled me by the hair to the sidewalk, then across the lawn and up onto the porch. As he pulled me inside the house, I felt my natural hair ripping from the roots. I never heard my mother contest the ass whupping he was putting on me.

"Duncan, oh my God, let me go! Please let me go!"

He pushed me to the floor and dragged me by the arm to my bedroom. I kicked, yelled, and tried wiggling my way out of his grip, but I was no match for his strength. Plus, my collarbone was damn near skinned from sliding across the carpet.

Chapter Two

Thomas Harris, aka Tom-Tom

"Make no mistake about it . . . I'm trying to level up and make some cash-cash! I'm starving out here." I clasped my hands together and begged Murk to take a chance on putting me down with his hustle. The few pennies I'd been able to put together hadn't been doing much of anything for my and Shayla's needs. It had been easier looking out for her when all she needed was some gummy bears and chips for survival, but now she was grown and needed all kinda shit I could not afford. I felt like crap every time I had to go home empty handed, because she did not have anybody else but me.

"A'ight, li'l homie. Pipe down," Murk replied, laughing, then gestured for me to have a seat on his leather couch.

I sat down and damn near melted into the butter-smooth material. From the massive flat-screen television mounted above his fireplace to the black-and-white gangster pictures hung on the walls, his crib was mad stylish, comfortable, and decked out like it didn't belong in the hood. Tom-Tom would have a field day up in this muthafucka if he ever got the chance. The shit was dope as fuck. Murk had a fly ride, a fly crib, and the lessons I needed to hold myself down like a man my age needed to be doing. In my eyes, he had the code to life cracked wide open. And I wasn't seeing him push dope, so I didn't think that was the key.

"So, let me ask you this, T. What's your goal? What are you chasing the almighty dollar for?" Murk sat down in a leather chair across from the couch, then dumped a few M&M's chocolate candies into the palm of his hand and chucked them back.

"Huh? Whatchu mean?" I thought Murk's questions were dumb as hell since I was sitting across from him in a dingy shirt and some winter boots, although it had hit eighty degrees outside. I was wearing the boots with the laces loose, like I was a New York nigga rocking some Tims, but everyone in the hood knew I was too broke to get a pair of sneakers. I was itching to go steal a pair, but I wasn't trying to go to jail behind no dumb shit, because I would not be able to make bail. Making some moves with Murk seemed like a smarter plan because he'd been hustling for as long as I had known him and had never been locked up.

"What I mean is, what are you trying to get down with at the end of the day? Do you want a few dollars to eat with? Are you trying to bag a couple of dollars to break off on a bitch? Do you got a baby on the way? Do you wanna jump fresh and floss for the block or move off this bitch? Or is you trying to look out for ya' pops so he can get off them corners? I'm trying to find out what tip you on, T. I wanna know where your head is at."

It felt like Murk was putting me through a ghetto-ass interview. Instead of answering the questions one by one, I kicked it to him as real as I could. "Look, big homie, at the end of the day, all I wanna do is make shit pop for my little sister. I made a promise to her eight years ago, when our moms abandoned us, that I would hold her down, but I ain't did shit but burn our last name and address up on all the jobs around the way."

"And how do I know you're not going to burn your bridge with me too?" He cupped his chin and stared at me with intensity.

I knew I needed to answer the right way, because I'd already given him a reason not to fuck with me. But I'd only said, "Fuck all the jobs around the hood," because they weren't paying me shit but a few pennies, but they were working me like a dog. The last job I had had was at the neighborhood market, and that clown had paid me six bucks an hour to clean, do stock, get the shopping carts from the parking lot, bag groceries, and even chop up meat whenever the butcher did not come to work. He had treated me worse than a modern-day slave because he was paying me, and because he knew I was trying hard to beat the odds.

I had barely got three hundred dollars every two weeks, and a hundred a month had to go to paying welfare back. In addition, I spent most of my money right back at the market on whatever the house needed. I kept us in toiletries, tissue, and cleaning supplies, and I made sure Shayla had whatever womanly products she needed. I was also the one who made sure the low-income payments were made on the light, gas, and water bills. I'd been the man of the house ever since my dad stepped down to the pipe and my mom decided being a wife and mother wasn't for her. I was twenty-two years old, with a thirteen-year-old's education. All I could do was get it on the streets, because I did not have the credentials—or the mental capacity—a muthafucka needed to hold down a real job.

"Because I respect you, and I already know you ain't the nigga to cross," I said, answering his question. I wasn't intimidated or proud, nor did I drop my head or avert my eyes from the intense stare he was giving me. The last thing I wanted to do was walk out of Murk's house without a hustle.

"Good answer," he said and nodded. "Very good answer, li'l homie." He pulled out a knot of money and peeled off some bills. "Look, I ain't even gonna lie to you. I know you done been around the hood a few times, doing dumb shit with them li'l niggas you call friends, but I'm gonna take a chance on you because I know you got a heart. You ain't out here doing stupid shit for kicks and some pussy, but so your little sister do not have to sniff up under no trifling-ass nigga such as myself. I been watching you, Tom. I knew your story before you even told me."

The whole time he was talking to me, I tried not to look at the knot in his hands, but it was hard not to. Even when my pops was sober and on his shit, his checks weren't fatter than a grand or maybe two, unless it was tax time. But Murk had about five racks in his hand, and he'd dug that from his pocket. All I saw was hundos and fifties. I knew he had to be sitting on way more than what I was eyeing, and that was probably why Bird's "hot in the twat" ass kept creeping over here.

"You ain't gotta worry, young Tom. This shit gonna be in yo' pocket one day as long as you take in what I gotta teach you and leave all that other shit you into alone," Murk told me. He must've read my mind or seen my eyes bouncing back and forth. "I know you got yo' li'l crew you fucks with, but you already know everybody ain't welcome to roll with me. The less accessible you are, the less accessible you'll be. Take this first lesson and keep it on your heart as long as you hustle."

Boon, Trey, and Jabari had been my homeboys ever since we were on the playground in elementary school, looking up skirts and shit, but them niggas didn't have a pot to piss in either. Boon was sleeping on Trey's mama's couch, and they were both about to get kicked out of the house. And Jabari was already homeless but was playing it off, because he didn't want us clowning him behind his baby mama kicking him out. I was the last person to judge them for failing to get right time and time again, but the shit never quite added up, because they all had diplomas. My struggle was built off me having only a middle school education. Although I had started ninth grade, none of that shit counted or was retained, because I had skipped during the one semester I was enrolled. I'd been out trying to get a few dollars to put food in my and Shayla's stomach when she got out of school.

"Them my niggas, and they are gonna stay my niggas, but I know better than to fuck up a blessing. What goes on between us will stay between us," I said. I wasn't the brightest man, but I wasn't the dumbest.

"You know what? I like you, young Tom. Real spit. I'ma show you some love and see how it comes back to me. Here. Go holla at Crisp at the barbershop and tell him I sent you to take my appointment. Then go cop you a new pair of shoes and a tee from ole boy who have the knock-offs. I'm gonna put you on today, but you gotta get cleaned up first." He gave me a buck fifty, which was a hundred and fifty dollars, and told me to keep the change. It was already on my mind to have Shayla meet me at the barbershop so she could grab a few dollars from me and get an Extra Value Meal from somewhere. I never got something and did not think of my little sister.

"Good lookin' out. I swear you're not going to regret it," I said as I stood from the couch. A minute later I walked out the door and headed straight to Crisp's. I wasn't about to miss out on an opportunity to get on my feet.

Crisp took me right away. When he finished his handiwork, he sprayed some oil sheen on my hair, handed me the mirror, then spun me around so I could check out the cut in the wall mirror too. It looked great.

"Oh shit. Thanks, Crisp man. I did not even know my hairline would be salvageable." I'd been doing my own haircuts in the bathroom, with some cheap-ass clippers from the dollar store. I simply hadn't been able to spot the twenty it took to get cut and lined up biweekly or even once a month.

"I saw where it was a little wrecked, but it wasn't that bad. You might fuck around and have a skill if you put some time into it," he told me as he patted me on the back and applied pressure to my shoulder. It was one of those man-to-man gestures that meant I needed to pay attention to him, so I looked up and tried to read between the lines.

"You really think there's still time for me learn a trade and put it to use, Crisp?"

"Why not? You think because you had a rough time finishing school that you've gotta have the same circumstances forever? Naw, son. Let me tell you a li'l something about this world. No matter who and what you are in life, you're supposed to reinvent yourself every couple of years anyway. I started cutting heads in my mom's basement, and then I got a booth at the Plaza a few years later, and now I've got this shop and employ five other people. All you gotta get is a starting point, then work day by day until you start seeing some shit shake." In one minute, Crisp had given me more knowledge about how to be somebody than my father had.

"Thanks, Crisp. For real," I said. I wasn't trying to wear my emotions on my sleeve, but it meant a lot for Crisp to pay attention to me.

"A'ight, young'un. That'll be twenty bucks."

I finished checking my cut out, then handed him one of the fifty spots Murk had given me, and told him to keep five for the tip. My cut was crisp as fuck, but I already knew it would be, because that was how ole boy had got his nickname. Crisp's real name was Jarell, but everyone that got cut by him always hopped out of the chair saying how crispy they looked. Damn near everyone around the way fucked with Crisp, even the chicks who rocked natural hairdos and fades.

"You good on the tip, Tom-Tom, but I appreciate it." I already knew he did not want to take what I barely had, and I appreciated it back.

"Good looking, Crisp," I said as I stood up. I wasn't about to force it, because the extra five bucks would indeed go to good use.

"Fa sho. And don't forget what I said," He told me as I stepped away from the chair. He nodded, then called over his next customer. There were about ten niggas waiting on him, and that was just right now. His shop slapped all day. Clearly, Crisp was getting hella cash by being a barber. At twenty dollars a customer, and that was just for a basic cut, he was killing the game better than a corner boy.

I went into the bathroom before I left, but not because I had to piss. I wanted to check my cut out without everyone looking at me. Crisp's cut had me feeling like a bitch fresh out of the beautician's chair. I looked like a whole new nigga. And I would look even better once I threw on the fresh kicks and clothes I planned to cop. I left the barbershop and took a dollar and played the lottery before I walked back to Murk's crib, because my luck was most definitely up today.

"Damn, young Tom. If you ain't got no bitch with a baby on the way, it won't be long," Murk exclaimed and dapped it up with me when I walked back into his house.

"Thanks, Murk. And thanks for the cut. It's been a minute since I been in Crisp's chair, and I forgot how good it feels to jump fresh." I rubbed my hands over my hair, then pulled out the brush I'd copped from the beauty supply store and started brushing my waves down.

"Look at you," he laughed. "But it ain't no thang. You can't be rolling with me unless you're rolling right. Ninety-nine percent of life is looking the part. Now, let's hit the streets, so I can show you how to rake in some cash."

I didn't ask no questions. I just went along with the opportunity I had asked for.

I was riding shotgun in Murk's all-black Infiniti truck as he pushed it up the highway toward the suburbs. I hadn't been anywhere outside the neighborhood since my dad started messing around with drugs. Before that, he used to take me and Shayla to all types of movie theaters, play places, and water parks. The further Murk drove, the nicer everything became and the more stores I saw. I felt like I was traveling out of town. The conversation between us was hella light, besides him asking me about Ricardo and even my mom. I never liked speaking about Rose, so I had backed off that topic quick as hell, not wanting my mind to start spinning off my unhealed emotional trauma.

As soon as he exited the highway, my stomach started bubbling, and then it twisted up in knots. Murk had gone over the plan about fifty times before we left the crib, and it had seemed cool, but now I was starting to freak out. I'd never crossed the Detroit city limits with a plan to do dirt, because leniency usually wasn't given to poor street punks from the other side of Eight Mile, but Murk had assured me his game plan was solid—as long as I did not mess up. His word seemed worthy of trust, since he'd never missed a beat. But that was him. I wasn't sure I could walk the talk I'd been swearing I could.

Murk had the air bumping and the radio banging a rap mix, but I was sweating bullets, and the beat was making my anxiety worse. There was a faint voice in my head telling me to cop out and work the money off that he'd given me for the kicks, the cut, and the shirt, instead of following through with the shit I was about to do.

"Yo, Murk, m-my dude . . . are you sure about this? M-my stomach is starting to hurt, and that usually means I'm about to fuck some shit up," I said, stumbling over my words.

"Tom, I'm gonna need for you to take a few deep breaths and calm down. It's normal for you to be nervous, because this will be your first time probably being in a bank in your adult life, but this is the game you asked to play. I do not like my time wasted. You knew what was up before we hopped in the truck." This was the first time I'd heard anger in Murk's voice, and it had me kinda tensing up even more.

"I—I'm not trying to have any issues with you, Murk." We were driving deeper and deeper into suburbia now. "How much farther do we have to go? We done passed about ten banks since you got off the freeway."

"Damn, li'l nigga! Do not make me regret taking a chance on you. Yo' grown ass better man the fuck up, so we can get to this money, Tommy. And that is on God," Murk barked. He was now showing me the side of him I had only heard about in the hood. Up until this point, he'd been nothing but like a big brother to me, but now this nigga was blowing up like a fireball.

"I'm G. I'm not going to make you regret fucking with me," I replied. I was like a stray dog begging for a bone. I wasn't about to stop barking up behind him until I got fed. Sad, but true, I needed Murk at this point because I did not have anybody else looking out for me. "I got this." I pulled out my brush and started brushing my soon-to-be waves.

"Yeah, nigga, I thought so. You must have thought about them beat-up-ass dress shoes yo' daddy run the block in, and come to yo' senses," he said. He capped on my pops like I wasn't his son. Murk was definitely on the nut and did not let up. "On the real, Tom-Tom, you do not have time to second-guess any avenues of money. Especially not one from a cat like me. I've been out here hustling, grinding, and I'm out the mud for a lot of years. And I've seen a lot of young cats fail for being scared. Scared money won't make no money, first of all. And, most importantly, a scared man will end up getting carried to the grave by one real friend, one associate, the murderer, and three friends of the family. You've gotta get your head in the game and learn how to maneuver in these streets if you're going to hustle in these streets. Period."

Although I'd held on to every word he spat with a fine-tuned ear, I did not have time to process them, because he was turning into the bank's parking lot. All I could do was cross my fingers and pray I'd be in this same seat when he pulled back out. After flipping the visor down, I wiped away the sweat on my forehead and the white ring of saliva that had gathered around my mouth. I was dehydrated because I hadn't been drinking water. The last thing I wanted to do was have a full bladder and piss on myself out of fear.

"Game time, Tom-Tom." Murk came to a stop, then pulled two envelopes from the middle console. "These are the two weekly checks from the industrial plant, with pay dates of today and last week. If the teller asks, tell her you saved up two checks, so you'd have more money at one time to make some movement with. Start opening the envelopes once you get to her station, and refuse to open an account but take a brochure. Do not appear rushed, do not hide your face, and do not brush off any small talk he or she makes."

"I've got it." I snatched the envelopes from his hands, ready to turn nothing into something. I was overly anxious to get some cash in my hands I could really spend. Both checks totaled a little over eight hundred bucks from eighty hours' worth of work—something I should've gotten my ill-bred, lazy behind up to do in the first place. That thought quickly went away when I remembered my dull reality of being a middle school dropout. I did not have much of an education, many skills, or the drive to much more than hustle. I guess you could say Rose had broken my spirits, because I had stopped going to school the same day she had stopped loving her family. Most of the time I had shown up to beat a li'l chump down over Shayla. I guess you could say a li'l nigga was rebelling. I stopped thinking about the past and focused on the moment. "I'll be right back," I said, then climbed out of the truck.

I reviewed Murk's instructions in my mind as I crossed the parking lot. The story I would tell inside the bank was that I worked at a light industrial plant only a few miles away, and I had come in to cash two payroll checks. The plan seemed easy enough to follow; at least that was what I told myself. As I approached the door to the empty bank branch, I greeted the security guard, feeling like his beady eyes were watching my every move.

I almost tripped over my feet as I walked through the door, but I knew Murk was watching me. My nerves were all over the place, and they'd gotten worse after Murk's so-called pep talk. All his words and warnings had done was make me more anxious. The bank was frigid inside, but that was a good thing, since my palms and underarms were sweaty. I had had no idea I'd be into a fraud scam when I woke up this morning, with the courage to holla at Murk. I looked around to take in the setup, and my eyes met the security guard's. I'd been so into my thoughts that I hadn't even noticed him lingering in the corner.

"W-what up?" I stuttered, with a slight head nod. He was a brother, and I had automatically assumed he'd be slightly relatable, but his posture tensed up as soon as he heard my slang.

"Good afternoon," he replied smugly.

Tighten up, Tom-Tom, I told myself as I got in line behind the few people who had arrived before me. There was an older white woman on a walker and a middle-aged white woman who was gripping the strap of her Gucci purse like I might be in the bank to rob her. I already knew I'd be typecast as a thief, because my swag did not blend with the rigidness of suburbia. But I was about to do my best at playing the hand Murk had dealt me. The line moved fairly quickly, and after about five minutes, it was my turn.

The teller politely waved me to her station. "Good afternoon, sir. How are you? How can I help you today?"

"Hi. I'm doing great. Thanks for asking. I'm just trying to cash a couple of checks from my job." I slid my ID through the slot and then quickly opened the envelopes. "I've got two instead of one this time," I said, insinuating that I'd cashed checks here before. "I hate cashing them week by week because it seems like it spends faster," I joked, knowing she would relate to the saying because my dad used to complain about that back when he was sober and employed.

"Oh, I completely understand. Would you be interested in opening a checking account that can save you even more? You can save on gas from coming in here, plus the check-cashing fee. It's free to open an account, and you can get an ATM card before you leave."

"Um, maybe next time," I said as I glanced down at my wristwatch, which hadn't worked in years. "Maybe you can give me a brochure to check out for the next time I come in," I added, playing it off like Murk had said I should.

"Sure. No problem." She slid over a brochure, then went back to typing on her computer, looking at my ID, and writing my ID number on the checks. Everything Murk had said she would do, she did. Even down to pulling open the cash drawer and counting out my payout.

A nigga's dick almost got hard when I saw her dropping all those crisp fifties and hundreds onto the counter.

"Here you go, Mr. Stewart. Have a nice day." She slid the money through the slot, and I snatched it faster than a whore off a blow job. I was feenin' to get to Murk's truck and run my fingers through the bills.

"Th-th-thank you, and y-you too," I stuttered over my shoulder, 'cause I was already skipping toward the exit.

I crossed the parking lot to Murk's truck at a brisk walk, not looking back, then slid into the front passenger seat.

"I told yo' scary ass my licks were foolproof, li'l nigga," Murk said as he tossed another sealed envelope in my lap and pulled off. "Pop a Tic-Tac, 'cause the next bank we hittin' is only a mile away."

It was on.

Chapter Three

Shayla

I was window shopping at the mall with a funky-ass attitude. I did not know what I was thinking by coming out here with Bird. I was way out of my element. With not one single slug in my pocket, not on any given day but definitely not now, I shouldn't have been anywhere but on the porch of my block. Bird was clearing racks, hangers, and shelves from every store we went into, making me feel even more inferior than I had earlier. As we meandered from couture boutiques to Bath & Body Works, I felt tinges of jealousy as I watched her swipe her mom's debit card balance down. Bird used the fucked-up shit that had happened to her as a child to her advantage when she wanted to, and most of these outrageous sprees came after one of her famous fake meltdowns. Between her mom and her grandma, she kept a wad of guilt cash.

Saving her generosity till we got inside Target to pick up her womanly personal items, Bird asked, "Want me to get you something, Shayla? See anything you like?"

I swallowed my pride before running down my short list, knowing Tom-Tom might not be able to come through. I hated not giving my brother credit when he tried hard to take care of my needs, but he was twenty-one, with no kids. I wasn't his responsibility. I couldn't wait to take the weight off my brother's back, so he would not have to rob Peter to pay Paul.

"It's no problem for you to get whatever you want." Bird was throwing her weight around.

I think this li'l bitch calls herself being funny, I thought.

As I walked around and grabbed up almost a buggy full of socks, underwear, and baby clothes for little Yani, it dawned on me that Bird was actually turning over a new leaf by trying to look out for someone other than herself. I also found it strange that she was even thinking of Yoshi after what had gone down almost an hour ago. But all three of us were strange like that, sometimes taking it too far. After making sure I hadn't missed the things I desperately needed, with me being in a rush and all, I steered the cart over to where Bird was standing.

"Here. Start throwing the stuff in bags, so we can get the hell up out of here. Jayson just called, so we can meet up for prom planning," Bird announced. After pulling out about ten old, balled-up Target bags, she passed me half of them before starting to bag up what was about to become stolen property.

I didn't move a muscle.

Bird paused once she realized I wasn't on the same game plan. "Snap into it, bitch, before we get caught!"

"Your ass is crazy! I'm not trying to get locked up behind no cheap-ass Target shit," I told her as I shook my head. I sure did not want to catch a case in suburbia. "You're on your own." Everyone knew cops and judges seldom cut young black women any slack for coming to their neck of the woods to steal. I did not know what thrill Bird got from being a thief, especially when she did not have to be one, but she was more serious than a heart attack as she tossed everything I had once thought we were paying for into the recycled bags. She'd only been swiping her mom's card, which meant the cash Murk had paid her for pussy was still on her person. I did not know what the hell his random act of attention was for.

"Oh, my bad. I guess you planned on passing the cashier your share of the bill," Bird said, taking a moment from stealing to clown me. She knew I did not have any money, so that joke did not have any humor. I was getting tired of her sneak dissing me. She'd just done the same thing to Yoshi. "You should be happy I'm putting you down with how to get on. I'm not gonna always be around to play Captain Save a Ho! Now hurry up and start bagging, before we get caught."

I did not want to . . . but I also knew I needed all the stuff that was in the cart bad as hell. "Oh, all right," I muttered. I opened two of the bags Bird had given me, and I started stuffing them as quickly as I could. "This is why Tom-Tom do not like me hanging with your daredevil ass," I huffed.

"Fuck you and yo' dusty brother, if you wanna be like that." Bird finished bagging up her items and darted off. She had dashed away like she already knew what route she was taking out of the store. And if I got caught, well, that was on me.

I thought Bird was a friend, but I could tell what she was thinking. She'd been the one cashing out for our meals, our weed, and our outings ever since we hit thirteen. So, it was about time I learned how to step it up and pull my own weight.

Chapter Four

Bird

"Bird baby, can you please get in that kitchen and wash those dishes today?" my mother asked me. "Not only does it reek like rotten milk in there, but we'll have maggots if any of them damn flies lay some eggs."

"Nope, I cannot clean the kitchen today. I got my nails done yesterday, and I am not about to mess them up in no dishwater. I suggest you call a maid service or off from work and do it yourself if you want it done."

She was fussing at my back as I got up off the couch and walked away from her. I went in my bedroom and slammed my door and dared her to invade my privacy. I was shocked she was even talking to me in the first place. She knew I didn't fuck with her like that.

I was worse than the typical hormonal teenage female who was grown and out of control. I was wild, disrespectful, reckless, and proud of being rebellious. The only thing I was not was sneaky, and that was because I didn't care about consequences or what anyone thought about me. Especially my mother. She'd lost the right to have an opinion when I was too young to even spell the word.

"Bird." My mother was now tapping on my door.

"Are you serious right now?" I yelled at the top of my lungs. "I wish you'd go about your business and leave me alone. What do you want?" I was hoping she did not say the wrong thing and irritate me even more.

"I was going to ask you if I can give you forty dollars to clean the kitchen. That way you can get your nails redone if you mess them up."

I couldn't believe her weak ass was bargaining with me about cleaning up my own mess. I'd been home alone for the past two days because she'd been chasing a check to take care of us and it looked like a week without care. My mother was a home health-care aide, and she worked seven days a week and sometimes overnight. She had just gotten off from a double of forty-eight hours straight and had come home to shit, shower, and change scrubs to go back for another eight-hour shift. I couldn't wait till she pushed the fuck on. Whereas Shayla yearned for her mother, I was happy mine was a workaholic and stayed away from the crib as much as she did. All I wanted up outta Beatrice was her check.

"Boost it up to sixty and I'll think about it," I told her. I already knew she was going to agree to my demands.

"Okay, but I only have a hundred-dollar bill." She slid it underneath the door. "Take the other forty and pay my phone bill, please."

"All right, whatever! Get away from my door." I snatched the bill up, then sat down at my vanity and started putting some makeup on so I could hit the streets.

I had no intention of stepping foot in that nasty-ass kitchen. At first, I was just being an asshole to my mother, and I was actually going to tough girl it out and clean up the kitchen when my mother left, but now I was about to take her crisp hundred-dollar bill and grab some Coney Island and get some Minx lashes installed by this lash tech I'd been following on social media for a few months.

She'Lash had a booth up in Greenfield Plaza, which was a mid-rise building of professional suites, with businesses ranging from jewelry stores to beauty bars, boutiques, and computer repair places. There were even studios and fitness centers on the lower level of the four-story building. Northland Mall used to be right across the street from Greenfield Plaza, and after the mall shut down, most of the small vendors moved across the street to the Plaza and brought their clientele along with them. The Plaza was the hot spot to go, and some of everybody and their mama could be there on any given day. I had to make sure my outfit was fly.

I decided on rocking a turquoise spandex short-set bodysuit, some fresh white Reebok Classics, and the white Gucci fanny pack I'd bribed my grandma into buying me. It was supersweet and had a rainbow spaceship with the same turquoise shade in it as my outfit. I had a closet full of name-brand clothes, purses, and shoes, all compliments of her ole pervert-raising ass.

My grandma thought she was making up for what sick shit my father did to me when I was a kid, but it was really making me despise her as well. She, my daddy, and my lame-ass mama were all abusers, as far as I was concerned. Not once had she ever sat me down and said, "Granddaughter, I know what my son did was wrong, and it's unforgivable, but let me love you." All she had done was toss money at the skeleton in the closet, hoping the truth would stay buried underneath all the name brands. Both she and my mother were delusional and deceitful, and karma would eventually find them for allowing me to suffer and carry their burdens. My thoughts drifted to one nightmarish moment in particular.

"I said you could taste her, not stick your penis inside her. Get your nasty ass up off my daughter," my mother cried and hit my father in the back.

He sat up, but he was still penetrating me. "Stop playing and go back to watching your soap operas, Bea. You knew it was only a matter of time before I took it to the next level with her since you promised her to me before I moved in here. Why did you burst through the door if you did not think you could handle it?" he calmly told my mother—too calmly.

I might had been only a child, but I knew his demeanor fit not that of a caught rapist, but that of a man who had been given permission to fondle and steal the innocence of a child. My mother was just as much a predator as he was, but because she was my mother, I still looked at her as a protector.

Instead of her answering my dad's question, my mother turned emotional. "Get off her and get out of my house, before I kill you! It's seriously something wrong with you that you'd rather fuck around in a virgin's pussy when I give you good sex every night."

"Stop playing, Beatrice! You knew it was only a matter of time and that I would not be able to resist. You knew what I liked when you asked me to move in here, Beatrice. You promised me I'd be able to have our daughter in due time." Nate was everything but remorseful.

Whereas some people blocked out traumatic events they'd experienced, I'd relived mine over a million times. For all the years that had gone by, I could still recall every word exchanged between Beatrice and Nate like it was yesterday. I was intentionally cruel to my mother because she had been cruel to me and neglectful. She had willingly sacrificed my innocence so she could have the presence of a man. In my opinion, Beatrice was just as sick as Nate was, because ain't no mother supposed to put her child in harm's way. Everyone had been busy protecting a predator while I had suffered in silence. Now another traumatic moment flashed through my mind.

I sat in the middle of my bed, wrapped in a bright pink blanket, crying, as my mom and Nate ran through the house, screaming and fighting. They were going at it like savages in the street. At first, I had thought my mom was throwing vases, plates, and knives in his direction because she was trying to hurt him for hurting me, but then I lost even more of my innocence, because I realized she was fighting over her own broken heart. She was more concerned about where he was going than about consoling me and calling the cops so he could be arrested for raping me. I even heard her ask him if he could get psychiatric help to fight the urges, so we could try to remain a family.

An hour later, after the screaming had died down, she came into my bedroom, locked the door behind her, and pushed my dollhouse up against it. "Bird baby, Mommy's going to need you to be a big girl, like you've been being all these nights this sick motherfucker has come into your room."

"Mommy, I'm scared of Daddy. I do not want to be a big girl anymore, please. I'm sorry! Please just make him leave and do not let him come back." My little body was shaking so bad that I peed on myself and did not know it.

"I know you're scared, baby . . . and I'm so sorry. None of this is your fault, and you did not deserve anything that has happened to you because of that mean-ass man. I promise that if you be a big girl one more time, you'll never have to worry about your daddy hurting either of us again." My mom pulled a gun from behind her back and told me to hold out my hands. I did, and she placed the gun on my palms. The steel felt cold like ice. "Here. You need to hold it up and steady like this," she told me. Then she stood me up and gave me a one-minute tutorial on how to grip, aim, and fire the gun.

Suddenly Nate tried to open my bedroom door, discovered it was locked, and started knocking hard. "Open this goddamn door and give me my car keys so I can leave, Beatrice. I'm done playing with you."

Nate banged harder on my bedroom door, causing my dollhouse, which my mother had slid in front of the door, to almost topple over. All the tiny furniture slid out, and I was mad about that, because I'd spent hours playing with it and decorating it perfectly. I played with dolls and dollhouses a lot, because it was the only time I could create a perfect family.

"I'm not giving you shit," my mother shouted bitterly in response.

His foot smacked against the door, and pieces of the wooden frame came apart, causing my dollhouse to topple over and crash to the floor.

"Mommy! I do not want him to come in my bedroom anymore!" I cried. I could barely see, because my eyes were clouded with tears.

"Then you've gotta stop him, Pooh. Pull the trigger back toward you and fire the gun."

"Help me, Mommy! Can you do it for me?" I turned to her, but she was backing away from me and nodding for me to do it.

"Do not make me kick this muthafucking door off the hinges, Bea," my father yelled, then kicked the door even harder. This time, the front of his steel boot pierced the door, and wood chips flew in my face.

"Shoot, Bird! He's about to hurt you again." My mother's words rang out before I pulled the trigger toward my body, like she had instructed me to do.

"Ah!" I cried out, in pain, as my body flew backward and smacked against my bed frame. I did not know then why that happened, but it was because I was too tiny to withstand the force of the gun's kickback. My mother had known I would fly backward when I pulled the trigger, but she hadn't warned me, because if I had braced myself, it would have proven she was in the room all along.

I ended up sending a bullet through my father's chest and killing him. One bullet. That was all it took for me to get a full night's worth of sleep and not have to worry about him creeping into my bedroom ever again.

"Make sure you do not tell the police officers I was in here when you shot him, Bird. Tell them that he was trying to break down your door to come back in here, and that you got the gun out of my purse. Do you understand? If you tell them I was in here and that I gave you the gun, I'll go to jail for a very long time, and there will be a lot of mean old men that can hurt you in foster homes."

"I do not want to leave you, Mommy! I want to stay home." I buried my face in her stomach, feeling myself starting to lose my breath, like I did when I was playing tag outside with my friends.

"Then you've gotta make sure you tell the story right, Bird. Tell Mommy what you're supposed to tell the police officers when they ask you what happened." She prepped me for the entire fifteen minutes it took for the cops to show up, and when they did, I saw why she had done that. She was making sure I didn't tell the cops about her involvement in letting him touch on me.

It was years before I learned what an accomplice was. But once I did, I started treating Beatrice like the snake she was. She was lucky I didn't cut into one of the homies around here to rob her on her way in from work one day. It was hard caring about a woman who had thrown me to the wolves.

My cell phone rang just then and snatched me out of my thoughts. I already knew it was my boyfriend, Jayson, calling, because I had ringtones set up for him, Shayla, and even Yoshi's ugly ass. Jayson's was a snippet of what used to be our song, "All my Life," by K-Ci & JoJo. You couldn't pay me to think I hadn't lived a full life at seventeen for all the shit I'd gone through. So yeah, I had really felt like Jayson was my happily ever after. We had gone to every one of our homecomings together, had stayed hugged up and kissing in the hallways, and had even won "favorite senior couple" for our class. But that bubble had since popped. I'd been beyond irritated as hell with him, with everything he'd done, and with everything that reminded me of him and us. I guess creeping around with a grown man had me ready to put this juvenile relationship in the past.

"Hey. What's up?" I finally answered, as dryly as I possibly could.

"Just left practice and am trying to see what's up with you. Why didn't you call me after you left the mall with Shayla? I wanted to kick it with you so we could coordinate our plans for prom," Jayson said. He was more excited about and involved with our prom than I was, and that was turning me off even more than I already was. I was supposed to be jumping down his throat about picking colors, choosing which type of car I wanted to rent, and deciding if I wanted to have a big send-off. But every word that came from his mouth was about prom.

"My bad, but me and my mom got to beefing about my chores," I lied, fudging the time frame. "I ended up taking a shower and crashing." I left out the part about me sending Murk a bunch of naked pictures of me in an attempt to bait him into inviting me over. "But what's the word?"

"My boss loaded me up with hours for the next few weeks, so I'll most definitely have the money we'll need to get a room at the casino." Jayson thought he was doing something major by getting us a hotel room at MGM Grand Detroit for after the prom, but I'd been down there two times with Murk last week, getting my back broken in. I had even been able to sneak into the casino's gaming room beside Murk, because he looked every bit of twenty-one and official.

"Oh, okay. Cool. Anything else?" I couldn't get geeked up over something that was easily attainable.

"I've got my tux rented, I got one more payment on the gators you picked out for me, and I got a hookup on some gas cards so we can have a full tank to ride out on."

I turned my nose up at how broke Jayson sounded. Murk was flipping fifty in the tank every time we pulled up at a gas station, not including the condoms and snacks. So to hear li'l fella talking about hustling up on ten-dollar gas cards had me annoyed. Plus, it was weak as hell that he was having to walk the bill down on some thousand-dollar shoes, which Murk could cash out on effortlessly. "Oh, okay. It sounds like that penny-an-hour job is really adding up."

"Why you gotta be acting like such a bitch, Bird? I've been busting my ass at that job to make sure you have the fairy-tale night you've been talking about since we were fifteen. You could scrape up some more appreciation to throw a nigga with your ungrateful ass!" Jayson's temper was in rare form. Even though I couldn't blame him, I for sure as hell wasn't getting ready to tolerate it.

I flipped the script and went off. "Bitch? Ungrateful? You're really showing your stank ass tonight," I yelled into the phone, ready to get vindictive. "I'll show you a true bitch, since you want to lie on me." I hung the phone up in his ear, then scrolled to the second name in my call log. I meant every syllable of my threat.

Tom-Tom

"A'ight, man, I'll slide through there in the morning. Good looking out." I jumped out of Murk's truck and slammed the door shut. We'd hit four more banks with the same made-up story, and each time I'd cleared over eight hundred bucks. Murk had split the cut with me fifty-fifty, leaving me with sixteen hundred big ones to feel like a real G with. I knew to Murk it was small time, but I was willing to be patient until my shine time came.

"No doubt, bro. Make sure you're mentally ready first thing come morning. No blunts or nothing! Like I said earlier, I've got some real heavy-hitting checks for a grand each, but you really gotta be prepped to play the part!"

"Running with you today has gotten me even hungrier for the come-up. I'm done with this training-day shit. I'm ready for the big leagues!"

"A'ight, playa, we about to get this money! Holla at me."

Chapter Five

Tom-Tom

I walked through the front door, several shopping bags in my hands, and caught the lingering smell of drugs, which I was, unfortunately, used to. Ricardo was playing a card game of solitaire on the coffee table. He was damn near sitting on the warped wooden floor, because the couch cushions were worn down and the frame was broken and held up by a set of bricks, but he did not care. He had stopped caring about furniture and appearances. We had the same fucked-up floral-print living room set that Rose had decorated our house with when my sister and I were kids.

Ricardo looked up from the cards. "I saw you getting out of Murk's truck. I done heard a lot of rumors about that boy up on the corner. You better be careful round him, son," he warned me. He was not welcome in my business, especially when it pertained to the come-up I was on. I leaned in with the quickness to correct his misunderstanding of our dynamic.

"First and foremost, Ricardo, you can call me by my government name and kill all that 'son' bullshit. You and I both know you have not been a father to me in a very long time." I hadn't shown him respect since he started showing the crack pipe more love than me and my sister.

To say I'd been carrying a chip on my shoulder and a grudge against him for his selfishness would be putting it lightly. His poor decisions had forced me to grow up before my time, before I was ready, and way before I could stand on my own two feet. Which was why I was struggling now to hold shit together. The older I got, the more it stood out to me that I was lacking. And the more it was pointed out that I lacked skills, the more vulnerable I felt. I was grasping at straws now, trying to get it out of the mud. Ricardo wasn't about to fuck that up for me.

"You have every right not to like what I dabble in, and I totally understand why you hold a grudge against me. But what I'm not going to allow is the blatant disrespect of me. I do not care how much drugs I pump into my veins. I am still a man, regardless of your judgment. There's only God that can put a stamp upon me," Ricardo shot back. He was trying to puff his chest out to command respect, but it was a failed attempt because he lacked muscle and mass.

"Yeah, whatever," I muttered, shrugging off him and his testimony. "I've got a better idea. Instead of peering through the curtains, trying to see who I'm rolling or what I'm doing, find a recovery plan and work the steps."

"You've got another thing coming if you think I'm about to tiptoe around my house, li'l nigga."

"Man, stop it. All you do is creep around this house, stealing whatever you can that is worth a dime. I can't even leave a phone charger plugged up in the living room, because your dusty ass will steal it and sell it for fifty cents. Me and Shayla have got dead bolts on our bedroom doors and bars on our windows to keep your crafty, cracked-out ass from stealing from us."

"I haven't stolen shit out this house in a very long time, boy. Do not stir no lie up on me. And as long as you are living underneath this roof, young man"—Ricardo emphasized the word *man*—"you're gonna have to find a way to treat your pops with a little respect. I can't have you coming up in here talking sideways to me. Next thing you know, you'll be thinking it's okay to go upside my head." Ricardo might've been speaking from true emotion, since his hands were wrapped tightly around a liquor bottle.

I set my shopping bags down on the floor and crossed my arms. "Listen here, old man. I do not give a fuck about what truth you're speaking with your drunk tongue. I'm not respecting no nigga that do not respect themselves. You better blow on that pipe and quit trying to call the shots around here."

"You hate the very nigga that made you," Ricardo snarled. "Them streets ain't beef you up with that hard head that got you thinking you can hang with me in the streets. I might stroke a crack pipe, but I'll still give your ass a swift ass kicking." My pop's eyes were bloodshot red as spit flew from his mouth. "Now, get the fuck on up out of my face before I forget the promise I made to Rose."

Despite me not knowing what his last comment meant, the mention of my mother's name triggered me to leap across the room and grab him by his scrawny throat. My hands were on him, but my mind was on her. A nigga ain't have no love for either of his parents.

Ricardo's eyes were bulging from the sockets as spit started to trickle from his mouth. He was trying to pry my hands from around his throat, but my fingertips were almost touching one another as I tried to choke the life out of him. "Get . . . off," he fought to murmur.

I pushed him with all my might against the floor before I stood up, dusting the wrinkles from my clothes. "Do not fuck with me again, old man."

"You'll regret the day you put your hands on me. God curses children that do not respect their parents," he seethed. He called himself cursing me, but his words fell on deaf ears.

If it weren't for Shayla, I would've completely disowned Ricardo and claimed both my parents were deceased. There wasn't shit Ricardo could do for me besides embarrass me further. I was good on the struggle, disappointment, and negative memories he represented. I was more than ready to come up off Murk's hustle. That was going to be my meal ticket up outta here.

I picked up my shopping bags and carried them to Shayla's room. I banged on her bedroom door, holding three bags in each hand. "Shayla, open up." I'd gotten myself a few outfits for the job Murk had for me in the morning, plus two pairs of gym shoes and matching outfits for my sister from Lady Foot Locker.

Now maybe her ass ain't gotta keep running up behind Bird's stale behind. Everything about that girl screams out trouble! I thought as I waited for Shayla to open the door.

"Give me two seconds. I just got out of the shower. I'm sliding some clothes on!" she yelled through the closed door.

I loved my baby sister more than anything in this world, and I always made sure she knew that. Before Rose had abandoned us, I used to be annoyed that Shayla wanted to play with all my toys and stay up under me when I was trying to hang with my friends. I had also been pissed whenever Ricardo and Rose made me babysit her or walk her home from school, because that meant I couldn't get into any teenage trouble. Shayla had a big mouth, and no matter how much candy I had bribed her with back then, she had always ended up telling on me.

But all that had changed when it became us against the world. I started keeping Shayla by my side wherever I left the house. So much so that I ended up losing a few friends because they did not want to be around a talkative eight-year-old. Back then, not only was Shayla scared to stay in the house with Ricardo alone after she saw him hitting a crack pipe, I was scared social services would show up while I gone and throw her in the system. Soon after Rose abandoned us, everything of any value that Ricardo had ever brought into this house, he marched to the pawnshop. We came home from school one day to find all the flat-screen TVs, laptop computers, and video games gone. The only reason I did not call the police and report a robbery was that my next-door neighbor told us Ricardo had had a yard sale and was probably nodded out in somebody's dope house.

I couldn't wait until I got a few licks under my belt with Murk and could afford to move me and Shayla to our own spot. All we needed was a two-bedroom flat, and since her name was squeaky clean, we could get the utilities on without a problem. I just needed to have some cash stashed away to pay the rent and bills. I knew there was no moving back to Ricardo's house once we moved out. Plus, I did not want to depend on Shayla for anything and have her end up seeking assistance from a savage-ass nigga from Detroit who did not have her best interests at heart, which was what both of her best friends had done. Duncan was only trying to smash Yoshi until he left for college, and Bird was letting Murk give her a bad name she would not be able to recover from. I wanted to give my sister better options.

"Come on, Shayla. Damn!" I was tired of standing outside her door.

"Oh shoot, my bad. I forgot you were out here," she exclaimed. Her goofy ass laughed, then swung the door open.

"Surprise, sis! Happy Birthday, Merry Christmas, and all the other holidays I missed over the years because I was broke." I stepped into her room, handed her three of the shopping bags, then closed the door.

"Oh my God! Are you serious, bro! All of this is mine?" She started peeking timidly in all the bags, like she was scared to look inside and touch the stuff for real. Her entire face was flushed red.

"Yup, and if anything is the wrong size, we can take it back to the store and get you the right size. Ain't none of this shit hot," I said. I knew she was used to me stealing.

"It's official? You're bullshitting, right? How, Tom-Tom? What job have you been secretly working that I did not know about?" She gave me a serious side eye.

I grabbed the remote to her TV and turned the volume up a few notches. I did not know if Ricardo was lurking outside her bedroom door, listening, but I wasn't trying to broadcast that me and Murk were hustling. "I went and got at Murk this morning, and he put me down with a hustle that will make it possible for me to take care of us. Let's just say I did well on my first day."

"This is crazy, bro! I swear, I keep waiting on myself to wake up. Are you sure this is all legit?" She finally started pulling all the clothes and shoes out of the bags.

"One hundred percent," I assured her. I went in my pocket and pulled out all the receipts. "Murk took me to an outlet mall, and they handle all kinds of fly shit for the low-low."

She pinched her arm until it bruised. "Wow. I can't believe this is really happening. Thank you so much. I swear, I do not know what I would do without you." She started crying.

"It's all good, sis," I said and pulled her in for a hug. "I do not know what I would do without you either. All we've had is us for a long time, and it's going to stay that way. Even if you bring some ugly-ass nigga into the picture, I want you to always know you can count on your big bro to look out for you. I do not care what I've gotta do to make it happen for you. I'ma chin up and take care of it."

Once I got on with Murk, I'd be able to provide my sister more than sporadic gifts or basic necessities. I'd be able to give her a nice lifestyle, which would make it hard for any man to come behind me. If Shayla was self-sufficient and got the best quality items on her own, no nigga on these D-Town streets would be able to control her with a dollar.

"Check the other bag, sis. That bitch Bird is gonna be sweating you hard off those other joints," I said. I loved playing Santa Claus to Shayla. If I could give her the skin off my back to survive, I would, no questions asked.

"These kicks are the coldest! Yeah, you're right. Bird is gonna be shitting bricks when I rock these boys! Everybody about to be jocking me come tomorrow, for a change!" I watched as she admired the ice-pink and silver Max 13s.

Those shoes weren't set to hit the shelves till next week, but Murk had had a special connect hook me up when we went shopping after hitting licks. He was the one who'd suggested them for Shayla—that nigga had taste fa sho.

"Where'd you get the money from to ball out on me like this? And what's in those bags?" She snatched the other three bags from me, dumped the contents onto the bed, and gazed at the dress slacks, shirts, ties, and the pair of Cole Haan dress shoes I'd bought for myself. I'd spent all but a few hundred bucks of the money I'd earned. As she admired my new shoes, I slid half of what was left into her palm.

"Murk put me on with a hustle that I can take care of us with," I whispered, just in case Ricardo was listening in. I knew that once he saw me flossing with Murk on a regular and getting my and Shayla's status together, he'd start coming for a few pennies too. But I had another thing in mind. He wasn't about to get fed off of me. "It's about to get real heavy around here, 'cause that nigga is on in a major way!" I sat down on the edge of her bed and got comfortable, about to kick it with my sister. We'd always been close, but ever since Rose left, we'd been damn near inseparable. I couldn't keep a girl for trying to keep my sister right.

She nodded. "Yeah, Bird let it drop a few times that he was working with a bank stash. What he got you doing, though?" She climbed on the other side of the bed and sat Indian style across from me.

I told her about Murk's intentions for me in the game. "It ain't much of nothing, but it's gonna have us eating hella right, sis. I made sixteen hundred in less than two hours by cashing payroll checks." After seeing the look of shock on her face, I continued on, giving her the rundown of how the trickery was set up. "They've got my name on them, they are replicas of the actual companies' payroll checks, and ain't none of my boys went up for fucking with him! His checks do not come back, 'cause they look too official to even cause an alarm."

"Damn. Everybody must've been on some hot shit today!" Shayla jumped up and opened her closed door. "Me and Bird went to the mall today and ended up stealing out of Target. This is my share." She hauled out a few large target bags, then dumped baby clothes, underwear, women's items, and even a stick of gum on top of the start to my new wardrobe. I knocked everything onto the floor, then grabbed her up.

"What the fuck you mean, 'your share'? Do not tell me that li'l bitch had you out there swiping this petty shit when Murk already said he gave her a few hundred for that ass this morning!" I shook her up without remorse. I'd been busting my ass to make her official, so for her to let Bird have her on some dumb shit had my head hot. "Do not be no dummy, Shayla! I schooled you better than that!"

"Let go of me, nigga! You can't judge me for doing on a smaller scale the same thing you're doing. You scamming checks, and I'm swiping spearmint gum." Somehow she managed to wiggle out of my hold, and then she stood across from me with her arms crossed, prepared for a word-for-word battle. I wasn't getting ready to argue with her young ass, though. My word was my bond, so she had no other choice but to follow it.

"Do not be a smart-ass, Shayla. I'll break your fingers off myself if I find out your ass is out there stealing again!" After picking up my clothes and stuffing them back into the bags, I left her room and slammed her door behind me, pissed all the way off.

Damn, we ain't even get to kick it about moving up out of this dump! I thought.

I stepped into my room and closed the door behind me. Then I lit the last blunt I'd be smoking till tomorrow night. From now on it was about to be all business—then pleasure.

Ricardo, aka Spiderman

With my ear pressed against Shayla's door, I listened as my disrespectful-ass son showered her with gifts that I couldn't afford to buy but was already itching to steal. Nothing was safe or sacred in this house 'cause I had a serious addiction to feed. Everything about me was a disgrace, just like Tom had said, but I couldn't admit that to his face. I would not dare. What man wanted to stand down as a fiend to his only son? I was supposed to be a man, a provider, a role model. Instead, I was the scum underneath everyone's shoes. I couldn't stomach my children thinking so poorly of me, but a day in the life of a junkie is a cold and lonely one. I'd grown accustomed to no one loving me but the white rock I broke down every chance I could.

Dabbling with drugs had started out as a necessity for me and a few other coworkers. Our boss had introduced it to his entire shift one night as a way for us to stay awake. Every night up until then, we'd gulped Red Bull by the cases and popped vitamin B$_{12}$. After freebasing for the first time, I felt euphoric, confident, and on top of the world. Not only did I and the fellas triple our production overnight from having increased energy, but I managed to work a double. In the beginning, crack wasn't working me; I was working it. Instead of refusing to eat on account of my loss of appetite, I forced myself to eat once every few hours to keep weight on my body. Soon me and the fellas started to freebase frequently, and we picked up marijuana to balance out our high.

At first, everything was all good. Money wasn't an issue, because I was working every shift the plant allowed me to pick up. The bills were paid up, affording material objects was no problem, and I was the go-to man in my family whenever someone needed a loan. Foolishly I thought I had control over my addiction. With the influx of cash, I was able to afford it all and still stay high. Rose was happy, my kids were living fairy tales, and I was feeding my secret addiction. But my whole world started crashing the moment my supervisor got fired. Our whole shift was approached with drug-testing paperwork, and we were fired one by one when our piss came back dirty.

The worst day of my life was the day I became a junkie. I went on a twenty-four-hour crack binge, then came home reeking of the gutter. It was weird, because going into a crack house sober, you damn near pass out from

the horrific stench. Those places reeked of human re-
gurgitation, musty body odors, and the strong chemical
smell of crack constantly being burned. Every step you
made had to be watched, 'cause you could step into a pile
of shit or stumble across a dope fiend laid out across the
floor in a crack-induced coma. Dealers did not care about
cleaning up the houses us junkies binged in. All they
worried about was pocketing our Social Security checks,
welfare stipends, and last few dollars in exchange for us
staying doped up and dependent. From time to time, I
made the crack spot my home. There were absolutely no
judgments at this level of the game. We were all living
rock bottom.

I went home to Rose one day and put my secret on
the table. She forced me to get up daily, look for a job,
and seek help for the addiction, which was starting to
eat me from the inside out. She was the model wife who
chose to stand by her man, in hopes I'd get my life back
together. She went hard at fighting for my recovery. But
the more she pushed me to be a man, the more I gave in
to the temptation of the pipe. I craved cocaine, and my
body started to reek of it. My complexion stayed ashy,
I no longer cared about my appearance, and the crater
bumps on my face were dead giveaways I had to be on
that stuff. Rose went from trying to help me stay strong
to partnering up with me in being weak. I guess I broke
her down by not being resilient enough to kick the habit I
had brought into our home.

Instead of seeing her crossover as a moment of crisis,
I pushed her deeper into the game. The only thoughts
on my mind were that she was finally off my back and
I could get high in peace. The higher she stayed, the
less she complained. But that was when the addiction
started to directly affect the kids. Rose started to nurture
them less, ignored their presence, and disciplined them

unnecessarily. She kept her appearance up, though, and from the rumors I heard around the hood, she used her body to finance her addiction. Since she was gone now, it had obviously worked. The monkey had chased her down quicker than it had done to me, 'cause she had the drive and audacity to leave her family. I'd beaten myself up every day since she left with our dealer. Then I'd cuddle up with my crack.

Chapter Six

Murk

Young cats from the neighborhood flocked to me like I was the second coming of Jesus Christ himself, so I was not surprised when Tom-Tom came to my doorstep, looking for an opportunity to get put on with a hustle that could put some real money in his pocket. I flashed nothing but hood riches—a flashy truck on rims, fresh sneakers to match every name-brand outfit I rocked, and crystal-clear ice on my neck, wrist, and pinkie finger. I kept my personal business and all the details about my background to myself, and most importantly, I kept my feelings close to my heart.

Not many knew the real me. That was privileged information I kept on reserve. I'd been out in these streets getting mine since I was twelve years old, and by the time I was fifteen, there was no stopping my wrath. By then I'd given up on loyalty and love, because loyalty and love had fucked me over the very minute I was introduced to this fucked-up world.

My mother abandoned me when I was two years old. The burden of raising me was left to my sixty-year-old, arthritis-stricken grandmother, and when I came along, she was already exhausted from trying to raise my wild and rebellious mother. My memories of my mother were very faint, but I did have nightmares about her from time to time, and these contained visions of her arguing with my granny. I did have one reoccurring dream that was pleasant. In it she was singing a song to me, and her voice was soft and sweet like the melody. I usually woke up humming the tune the next day. One time my grams asked me about the tune, and I told her about the dream, and she confirmed that my mother used to want to be a singer and could sing very well.

Old Ruth Mae did the best she could do with raising me and providing me the most normal life she could as a senior citizen. I remembered her limping on her cane as she walked me to the park, taking me to the penny-candy store and making it seem like two dollars was two thousand. Somehow I turned out coldhearted and ruthless. There was not a day that passed when I did not regret stealing from her, cursing at her when she refused to give me money for bullshit, and even running away and running her blood pressure through the roof. I had acted out and been rebellious with the wrong person, and I still had not forgiven myself for being young and dumb.

During her last days she begged me to make a change and even to forgive my sorry-ass mama for her wrongs. The last day I saw my grandmother alive, she was rubbing holy water on my forehead and praying for a positive change. Me and Ruth Mae had a real-ass relationship, but she never should've told me the truth about Marilyn leaving me the way she had, 'cause that shit was brutal for my young mind. But I didn't blame her. At the end of the day, her role should've never been my guardian. Anything that Ruth Mae may have done wrong was Marilyn's burden to carry, as far as I was concerned. My granny had died trying to right Marilyn's wrongs. But I had been too self-centered then to pick up on the red flag and wave my white one. I had been too busy trying to break out of the crib so I could hang with my homeboys and get high. And these were the same homeboys who were nowhere to be found when I had to help carry my granny to her grave.

I still had not forgiven God for taking the only woman who had ever loved me, and had loved me unconditionally. My rotten ass did not know what I had until I did not have anyone, which was exactly how I had started out in this world. Her death had made me colder and more rebellious. Even my rights became wrong, and I was swift enough with my tongue to rationalize my ill-bred ways. Since Ruth Mae was not here to see the kind, forgiving, and well-mannered young man that she had prayed to God for me to be, then there really wasn't a reason for me to try to be that type of man. I was more comfortable not giving a fuck. Especially when Marilyn brought her unwelcomed ass back into the picture.

My grandmother's best friend and two of her neighbors put a burial service together for my granny and hosted the repast at our apartment. The only people who came to the service were a few people from our building and some people from her church. We did not have a lot of family, which was why I had begged my granny's people not to call social services on me. I knew how life went for boys in the system, and I wasn't trying to get raped or jumped in a gang. I might've done a little dirt with my homeboys, but we weren't savages, and I definitely did not have the mentality to compete with one.

The first week after we buried Ruth Mae was the hardest days I'd ever walked down in my life. The memories either kept me awake at night or had me crying in my sleep. Regret was a tough pill to swallow when you couldn't at least make a call to apologize. The only good thing that came from all those hours of me being awake was that I'd gotten several call-backs for job interviews.

The rent and bills were subsidized enough for me to get a side job after school to cover them and have a few dollars left in my pocket. I knew I hadn't budgeted food into the equation, but I could live off boxed corn bread and greens, sandwiches, and noodles. I would have eaten scraps out of the dumpster after watching a rat nibble on them just to stay in the apartment Ruth Mae had brought me home to. She had made it my home, our home. The memories hurt, but I felt her presence in the apartment, and that soothed me. And my homegirl made sure I ate and kept my head up when I was ready to go reckless and wild.

A month after Ruth Mae made her transition, Marilyn showed up at the door with a lawyer. At first, I thought it was child protective services, so I dodged the first visit, but Marilyn flat out started banging on the door the second time around, yelling that I better open up before she kicked the door down. In order for my mother to collect what had been left her in my Granny's will, there was a clause that stipulated that she had to take back custody of me first. What fucked me up in the head more was that it took only thirty days and some money on the floor for her to pick me back up. By that time, I was a wild child adolescent who had a vendetta against the world. Life for both of us turned into a hotter version of hell.

I think growing up a ward of the state would've been better. At fifteen, I already felt like I was the man. Being left behind and raised by a half-crippled woman had left me no other choice but to grow up way beyond my years. But in spite of me running wild through the jets, me and Grams had had a dynamic that worked for us. I'd done my dirt while she'd prayed for me, and she'd also taught me how to survive on my own, in case something happened to her. She had prepared me for the real world and had not babied me, because she'd known I'd get murdered in my environment if I wasn't tough as nails. I knew how to run a household as far as cooking, paying bills, and balancing bills were concerned. And I also knew how to rob Peter to pay Paul till the next Scheck came in. Plus, I knew how to kick a nigga's ass and rob him. Like I said, I was a savage in these streets.

So, after Grams's death, I had to go live in my mother's home, which was actually some overprotective, controlling pimp's home, and that move threw me more into a downward spiral. Especially since the hood was worse than the jets and was infested with gangs. I wasn't trying to give my blood, sweat, and loyalty to no stranger. So I stayed in the crib most of the time to avoid having to fight or die, and then I tried to make it out of my mom's crib altogether, which was another battle in itself. Me and her dude didn't get along at all. He flat out hated me. And truth be told, all he wanted was the money my grams had left behind, not me. He beat my mama's ass the day she brought me home, the whole time screaming that she should've left my stupid ass where she found me. To this day, I couldn't say why I didn't turn around and walk right back out that man's front door. It wasn't like Artavia would've turned me away if I showed up on her doorstep.

During the first six months of me staying with my mom, we got into arguments daily. Then he started stepping in and shutting her down altogether, and trying to control me in the same way that he had her whipped. She thought he was providing much-needed discipline and getting me in line, but what he was really doing was pushing me over the edge and putting even more of a wedge between me and her. He thought I was about to be a live-in slave, while he prostituted my mother out to the highest bidder, but that shit was weak as hell.

Marilyn's pimp went from putting his hands on her, to flat out fighting with me over bullshit almost on a daily basis. If the dishes weren't washed and dried properly, he went crazy. If I missed a few lint balls when vacuuming, he'd trip me with the cord after making me redo it. And I swear, I woke up to him trying to choke me with the phone cord when I fell asleep caking with Artavia, but he denied that when I told Marilyn and she confronted him. I was shocked she had even said something to him, because my intent was really for her to leave him, for us to finally go be a family, with just the two of us, even if that meant we had to go live back in the jets. I knew they'd get us a unit if Grams was gone. But no, Marilyn bucked up to her pimp, and he spanked her with the same phone cord he tried choking me with. That was when I knew there was no saving my mom, or the fairy tale I was still holding on to, and it was time for me to find my way back to the jets solo dolo.

Three months after that incident, the explosion finally occurred. I was doing my chores, and he was being an asshole, following behind me each step of the way. I hated walking on eggshells and being antagonized. He was poking me like a bear on purpose. And when he tried pushing my face into the toilet bowl, saying he couldn't see his reflection in the water after I scrubbed it, I blacked out and beat his ass. Then I took his gun off his holster with a washcloth and wrapped his finger around the trigger and blew his brains out.

My fingerprints weren't on the gun, so they couldn't prove I had murdered him, but I indeed caught my first body on my sixteenth birthday. I never asked Marilyn what had happened to that nigga's dead body after I stepped over it—'cause I walked right out of the house and her life for good after that incident. Stockholm syndrome was real. Her dumb ass would've probably

painted that demon as a saint and had me rotting in jail
for his murder had I stuck around. That was about ten
years ago, and I'd been getting it out of the mud ever
since.

I pulled down on the corner boy. "Let me get a dime
bag."

"Not Murder Murk! You on this shit too?" he exclaimed
with a look of bewilderment on his face.

"Nigga, naw. Do not start no fucking rumors yo' ass
ain't willing to die behind." When I pulled up my shirt
and let him see the handle to my chrome piece, the boy's
knees started to knock, as he knew my body count hinged
on my quick temper. When it came to proving a point
about my pride, taking a moment to rationalize wasn't
part of my pedigree. I did not have time to think about
what a nigga might've been contemplating.

"That is your word, and I'm living by it, chief. We ain't
got no problems." The small-time dealer threw his hands
up in defeat, then nodded, which meant we had a clear
understanding. "Here you go," he said, tossing me the
small plastic bag with the Devil's dandruff in it.

I slid the bag into my own jeans pocket ,then returned
to my truck. By the time I pulled off to head east, the li'l
nigga had gotten ghost.

Wise choice, grasshopper. That was a wise choice.

"Marvin, is that you?" my mother called, her voice
weak, as soon as I pushed the door open.

A cloud of funk spilled out of the room. The place
reeked of urine, feces, and crack cocaine. A normal person would've died if he or she had to endure these living
conditions for a week, but my moms wasn't easily broken.

"Who else would it be, Marilyn?" I pulled the thick, dirty curtains open so some sun could pour into the room. I knew the sunlight would hurt her eyes, because she'd been locked up in the dark room for over twenty-four hours. I starved her for light and the blessing of voices to help drive her even more psychologically crazy than she had already been when she came for my grandmother's money. "How are you feeling today?"

"You know how I'm feeling. Got my shit?" Her hot dragon breath hit me as soon as she turned over. Her sunken face told she was living with skeletons in her closet and an addiction through her veins. I couldn't say I felt bad for her deteriorating appearance. Everything about this woman looked rotten. Her eyes were blood-shot red, dilated, and glassy. And her skin was covered in picked-at scabs and tracks. You could easily tell by eye I'd been starving what little meat she had left on her brittle bones.

Digging deep into my pocket, I found what she was after. I tossed her the dime bag, which I rationed out to her once weekly. The rest of the days I kept her locked in one of the many half-abandoned houses I owned, and she lay in the back room, decaying, withdrawing, and wishing she was dead. No one came here but me. No one knew my mother was still even living. For years, my story to folks had been she kicked me out for her husband.

I watched the woman who had given birth to me get stoned. She ripped the hard rock she craved from the plastic baggie, then packed it into her burnt-up glass stem pipe. Her eyes were bulging wide at seeing her prized possession finally full of blow. She took a few deep breaths to clear her lungs so she could inhale and hold more vapor. It was just like reliving my teenage years as I watched Marilyn place the lighter underneath the pipe, then take hit after hit, chasing the running rock. The whole scene was disgraceful. As she leaned back against the wall, letting the only high she'd get all week seep into her system, I shook my head in disgust. It was hard to believe we shared the same genes. Marilyn was weak, feeble, and a disgrace to everything that was Marvin Vassar. It sickened me to even have her blood runnin' through me.

"You're just like your father, believe it or not." Marilyn kept her head low as she spoke while lighting a cigarette. "He was able to break a bitch down to her lowest point too." After she took a long drag, then puffed out the stale-smelling smoke, I watched her bony arms hang at her sides, as if she was slowly admitting defeat.

"Fuck being like a nigga I ain't even met. Neither one of y'all disgraceful pieces of shit cared enough to look back for ole dirty Bert Murk. If I ever cross paths with this nigga you speak of, its light's out for him too. Believe that."

"I knew that woman had it in for me." Marilyn took a puff of her cigarette. "I should've never left you, and I know there's no excuse for that, but I was too young and twisted up. Since it seems I'm gonna die in this hellhole and meet up with Mama anyway, I might as well release some skeletons. I called daily for months, only to have Ruth hang up in my ear. She told me that you didn't need the disruption and you were her son. She begged me to leave you content and not stir up mess and confusion in your life. I wanted you back, Marvin. I just wasn't allowed those privileges."

"Do not lie on Grams. She ain't do shit but save your sorry ass from your responsibilities." I was boiling with bitterness and hate at the nonsense flying from Marilyn's mouth. It was weak as hell for her to blame anybody besides herself for abandoning me. I didn't want no seeds out here, thanks to my emotionally unstable upbringing, and that was thanks to me missing out on my mother's love. No matter how tough I played it, her absence had screwed with my head. "You ain't shit but a weak-ass bitch. I wish God would've picked you instead of Grams," I snapped. I really wished I could change the past and rewrite the future.

"You're just about as cold and heartless as your father. You've got that same demon spirit controlling your soul."

"Naw, I've unfortunately got that same selfish 'I don't give a fuck attitude' you put your mother in the grave with. Grams was too old for me and the shenanigans I put her through 'cause your messy ass was blowing in the wind. Now it's payback time. This is just karma coming back for you."

"You're right. I'm more than sure this is karma's way of letting me know it can't be outsmarted. I did way more wrong to a lot more people than you know. But what do you think is going to happen to you for all the wrong you running around doing, huh?"

"Don't waste your last days worrying about me. That ship done sailed. I got me, and if there's some consequences I gotta deal with, I know how to chin up and handle shit. Especially now that you're officially dead to me." I was just as grim with Marilyn as she'd been to me for most of my life. Readjusting my *D* fitted cap so the brim was back covering my face, I nodded my head as a last farewell, then slammed the door separating us. I didn't have any plans on returning either. Once she got done nursing her high, she could struggle through withdrawal and die for all I gave a fuck.

The projects hadn't changed since I'd slummed in them as a kid with Grams. The basketball courts were full, with the fellas tossing the pill around probably on a bet, and a few knuckleheaded kids hanging from the lead pipes they'd turned into monkey bars and bouncing up and down on a filthy, pee-stained mattress as if it were a trampoline. I used to be on the same make-believe bullshit. I damn near had an imaginary life back then, as much as I lived in my mind to escape how poor we were. But I knew Grams was giving me all she had and was doing her best. She was one of the few people in the community who didn't have a drug or alcohol addiction. My grams having to check out early still seemed hella unfair to me, and this was some shit I hadn't forgiven God for. It was like He had taken the only person who loved a young nigga. Fresh off the emotional trip down memory lane with my moms, I really didn't want to be in this place, but business for me was a priority, and my partner was still living here. Artavia had grown up a few floors underneath me and Grams, and we'd been cool as fuck as teenagers. She was the only person I had truly connected with. She had listened to a nigga, had held me down at all times, and had been my grandmother's keeper before she died. I considered her family, but I couldn't stop fucking her fine ass.

After hopping out of my ride, I hit the car alarm and then pushed past the group of dudes who were bent over shooting dice in front of her building.

"Yo, Murder Murk! You want in? Let me take a few of them dollars out ya' pocket," one of the fellas called out to me.

"Naw, I'm good. I gotta holla at my shorty. But I might fucks with you fools on the way down." I punched in the five-digit code at the front door, rushed inside when the door buzzed, and hurried to the staircase to take the eight flights up.

There was no way in hell I'd be caught in a death-trap elevator in any of the buildings in the jets. If they didn't stop working midway up or down, you could get caught slipping and be stabbed and robbed in one of them muthafuckas. I remembered they once dragged a body out of the elevator in the building I grew up in, and it was half-ass melted. By the time the property manager got around to having a maintenance man even look at the out-of-order elevator, ole boy had been dead in that box for damn near a month. The sad part was that it stunk so bad in the building on a regular basis that no one had even noticed the constant smell of death lingering in the air. The shit was normal. I done seen so much foul madness go down in these buildings that living off Linwood was living in the burbs. Halfway up to Tay's floor, I whipped out my cell to have her open the door. Even with my piece only a finger movement away, these thirsty cats in these towers were always shiesty, reckless, and on lurk mode to come up.

Artavia swung the door open as soon as I walked up, looking delicious, as always. And I was happy she was already undressed, as this took my mind off Marilyn. I'd smoked a blizzy on the way over here, but you would've thought it was trash, 'cause I wasn't buzzing at all.

"It's about time you showed up. I was about to start playing with my own coochie in a minute." As soon as I stepped inside and closed the door, she jumped in my arms and wrapped her legs around me.

Shorty wasn't lying, either; 'cause I felt the heat radiating from her hot box. Tay stayed ready to freak, and I wasn't complaining. "You can still play with that pretty kitty while I watch. Then you can take care of me," I told her.

I cupped her juicy booty cheeks, then started walking her to her bedroom. Her Dolce & Gabbana perfume was intoxicating. I sucked on her neck, then licked a trail down to her D-cup breasts, and all the while she was moaning in my ear. The chemistry and attraction we had between us was undeniable. I couldn't wait to slide my inches up in her and wreck her guts. Fuckin' Tay was different than when I banged off Bird, 'cause me and Tay had history. She knew how to snatch my soul from my body, plus put money in my pocket. I might've wifed her were she not so possessive and crazy. For instance, back in the day, she bent this bitch into a pretzel and broke her leg 'cause she'd caught the girl giving me a li'l head. I had to push the memory out my mind because it made me think of Grams and I started going soft. She was the one who had let Tay in the house that day, despite knowing I had a girl in the room. Like I said, me and Tay went way back. But right now, we were about to get down in the freakiest way possible. Of course, I had every intention of getting straight to business after I unloaded this stress.

Two hours and a shower later . . .

"So, what's up? Have you found a sucka to help us expand or what?" she asked as she strolled out of the kitchen with me after we enjoyed a bowl of her fine-ass jambalaya.

"Yeah, I think so. Matter of fact, I'm 'bout 99.9 percent sure I have," I revealed as we headed into her office. She plopped down at her desk. "This young cat Tom from the neighborhood came to holla at me about some work yesterday, so I took him on a trial run. He popped one account wide open on his first try."

"Damn! For real? That's impressive. When are you going to bring him through here so I can give him a once-over?" Tay swore she had an eye for snakes, and she just might've. Living in the jets wasn't no easy feat, so staying on your toes was a must if you wanted to stay alive. And Tay was living like a queen up in this plush muthafucka. Her unit didn't compare to none of the others. She had flat-screens mounted in every room, including the bathroom, and she had even knocked down the wall to the next unit and had had her crib transformed so she'd have almost nine hundred square feet of living space, instead of the four hundred square feet everybody else was stuffed into. I wasn't hating, though. She was banking enough cash to move out of the belly of the beast if she wanted to. And this link up with Tom-Tom was about to rake in even more cash for the pot.

Tay was valuable—and skilled when it came to making fake documents, such as checks, and forging paperwork we needed to open accounts. Shorty stayed working the system. She was living in a subsidized community, she easily qualified for welfare, and she had access to free classes, which most people around here turned down. Artavia gave her food stamps away, so she had a good reputation around here, but she fa sho stayed in a computer class or some nerdy shit. Again, I wasn't hating, 'cause she was the truth when it came to getting us to the bag. Now we just needed to expand.

"I'm gonna swing him by here in the next day or so, but I know he's solid and ready to put in some hella work."

"Okay, well, you know I trust you with my life. Any nigga you ride with can roll with me. You've been beating bullies off me since we were little." Artavia was one of those down-ass chicks that every dude wanted to be around. I considered myself lucky to have her.

For the rest of the night, we got down to business in a major way. Tom had run through the stack of checks I had on hand, so it was time for me to re-up. Tay loved re-up time, because she always got fronted her share, which was 10 percent of each check she printed. The second bedroom in her apartment was set up like a high-tech office. There were advanced copiers, several laptops, and scanners conveniently placed, so our fast-paced operation could go smoothly. Since we had a business account, every piece of equipment a company desired, we could purchase at a discounted rate. We used this all to our racketeering advantage.

Not only skilled at duplicating checks, Tay could create them from scratch if need be. The company we'd created was called 5-Star Consulting. There were no real employees, no real jobs to complete, and no real income. What we did have, however, was the ability to set up business accounts and act as a legitimate enterprise. But the only thing official about what we were doing was getting money.

"Roll up some of that good stuff, Murk. It looks like we've got a good reason to celebrate," Artavia said, smiling and waving me toward the computer. "Our site is doing major hits. I put an ad on Craigslist yesterday that said we were hiring a few administrative assistants, and people having been applying all night."

"No joke? That is why I'm hooked to your ass, baby girl. You stay thinking on your toes."

I looked over her shoulder as she scrolled through a hundred or so emails, with applications and résumés attached, then emptied the email account so we could start fresh on the next print down. We were about to use all their personal information—Social Security numbers, identification card numbers, and previous addresses—to run their credit into the ground for our gain.

"Once again, you've done your thang, baby girl!" I exclaimed.

"Yeah, so like I said, light up, so we can celebrate."

I did not waste time obliging. Before getting caught up in my racketeering world, Artavia had been a computer science major at the local community college. While growing up, she had kept her head in the books and had made school a priority. She had had high hopes, aspirations, and dreams of running her own small-time IT firm, but I'd turned her into a criminal. When we linked back up years after me being on a complete hiatus, I'd manipulated her into getting down with this check-scam brainchild we were now living comfortably off of. One of the benefits of our business relationship was that we both got full benefits to the good-good.

Chapter Seven

Artavia

Me and Murk were supposed to just be friends with benefits, but as long as I'd known him, it had been much more than that to me. I'd never been that innocent girl he was fooled by back in the day. Murk thought I was just his ride-or-die sex/business partner who got down with hooking and crooking, but I was much more devious than that. I wanted him to be my man, and I'd given up far too much, including a college degree, to stay his side piece forever. He was the Adam to my Eve, the Clyde to my Bonnie, and the Kanye West to my Kim Kardashian. Me and Murk complimented one another well. We were both skilled in the art of being manipulative, conniving, and unscrupulous. There was no one else in this whole wide world I'd rather be with. I'd done some things God was gonna judge me harshly for, so I at least had to get what I desired on Earth till then.

The business that Murk and I shared was sacred to me. I loved to see him coming but hated to see him go. Everything about his demeanor, personality, and physical features turned me on in the type of way that made me crazy. But I had no other choice but to play my position by keeping my feelings tucked deep inside. No matter how deeply I loved him, Murk wasn't the type of guy who could commit. When we were kids, he never paid me any attention. I was always the geeky girl who couldn't do much for a boy like Marvin but his homework. He was the bad boy I wanted but couldn't have. I'd never thought he would pay me a second glance, but when his grandmother got sick, I became just as important to him as he'd secretly been to me.

Ruth Mae became too ill to stay home alone and needed a home health aide. Marilyn was too trifling and Marvin was just a dumb boy running with bullies in the streets to be of any real help, so I became his grandmother's keeper. Anything she needed around the house as far as tending went, I took care of it. If she needed errands run, I ran them. I took on the responsibility of making sure that she was wheeled to church every Sunday and that her meals were prepared, then frozen for the upcoming week. In Marvin's eyes, I was a lifesaver, 'cause he couldn't let the streets go long enough to tend to his dying grandmother, and I was there to pick up the slack. But only the Lord knew I was the one who was really responsible for Ruth Mae's death. That would be a secret I hoped to take to my grave.

He rolled up several blunts, and we worked and smoked until daybreak. Not being able to help myself, I pounced on his dick each time he dropped a hint that he was slightly horny. Murk had me whipped in all type of ways. By the time he walked out of here, my pussy was sore and his roll-around suitcase was full of fraudulent checks, all made out to Thomas Harris. It was a night well worked, and I couldn't wait to punch in for our next shift.

Yoshi

The hot sun had risen and was peeking through my tattered blinds. I couldn't believe it was daytime and time to get up, because I'd dozed off only forty-five minutes ago. I was not ready for another day full of the same depressing shit. All I wanted to do was lounge my exhausted ass in the bed all day—but without Yani. I'd spent nine months anxiously waiting to meet my first daughter, but now I was spending every minute that she was awake wishing I'd waited on getting pregnant. This shit was harder than I had ever imagined it would be.

I guess I'll need another five-hour energy drink to make it through the day, I thought as I rubbed my aching neck and peeled myself off my mattress. From head to toe, my entire body was sore from how Duncan had manhandled me; but my neck and head were hurting the most. I swore it felt like he was trying to snatch the skin off my skull when he dragged me across the sidewalk. Digging through my nightstand drawer, I was praying to God that I had at least one Motrin 800 left over from when I got discharged from the hospital after having Yani. My shit was throbbing like a muthafucka, and the pain was damn near intolerable at this point.

Right before I got ready to give up, I found a tablet, and though it was kinda dirty from being loose in the drawer, I rubbed the dirt off and popped it down my throat as quickly as I could. I was feenin' for the ibuprofen that was packed inside the capsule to hit my bloodstream and give me some much-needed pain relief.

I was about to get up and sneak a shower in when I peeked over my shoulder and saw that Yani was stirring and was about to wake up. *Please go back to sleep.* It felt like her little behind had a LoJack on my body or was still in my tummy.

"Come on, baby girl. Please give Mommy a break, so I can be good for you and to you," I whined, wishing I could get some time to myself so I could cater to myself. All I wanted was a few minutes in a hot shower to let the steam soothe my headache.

Yani had been up every other hour with gas and crying fits. I'd tried rubbing her belly, giving her a warm bath, and even administering Mylicon, but none of those remedies had soothed the gurgling gas in her tiny tummy. I had felt so bad I couldn't stop my baby from suffering.

I felt like shit for wishing I'd never stopped taking my birth control pills, because that meant I was wishing Yani had never been born, but, as I said, being a mother was harder than I had imagined it would be. Especially since Duncan had started to come around less and my mom refused to look out and give me a break.

I thought back to when I had first brought Yani home. It had been all smiles for the first few weeks, when I was in love with her baby smell, the soft curls that graced her head, and the way she smiled in her sleep. Duncan had even stayed overnight on the weekends then, and he had dropped in after school and basketball practice during the week. Then the newness had worn off and I'd realized how stuck I actually was. Yani wasn't on a schedule, she kept me from hanging with my girls, and she hadn't changed my and Duncan's relationship for the better one bit. Her arrival had actually made me and him grow further apart.

I got ready to scoop Yani up, but then I realized she was soaking wet, so I started getting her stuff together for a bath so I could take care of everything at once. Plus, I did not want to waste any diapers. Duncan had been tripping lately about having to go in his pocket for this, that, and anything I asked for regarding Yani, and Lord knows I wasn't trying to piss him off even more.

After I bathed, dried, and dressed Yani, I stretched out my legs on the bed and laid Yani on my chest, trying to give my overworked body a rest. Yesterday had been crazy as hell altogether. I thought about hitting up Bird and Shayla in a three-way message, but I was salty over how them hoes, who I thought for sure were my girls, had pulled up yesterday, expecting we'd hit the streets like we used to do before I got preggo. And then Bird had tried to come for me by slick dissing my relationship with Duncan. Hell yeah, I took it personally, 'cause she was supposed to be my girl. Me, her, and Shayla had shared each other's most private secrets, so Bird's trick of using what I'd confided as ammunition against me was foul. I guess my mom's slimy-acting ass was right—Bird couldn't be trusted. It took a snake to know one.

As far as my heavy-handed baby daddy was concerned, his ass was out in the living room, asleep on the couch right now, 'cause Yani had been too loud last night. He had a lot of nerve, seeing as it was his fault she'd been up anyway. If he hadn't woken me up with a stiff dick, then cum all loud, like he ain't never had none, she'd still be sound asleep. Or at least I thought so.

After the whole ordeal, and after he'd calmed down upon hearing my side of the story, Duncan had stripped me naked, then rubbed down my tender body. He'd fucked me hard, raw, and without remorse, and I'd eventually got into the groove of his pace and enjoyed each stroke. The more sexual pleasure he brought me, the more I forgave him for humiliating me. What else could I do? I needed my little family to come together. I welcomed each ounce of loving, fucking, sexing, and abusing Duncan put on me before leaving a trail of nut leaking from my coochie. As I'd drifted off to sleep, happy to have him totally consumed with me again, I hadn't been the least bit concerned about our past, 'cause I was too busy praying for a better future.

Light tapping on the door pulled me from my thoughts. Duncan peeked his head in, then walked into the room. I watched every move Duncan made, not knowing what tip he was on. Yani had been up most of the night and my mom slept with the TV blasting, so I knew he had barely slept, so the odds of him being pleasant toward me right now were slim.

"Damn, Yo-Yo. Is your motherly instinct off or some shit? How come you couldn't quiet Yani last night?"

"Naw, that's babies for you. Plus, I was just exhausted, and my head hurt from earlier," I snapped, my neck rolling and my eyes making sure to dish him much attitude. "Maybe you'll think of the effect your ass kickings have on me next time." After getting up and handing our daughter over to him, I fell on top of the bed, ready to do some serious drooling on my pillow.

"Look, Yoshi, I already told you that is my bad about yesterday, but I'm not gonna keep apologizing. I was tripping off the vitamins I've been taking to keep my stats up, and you know they give me a mean streak I have a hard time controlling." He could call what he was popping everyday vitamins if he wanted to, but I knew he was taking steroids.

I'd gone through his gym bag a while ago on some insecure shit and found the bottle of enhancers. Although I had agreed to keep his secret, I hadn't agreed on being the person he took his emotions out on when the world became overwhelming. I'd turn from Duncan's heart into his punching bag.

"I get that you're stressed, bae, but you can't keep putting your hands on me. Especially now that Yani's here. You promised me our dynamic would get better." I was careful with my words, so I did not upset him.

"And it will be after I secure this scholarship. All I need you to do is act right and quit making a nigga mad when you know I got everybody on my back about fucking up. I gotta hear my moms talking smack in my ear every time I come chill over here, and then I got my coach trying to throw me on the bench because he do not want me to fuck the scholarship opportunity up and make a waste out of what could be someone else's shot at success."

"Wow! So, they feel me and Yani are distractions?" I kinda got in my feelings, because his mother always smiled in my face, and she'd even shown up at the hospital a few hours after I had Yani.

"Well, y'all kinda are. I've been showing up late to practices, and the last few games I had were off because you been in my head off some bullshit. That is why I'm asking you to fall back and let me lock my deal in. Ball is my world. If my stats slip again, or I mess around and fail one of these finals, I won't be eligible for a top ten school. Florida has still been reaching out to Coach, so I've gotta show him I'm worth the referral."

He went on. "Look, that is my bad on yesterday. All the stress I've been under just got to me more than I could bear. If I do not get this scholarship and get up out the hood, I'm gonna be fucked. Ball is my world, and it's the only way I know fa sho I can take care of Yani in the long run."

"I feel you, baby, but you can't keep using me as your punching bag. I'm supposed to be your girl, your confidante, and the one to massage that stress up out of you, but it's like I gotta carry your burden with these bruises. And that ain't fair. I've been holding you down since the night before you tried out for his ho-ass squad anyway!"

Getting amped up, hating that people were speaking against the love I yearned for so deeply, I hoped my words went further than his hating coach's words did. No, no way in hell I'd let Duncan's life go any further than this bedroom without me. Me, him, and Yani—we were a family. I'd taken enough blows to ensure my position in life forever. Bird, his coach, and whoever else wasn't riding for us might as well get ready to be run over.

"Don't you think I know that? A nigga be trying to do right, Yoshi, but it's like the shit is extra hard now with you riding my back about being a family. I'm just trying to get used to being a father!"

"It ain't like I've been a mother before," I mumbled under my breath, starting to get angry. "You should've thought about that before you started selling my ass all those happily ever after dreams. A bitch got thirsty," I admitted accidentally.

During the whole pregnancy I rode it out that the birth control shot must've gone wrong, but now the truth had slipped out of my overly tired mouth. The cat was totally out of the bag. There was no way I could take the words back or turn them into something that did not make me seem as trifling or conniving as I actually was.

"Thirsty?" His head snapped. With a pure look of confusion on his face, Duncan walked over with Yani in his arms, then laid her beside me in the bed. "Bitch, sit up, so you can explain what the fuck you mean by *thirsty*!" Grabbing me by the back of my neck like I was a cat, he applied pressure and pinched my skin together, making my neck burn, as he snatched me up into a sitting position. "I thought your sneaky ass was on the shot? Were you lying all along, ho? Did you intentionally set me up to trap me?" he yelled, louder than I had ever heard him before. I was sure my mother was wide awake now and was listening with a nosy ear. She'd never been a fan of mine, but she'd always been a fan of Duncan putting his hands on me.

"Please do not hit me. I ain't mean it like that!" Jumping up, guarding my face, I prepped myself for his wild blows.

"My mama was right about taking Yani from yo' trife-life ass. She said your slimy ass probably set me up in the first place, 'cause I had a future." At first, Duncan stood over me, with balled fists, spitting rage, but now he was running around the room, grabbing everything he could fit into Yani's diaper bag.

"Quit touching her stuff! You ain't taking my daughter nowhere!" I reached out to grab her onesies from his hands, but he snatched them back, then roughly pushed me down onto the bed.

"Bitch, back up off me. I'm not about to leave her here so you can play that childish game about me not seeing her. Me and mine about to leave your wannabe entrapment ass. The joke is about to be on you!" He scooped up the diaper bag and then Yani, and I jumped on his back, refusing to sit by while he walked out of the house with my daughter. It wasn't no secret his mother hated me but adored Yani. She's been wanting to get her tubal ligation–having hands on my little girl ever since I had brought her home from the hospital. Who knew when he'd bring Yani back if he got her out of here with us on bad terms.

"Put my daughter down, nigga! She ain't even yours!" I said the only thing I knew would get him mad enough not to go through with his intentions, but I wished I did not have to. It would be hard to come back from the lie, but right about now, it was worth it.

"Oh, okay then." After backing me up into the wall, he knocked the wind out of me, giving me no choice but to let go, then slide down onto the floor. "Your lies done caught up with your ass today!" He tosses Yani onto the bed. I could see that she was beet red. She was screaming at the top of her lungs from being caught up in our fight. "Do not call my phone no more with ya' sack-chasing ass! Find ya' kid's daddy!" With that, Duncan stormed out of the house, but this time I did not chase after him.

I quickly grabbed my baby and cradled her in my arms. I'd never held her so tightly and regretfully in my life. I loved her so much, but I was so sorry for bringing her into a fucked-up world, with so much hate between the people who were supposed to be nurturing and protecting her. I knew I needed to get mentally stronger for the position I'd signed on for.

"I'm sorry, angel. I promise to try my best to fix things with your father so we can be a family, but if he doesn't come back, I promise to never leave you. Mommy's got you." I was making promises I was not sure I could keep.

As if my world wasn't spinning enough out of control, my mother came along just then, and everything got nastier.

"I see you have run that child's daddy up out of here." My mother stood in the doorway, with a condescending grin on her face. "It's gonna be hard as hell to raise that child on your own, Yoshi. Between all the whining, tantrums, and bullshit she's gonna take you through, you're gonna know how it feels to be me in no time. Ain't no man checking for no li'l hot ho with kids. They barely want the responsibility of what they make, let alone some other nigga's seed. I can't believe you're that damn dumb!"

"Me either. Now, can you please close my door back how you found it?"

She just stood there and looked at me.

I went on. "The only thing dumb about me is that I thought you'd finally start to have my back. Why do you always have to cut into me so hard, like you hate me?"

"Aw, girl, being dumb and so emotional. Just because I don't like you doesn't mean I hate you. And you know me better than anyone else out here. I don't sell fairy tales or pass out lollipops and gumballs. There ain't no way around shit stanking! Tell me something, Yoshi. Humor me for a second, if you don't mind." As she shifted her weight to her right foot and folded her arms, I could tell Karen was in rare form, ready to read me up and down.

"Did you think Duncan was gonna stay fooling around with your ass once he went off to school?"

I rolled my eyes, not wanting to be bothered with the conversation, since I knew exactly where the banter was going. She was getting a kick out of my heart breaking. I didn't believe what she'd just said about not liking me: there couldn't have been nothing but hate in her heart for me, because she had never shown me love. Hell, I barely ever got a piece of pity. She had always said Duncan was using me for nothing other than to keep his nuts warm while he got scouted. The truth hurt bad as hell, probably more, because she was right.

"Whatever. Ma. I ain't trying to hear all this right now," I finally said. I was trying every way I knew to soothe Yani and quiet her whimpers. I was sure she could feel all the tension bouncing around in this house.

She ignored my plea. "I mean for real, tell ya' mama, did you think you were the star-pupil hood rat that came up with the secret recipe for a golden egg? That boy wasn't never gonna take you out the hood. You were searching for love in the wrong league. You best start checking for one of these corner boys who don't give a fuck about a loose coochie, 'cause I know what steroid-taking mutha-fucka done wore the elastic out that cat."

I wanted to get up and swing on her ass, but, of course, I dropped my head and cried instead. I was too tired of pain.

Chapter Eight

Artavia

My stomach grumbled from anxiety and irritation as soon as I heard Murk's phone vibrate on the floor. I knew it would be only a matter of moments before he slid from beside me, out of the bed, and into his drawers. Sadly, I'd grown accustomed to him sexing me like a savage and then leaving me like I wasn't shit but his side slut. Reality stung.

Why can't this nigga love me the way I love him? Damn. I thought.

I considered play drooling, like I was knocked out from the massive nut I'd just bust, but he was tugging at my heart on his way out the door. I couldn't keep my fronts up. With Murk, I'd always worn my emotions on my sleeve. "I hope you weren't planning to dip and not at least tell me goodbye," I said. My voice caught him off guard, 'cause I saw him rush to slide his phone back into his pocket. It was too late, though, as I'd already caught the quick li'l smirk.

"Aw, shit, Tay. I didn't know you were awake." Murk looked over his shoulder at me, then leaned back over the bed and kissed my quivering lips. Each time he kissed me was like the very first time all over again, and it had been years since he stole my innocence—and virginity. I had history with him that was much deeper than that of whoever was hitting him up. I knew that for sure.

"I was dozing off—until you got out of the bed. You know I'm a light sleeper. And you know I toss and turn without your big-head ass next to me."

"Yeah, I know. But all this heavy-ass dick that I dropped off in yo' guts last night should've had you tapped out for the count," he replied. His thuggish ass had the nerve to be smirking because he knew I was sprung off his sex.

"I could say the same for you. I mean, if you put it down and all, shouldn't you be knocked out in this comfy-ass bed you bought me?" I slid around the bed, making it seem extra comfortable, warm, and inviting. "Why'd you get a new one if you weren't going to break it all the way in?" I was throwing hints and innuendos but he was ignoring them or refusing to pick up on them. Either way, it was starting to look like I'd be spending yet another day alone.

"Damn. You're cutting into a nigga real raw, like I just did not have you climbing that headboard, screaming my name. Go on and take that pretty self of yours back to sleep so you can be well rested for this afternoon. I'll be back through here with Tom after we get down in the streets."

"But, damn, it's barely seven in the morning," I said. "You and I both know ain't no banks open this early, and when they do unlock the doors, your ass will be puffing on Kush or snoring. It's too early for you to be playing games."

"Whoa. Slow down, Tay. Since when did me and you get on the level to where you could start checking me on some relationship-type shit? If you cannot handle mixing business with pleasure without giving a nigga a hard time, then I can take this dick right up out your life. I ain't got time for confusion, Tay. And you already know that." I could tell by the creases in his forehead that he was irritated and pissed, but I wasn't in the mood to have my feelings dismissed.

"I beg to differ about you not wanting drama in your life, Murk. You're the one who has got bitches blowing up his phone all night and then at the crack of ass in the morning. But whatever. We will see how you act when I start passing out this pussy." I purposely crawled out of the bed and let all my juicy ass hang out in his face before I wrapped my silk robe around my body.

As quickly as my ego had shot up, Murk stuck a pin in it and deflated my spirits. This nigga always went for a gut shot with whomever he had a beef, and heartbreakingly, I was finding out my loyalty wasn't giving me a pass. "If you want to make that pussy for everybody, shorty, be my guest. It ain't got my name on it, and I'm not trying to stop you from doing yo' thang or finding your forever-after nigga or whatever. The only relationship me and you got going on that you need to be faithful to is 5-Star."

How dare he come at me like this? I've devoted my life to him and his family. This is some straight bullshit, I thought.

"I haven't forgotten, and that is why I'm about to go hard on you, nigga," I told him. "I'm a woman with needs, and they go further than just us staying cooped up behind these four walls, ruining people's credit." I was dishing him back the same attitude.

"I ain't stopping you from getting your needs met. The only relationship you've gotta be faithful to is 5-Star. That pussy ain't got my name on it. We good on that?"

Murk was leaving me looking stupid. With him stating his position with so much authority, what else could I do but agree that we were good?

"Good. Now, have your shit together by the time I link back up with you tonight."

He dropped my commission on the dresser, as usual, then picked up the stack of checks I had printed last night. Then he headed to the front door. I went into the hallway and observed him from there. I wasn't about to chase after him. This nigga had my heart racing with so much negative emotion.

I was seething with hate and bitterness as I watched the front door open and close and separate us. I went back into my bedroom, Instead of searching for the Zoloft that my psychiatrist had prescribed for me to take daily, I reached for the Kush-filled medicinal weed I'd chosen to medicate myself with instead and lit a blunt. I hated the way the oblong blue pills made me feel. Though they were tiny in size, they were potent and had me too mellow and calm through Murk's bullshit and disappointment. It was time I started facing the pain and making his ass feel some too.

"Naw, nigga, we ain't good," I mumbled under my breath as the anxiety in my chest started building. Puffing out a large cloud of thick gray smoke, I rocked back and forth as I waited for my phone to power back on. "You can run, but you can't hide."

Naw, nigga. We are not good, as a matter of fact. I leaned against the wall and then slid down it in a dazed-like state, but I was very much aware of my feelings, my surroundings, and my future intentions.

Chapter Nine

Shayla

Tom-Tom tapped twice on my door. "Sis, are you up?"

"No, I wasn't." My eyes were heavy, but I managed to pry them open and wipe the crust from the corners. "But you know it's cool. Come in, bro. Is everything okay?" I sat up against my squeaky headboard, yawning, and stretched. I hadn't too long ago gone to bed.

"Yeah, it's actually never been better," he responded coolly, sounding shocked that for once there was not bad news on the floor. Then he continued, "But, anyway, you can go back to sleep, 'cause I did not want shit serious. I just wanted to let you know I was about to make a few runs with Murk and would be gone for a couple of hours. I did not want you questioning any of the fellas about my whereabouts."

"Your whereabouts? And where will that be at exactly?" I was curious about how he was getting money with Murk. Very curious. I was planning on doing a little low-key snooping with Bird whenever we hooked up to see if I could find out more about Murk's get rich scam. I did not want Tom-Tom in way over his head.

"Do not worry about all that, li'l sis. All you need to worry about is jumping fresh today. Have you figured out what you're going to wear?" He walked over to my closet and started inspecting how I'd hung all the clothes up since last night. "Well, shit, I see you went off and did a whole redecoration in here. It looks hella nice."

Along with all the stuff from the mall Tom-Tom had purchased for me, he'd also put some money in my pocket and paid my phone bill. I had taken the money and walked to the local store for some peel-and-stick inspirational quotes, a new comforter, and some other cute girly things to make my room more comfortable. My hands had ached on the way home because I had so many bags. But I had smiled through it.

"Thank you, and thank you for the money that paid for it. But nope, I have not figured out what outfit I'm popping the tag on. I've never had so many options." It was a good, yet overwhelming feeling to have.

"It's 'bout time we have more than none." We shared a second of silence, probably thinking the exact same thing but not wanting to speak on it and curse the good streak of luck Thomas was coasting on. Luck hadn't lived in our lives in a very long time. The feeling was uncommon.

His ringing cell broke that silence. After pulling out a brand-new iPhone, he started moving his fingers across the screen, typing what I assumed was a text message.

"Oh, okay! I see how you're stunting, but I'm still out here with an outdated free phone," I huffed. "I'll take the purple iPhone since you're out here doing upgrades." I smacked my lips, kinda salty that he hadn't copped me one with his.

"I see you're learning the game fast, brat. We can hit the cell phone store up later. I got you." He shook his head, laughing.

It was then that I paid attention to how Tom-Tom was dressed. In a pair of khaki-colored slacks, a button-up polo shirt, dress shoes, and a grown man–looking watch that looked like it cost a grip, he was casual and clean-cut.

"Where are you about to go? To get baptized or a job interview?" I raised my brow, low key doubling back to the initial question.

"Neither, but I see you've got jokes." He chuckled as he smooth talked his way right around answering my question again. "But I'll be back in time for the block party. Hit my line if you need me or if it's an emergency. I love you, sis."

"Love you back, bro. And be careful doing whatever it is you're about to do," I warned, feeling even more uneasy about him hustling with Murk since he was being overly secretive about it.

"I'm good, sis. Trust. The last thing I want you doing today is worrying about me. So get up, cute, and do whatever it is that you do with your girls, without all that worry on your back we usually have. I'll see you in a few hours, a'ight?"

Tom-Tom wasn't about to take heed of my warning, nor was I trying to mess up his mental for whatever hustle he was about to go do with Murk by stressing him. Instead of me continuing to harp on it, I let the whole matter go and leaned in for his quick forehead kiss. "All right. I will see you later, and then we can go get that phone," I said. I threw the last part in for good humor, letting him know I was done tripping.

"You got it. I gotta bounce before we be late, though," he replied, then started rushing. His phone rang as soon as he got on the other side of the door, and he answered with the quickness. "My bad. I was talking to Shayla, but I'm about to walk out the door right now. I'll be at your crib in a hot sec." His words drifted off; then the front door slammed.

Ten seconds later, my father's record player tuned up and had me jumping out of the bed to get out of the house. In between him staying up all night, blasting old blues records that him and Rose used to spin all the time and banging his bag wife, which was what I called his drugs, I'd barely slept. I wanted to chase some z's for a few more hours, since the picnic wasn't till late this afternoon, but that was a dream deferred, literally. I was learning all about misery loving company the hard way. And Ricardo's grief was intense. Ricardo had never remarried or even got serious about another woman after my mother left, at least that I knew of. And he always drowned himself in alcohol, drugs, and memories of him and my mom around this time of the year. My pops had that graveyard type of love for Rose, even after all these years. I never wanted to love a person that hard. I was planning on staying as far away from this house as possible today. Even if that meant posting up at the park all day.

I ended up trying on three different outfits before finally settling on a pink-and-white Nike short set with a matching pair of Air Max sneakers that jumped off the set perfectly. It was a simple and chill, yet very cute outfit for the occasion, and it did not scream, "Look at me. I've got on some new clothes, and I'm trying to stunt." I wasn't trying to apply pressure, just finally fit in. It felt good not having to rearrange and remix the same tired-ass clothes Bird had made sure to take a picture of herself in before she handed them down to me. I couldn't help but wonder if she'd be happy about my glow up or if she'd think my shine dimmed hers. Bird had always been a wild card, but her behavior as of late had me thinking it was always rooted in hate. Especially the way she had turned on Yoshi. I was planning on paying very close attention to her first reaction when she saw me, because it'd be the most real. That I knew for sure.

Dialing Yoshi's number, I was hoping that I'd given her enough time to calm down and that she wasn't about to start snapping off as soon as she answered the phone—if she answered. Out of us three, even though we all had personal drama within our families, Yoshi was the only one who was actually going through it on a daily basis by getting shit on by her moms *and* her nigga. Duncan was supposed to be her happily ever after out the hood, but he was turning out to be her graveyard love. There wasn't much I could get in the middle of, but I knew I needed to be more supportive of her as her friend. Especially since Bird was flopping like a fish out of water in the friend department.

"Hello," Yoshi answered dryly.

"I know I'm not your favorite person this morning."

"Nope, not really. But you're not as high up on my shit list as Bird." She said her name with disgust.

"Well, at least you're being honest," I replied. I wasn't bitter about what I already expected and deserved. I would've felt the same way had she and Bird pulled off on me while I was getting slapped up by my boyfriend, if I had one. "But that's why I was reaching out to you. I wanted to apologize for not being able to break you and Bird up, as well as not stopping it before it escalated. I can't really apologize for not jumping in between you and your baby daddy, but you already know I try to stay out of y'all beefs." I was sincere.

Unfortunately, yesterday was not the first time Duncan had put his hands on Yoshi in a physically abusive way. I had made the mistake of trying to break them apart once by physically inserting myself between them and trying to push Duncan back from choking her, and he had ended up shoving me across the room. I couldn't lie and say he did not knock all the spunk and energy out of my body, but I would've been willing to get up and defend my friend again had she not begged me to leave the situation alone. I had felt dumb as hell and had got cursed out by Tom-Tom later than night, once Duncan had told him what happened. "You can't fight no couple, sis. You'll get hurt while trying to fight for Yoshi, and then she'll be cuddled up with that nigga and treating you funny." Tom hadn't been lying, because the very next morning, I'd seen a picture of Yoshi and Duncan booed up on her social media story.

"Girl bye, it's a little too late to act like you care. I feel like a whole fucking fool for believing you and Bird were my best friends." Yoshi wasn't letting up.

"Whoa! Why are you coming on me like that? I know I got a little shade coming, but damn! You're going off on me like I was the one beefing with you and trying to fight. I was the one trying to keep the peace and break you two up, if you do not remember," I told her. I was about two seconds from hanging up on Yoshi and letting her come around when she was ready. I had almost got hit while trying to keep Bird from choking her up, but she wasn't giving me credit for that.

She sighed. "That is my bad. I'll give you that. And I'm willing to admit I'm probably taking everything out on you. But I'm stressed to the max. A lot has gone down since we last kicked it. I'm convinced Karen has a life insurance policy on me and Duncan is helping her take me out the game. They are making me so miserable."

"I'm sorry, sis," was all I said. I did not know what else to say, but I did allow her time to throw a "woe is me" party and vent. It was beyond crazy how her mother treated her, but more so how she allowed her daughter to be treated by Duncan.

"What are you about to get into within the next hour?" I asked her after she had vented. "If ya' crazy-ass moms is gone, I want to fall through, so maybe we could get a session started or just kick it on some chill shit. I know you don't have a babysitter for Yani, so your options are

Starving for Love 109

limited." It wasn't like I had a plethora of options, either, so her situation kinda worked for me as well. Her and Bird had always been hitting the streets before she got pregnant, which was another reason Yoshi felt that Bird had abandoned her and that she wasn't a real friend.

"Yeah, thankfully, she's gone to work a double shift. God heard my prayers last night to get her out this house so I could get some hours of peace. I swear, her mean ass can't get through one twenty-four-hour day without doing something that's spiteful toward me, and I can't figure out what made her hate me so much. So please, please, please come save my mind from wandering. Between Bird's bullshit, Duncan's temper, Yani's neediness, Karen's hatred, and this large-ass packet of make-up work I have to turn in so I can graduate on time, I'm thinking about taking a handful of these damn pain pills and ending it all . . ." Her voice trailed off.

I didn't know if she was serious, but I wasn't about to ignore her mentioning suicide. "Well, try to hold it together, boo. I got you. Once I get out of the shower, I'll grab a bag of some good-good and be that way. Do you want me to call Bird, so y'all can make up?" Not sure if I should jump back in the middle, but I was used to our dynamic trio.

"I'm good on that. I need a break from that bougie bitch. But I'm about to feed Yani, so she can go down for her nap, so me and you can chill. See you in a minute, but hurry up. I'm antsy and bored as hell."

"Okay, see you in a minute, and I have a surprise for you." I couldn't wait for her to see all the cute little outfits I'd gotten Yani from the mall. Plus, I needed to spend some time with my goddaughter.

As soon as I hung up with Yoshi, I picked out my favorite-smelling shower gel and lotion set that I'd stolen from the mall. After showering, I put some pep in my step so I could make it to Yoshi's before she got too deep in her thoughts and hurt herself for real. I'd never heard her mention depression in all the years she'd been dealing with her mother's abuse and in the briefer time she'd endured Duncan's physical and emotional abuse. But that didn't mean she wasn't about to break from the pressure.

As soon as I walked out of my room after getting dressed, I wanted to duck back in, but it was too late.

"Morning, baby!" Ricardo exclaimed in a booming voice as he walked down the hallway. He was high as a kite for sure. You could always tell from his loud, hyper, explosive behavior.

"Good morning," I responded dryly, hoping he kept it moving wherever he was going.

"I was thinking that we could spend a little father-daughter time together today. We haven't done that in a long time." He tried hugging me, but I backed away.

Ricardo repulsed me. Plus, I knew his hands had been all over some random dirty street walker all night. And ain't no telling where her hands had been. I would've asked him whether he was high, but we both knew that was a given. He was a walking germ, which was why most days I wished he'd just move into one of the dope houses he liked visiting so much, so he wouldn't bring something home with him.

I might tell Tom-Tom that he should start making him strip down in the backyard before he comes inside the house, now that I think of it.

"Come on now, Pops. Let's not even go there. You know I'm straight on us spending time together, especially till you get into a meeting at least. I'm trying to bite my tongue, but you're high right now, so the shit you're saying ain't even *you* talking, but the dope." I pushed past him and dashed into the bathroom, then slammed the door so hard, more of the plaster fell from the ceiling. This entire house was in terrible condition and was going to end up falling on our heads.

Ricardo irked me. His breath, body, and clothes reeked of Paul Masson. Not to mention the residue from his chosen passion was still underneath his nose. I was doing him a favor by keeping my feelings bottled up, because I didn't want him overdosing off the truth. In terms of my age, I was damn near grown; but on the inside, I was still harboring ill feelings for all the shortcomings, embarrassments, and lies I'd had to deal with from Ricardo. It didn't matter that he was chasing forgiveness *now*. I was still hurting from the *then*. And a large part of me kinda wanted him to hurt just as badly as he'd made me hurt with the little support he'd given me. I wasn't applying the same level of disrespect and pressure that Tom-Tom was, but our walks through childhood were vastly different because of our ages. Either way, I wasn't fuckin' with Ricardo.

Ricardo

Shayla's behavior reminded me of how Rose had acted right before she left me and this family. I knew my daughter was not using drugs, but I knew she was mad at me for using them. I used to be her superhero. Every man that was in his daughter's life was her superhero. I had been so successful at the job I had, and so proud of the lifestyle I'd built for Rose, Thomas, Shayla, and myself, that I'd become one of the guys old folks bragged about in the hood and a guy young bucks looked up to. But I had fucked all that up on a rock. But I did not know what else would numb the pain Rose had caused my soul. Her wrongs had done more than break my heart, and to preserve her conscience, I had never told her that I started hitting the pipe the day I found out she'd lied about Shayla being my kid.

During one school day years ago, the school had tried calling Rose and hadn't been able to reach her. It had turned out that Shayla had a temperature that had shot up too high for them to keep her on school grounds, and they had her transported via ambulance to Children's Hospital. They'd called me by that time, and I'd jumped off my line and met the ambulance at the emergency-room entrance. Rose was still unavailable, and the next-door neighbor did not see her car at home, so I was double worried about my wife's safety.

Shayla's temperature was so high that the doctors took my blood for "just in case" purposes, and then they had to save my life when the results came back with 99.9% certainty that I did not have a daughter at all. I had never thought I had to question Rose about being sure I was her children's father, and having the legal right to deny Shayla had me wondering if my blood ran through Thomas's veins. I couldn't help wanting to know how deep my wife's betrayal had gone throughout the years. I had thought I was an upstanding and responsible man by keeping a job, spoiling her and the kids with everything their hearts desired, and never cheating on my wife, but the bitter truth was that I was a fool. As a man, I knew I'd brought this all on myself, but it did not make the punch to the gut seem any less severe.

With the pit of my stomach bubbling now over the past, and my mind thinking too much, I had to get high, but my resources were scarce. It was too early for me to scrape up bottles; plus, I'd spent all the loose change I'd collected yesterday on drugs to share with rock trick. This might've seemed low, but times were hard. Desperate times called for desperate measures.

I had heard Shayla lock the bathroom door behind her, and I knew Tom did not come out till at least waking or baking first. As soon as I heard the shower curtain slide across the rail in the bathroom, I ran down the hallway to Shayla's room to find something I could steal and then sell for a quick few dollars. All I needed was five dollars to drift off to a pain-free place. Once again, I was hitting rock bottom, but being down there did not stop me from entering my daughter's bedroom. When she was a little kid, I used to read her bedtime stories, play make-believe tea parties with her, and scare away all the monsters my little girl saw in this bedroom. Bit if she caught me in here today, she'd scream and go crazy, since she'd know I was in here to steal.

Her bed was covered in brand-new boxes of soap, lotion, women's body products, baby clothes, undergarments—enough stuff to get me a bottle of Paul Masson to wash my rock down. After grabbing one of the Target bags that lay next to the bed, I rushed to fill it all the way up. With all I was taking, you still couldn't tell anything was missing. Li'l Tom's ass sure was looking out for his sister. Good thing Shayla had him, 'cause I've been a sucka sold to the game for years.

I darted out of Shayla's bedroom, then ran out of the house in just my tattered house shoes, worn-out flannel print pajama pants with holes all over them, and a stretched-out yellow, stained undershirt. The convenience of living in the hood was that there was always a dope spot a few feet away. I half tripped up the spot's driveway to the side door, tapped on the window, then was told to come in. It was time to do some bargaining to see what I could get for this stuff I'd just clipped from Shayla.

I held up the Target bag. "Hey, my manz, I know you said not to fuck with you on no nickel-and-dime shit, but this might be good. Can I get a twenty-dollar spot for this whole bag?"

Chapter Ten

Bird

"Right there! Please do not stop or slow up. I needed this so bad, Jay." I grabbed at Jayson's head and pulled him closer to me, giving my hands a break at the same time. My fingers were aching from clawing at the mattress as his tongue danced with my clitoris. Jayson was giving me some all-star head. "I missed you so much. I swear I'm done tripping." I was willing to apologize and make whatever promise necessary for Jayson to keep my body on the flight of pleasure it was on. So caught up in Murk's stroke game, I'd forgotten all about Jayson's attentiveness and desire to cater to my body. I was being worked out instead of overworked.

There was a thin line between love and lust, and it was obvious Jayson wasn't the one. I had been irritated to the tenth power when he popped up on me while I was on the porch, because he wasn't the one I had wanted to see, but now that feeling had passed and been replaced with pure pleasure. I'd been so twisted up with Murk's stroke that I'd forgotten all about Jayson's head game. If I could put Murk and Jayson together, I would have the perfect boyfriend.

"It feels so good," I purred as I finally felt a wave of hotness rush over my body.

"Yes, baby. Damn you taste good." He was slurping my juices up as the orgasmic wave rode through my body until I was limp.

Though I grabbed his head so he couldn't move, Jayson did not even try to budge as he loved the taste of my milkshake. From the convulsions my body was going through, I thought it was even obvious to him I was glad he'd popped up. Lucky for him and, I guessed, for me too, I'd been at home. I'd been checking for Murk's truck to pull back up when Jayson surprised me.

"Whose pussy is this?" He was rightfully cocky as he lifted his head from between my thighs.

"Yours, Daddy! I love you," I squealed as he whipped out his hard manhood, thinking he was working with a monster. Murk was thicker and bigger, but I wasn't getting ready to turn down another nut. No way! After stroking it a few times, making sure it was hard and ready, he held my pussy lips open with his fingers, then guided his dick inside me.

"I love you too, girl!" As he rubbed my G-spot with his fingertip, I realized he must've been watching pornos, 'cause his sex game had been stepped all the way up. "Spread them legs out wider. Let me dig them guts." Now Jayson was just wishing. His stroke might've been better, but my guts were still gonna go untouched.

"Beat this pussy up, Daddy!" I grabbed his back, show-ing him I'd learned something new too. Murk liked me to talk dirty and take it rough when getting dicked down. In the few times we'd done it, I'd been turned on to the point of squirting, so yeah, I was a downright freak in the bedroom.

Sweat gathered around Jayson's forehead as his mouth hung open in his desperation to hold on. I could tell that the way I was working my pussy muscles around his dick now was too much for him to keep stroking me with a sac full of nut. He was only seconds from cumming.

"Shit. You feel too good!" he yelled.

The tighter Jayson squeezed his eyes closed, the more I left scratches across his back. Any chick that came after me was gonna know I'd been here fa sho! "Get up in this pussy, Daddy. It's yours!" I yelled. My mother was working a double, so I knew she wasn't home, but if she was, it would not matter, since she had turned me into the sex fiend I was.

I felt his dick going soft as it pumped thick semen deep into my walls. "Aah!" He continued to enjoy the warmth as he made good on his word to fill me up with cum. "You on the pill, right?" he panted near my ear, still letting his cum flow freely.

"It's a little too late for that question, don't you think?" I pushed him up off me, now totally turned off.

"Oh my God. Lay back down, so I can fuck your ass back quiet. That is the only time we get along!" Sitting up, trying to stroke his dick and make it hard, he was serious as ever, but I wasn't getting ready to give him a drop more.

I laughed. "Boy, you sound silly as hell. I'm not even in the mood anymore. I'm not turned on with this whole situation anymore," I huffed. "What type of dude asks if they girl is on the pill during the climax of sex? I couldn't even get my nut!"

"What was that tsunami you just made happen on my mouth? Your ass is tripping!" As he slid on his boxers, I figured Jayson might as well get fully dressed, 'cause he wasn't about to lie up around here. I had plans for the day, which did not include him.

"I'm not the one tripping, but whatever!" I retorted. "If you think I'm trying to end up like Yoshi's ass, you've got me all the way fucked up. I've got plans for my life, and being tied to you and some crybaby kid for the rest of it ain't part of 'em!"

"Hey, you ain't said shit but a word. I'm tired of dealing with your psycho-ass mood swings anyway. There's only so much of Beatrice a nigga can take. I'm out!" Just like that Jayson was dressed and heading for the door.

"Make sure you turn the bottom lock on your way out, you clown-ass nigga!" I wasn't into chasing no nigga with lightweight pockets, and since Jayson was the number one candidate in that category, he wasn't worth the energy.

After entering the passcode to my phone, I dialed Murk's number from memory but was sent straight to voicemail. Just as I slid underneath the covers, thinking I'd struck out, my text notification went off.

Send me a picture. Make it good. This nigga loved to play nasty.

As I pulled my spaghetti-strap shirt down, I saw my nipples were still hard from Jayson playing with them earlier. I snapped a few pictures, looked through them to see which was the best one, then sent him one with a reply. Send me one back and make it better.

Two seconds later another text came through. Send me a video with your clit. You know I like it slippery and wet.

This nigga was playing. Where was my naughty picture? Nope, 'cause I see you do not play fair.

After waiting for five minutes and not getting a response from him, I got busy making the video. For some reason, Shayla's words about him getting bored with me had stuck in my mind. Every girl wanted a piece of Murk, so I had better do all that I could to keep him wanting a piece of me. Once the video was ready, I wrote him a text. This is the best you'll ever have. I hit SEND on the video message, then slid my finger back into my vagina. I'd gotten myself worked up while trying to entice him.

A minute later Murk texted back, with an attached picture of his hardened manhood. Bring ya' ass down here, girl. This dick is waiting for some mouth and lip service. When I read the text, my coochie walls softened up even more than they already were. It was crazy how much I stayed feenin' for this man. Since I was already thirsty for his attention, he did not have to beg me twice or make me any promises to get me out of my bed and into his. And, of course, I gave less than two fucks that Jayson and I had just been laid up.

I couldn't jump up out of my bed fast enough, in fact. Jayson hadn't been gone ten minutes, and I was already on to the next. "Well, Dad, I know you're proud. You made me this way," I said aloud as I peered up at the slice of sky visible through my bedroom window. Every now and then, I talked to my dad about the sexual promiscuity he had single-handedly taught me.

Artavia

As I slid farther down in the driver's seat of the Toyota Corolla that belonged to the crackhead in my project tower's lobby, I was glad he loaned his car out for rocks. The ten-dollar spot was well worth it not to be identified by Murk and possibly fuck up what we had. I'd heard what he said earlier, but I knew he did not mean it. We had too much of a history for him not to be in love with me. And what I was doing now wasn't stalking; it was watching my investment. I surveyed the neighborhood to see who might be watching me. In the hood, there were always bird-watchers and nosy neighbors on the prowl for gossip or an opportunity to snitch. This might not have been my hood, but the same rules were applicable everywhere.

Murk's house was completely still and quiet. You would not have thought he was inside, but I was crafty with my shit. What was the purpose of being a computer geek if you could not use those skills to your advantage? I had installed a GPS tracker on his phone when he first got it, and it provided me his location points at all times. These Androids were on a business account, so, of course, they had arrived at my house first. He knew nothing about this, of course: the application was installed privately, and he had no way to recognize it. He always thought he was one up on everyone around him, but I wasn't to be slept on—believe that. Most chicks were juveniles when it came to blowing up their man's spot. Naw, not me. I moved on a much craftier level.

Chapter Eleven

Shayla

I wanted to cry as I looked at the reflection of myself in my bedroom mirror. I couldn't remember when my feet were graced with a pair of new sneakers that I hadn't crept out of a store with because they were stolen. I'd lost count of how many times I'd switched my worn-out shoes for a new pair and left the box tucked away in the store. Still, none of them went as hard as these kicks went. The price on the box and online was a buck fifty, and that alone had me feeling like I was walking on clouds. Plus, the outfit was cute and fresher than ever. My brother had good taste.

I was hoping Yoshi was prepared to forgive me, so I could beg her to flat-iron my hair or put some curls in it. I normally did not care about stuff like that, since my clothes were raggedy, anyway, but I wanted to be sweet and neat from head to toe. I had never caught on how to do hair, apply makeup, or do all that girly shit that a lot of girls learned from their mothers. I was more of a tomboy and comfortable with my hair tied back in a ponytail.

In a house with two men, one of whom could care less about his hygiene, I was lucky to have picked up my hygiene skills from Rose while she was here. But I hurried up and pushed the thought of her cowardly ass out my mind. I did not want anything ruining my day.

After pulling my hair into yet another ponytail, I found the lip gloss and fashion hoops I'd gotten from the dollar store yesterday.

Once I was all ready, I grabbed the Target bags filled with clothes for Yani off my bed and left the room. I headed out the front door, and when I hit the sidewalk, I saw Bird's car pulling over to the curb.

Bird hopped out of her car, dressed in her pajamas. She was obviously making a booty call run to Murk. "Where are you about to go?" she called.

"Around the corner to Yoshi's." I held up the bags full of Yani's clothes and opened my arms wide enough for her to see my crispy pink shirt. I'd decided against the white one, not wanting to get it dirty at the park later.

"Oh, okay, call me later, You might want to go the other way to her house. Your dad is nodding down that way," was all she said. Then she rushed past me, hurried up Murk's steps, then disappeared behind his black steel security door. Not only had she not given me grief about hooking up with Yo-Yo, but she also hadn't noticed my new kicks or outfit.

At least she'd warned me about Ricardo. To avoid a potential scene, I turned the other way and kept it moving. Seeing the man who had given me life doped up wasn't really how I was trying to start my day.

Artavia

Murk had me all the way fucked up. As I watched the girl damn near break her neck to get through his front door, it took everything in me not to jump out of the car and beat the bones out of the skinny bitch. She ain't have nothing on me, believe that. "Oh yeah, Murk? So it's like that? Fuck me, huh? My pussy ain't enough?" I muttered out loud. Rage was taking over me, and all I could see was red. I couldn't believe that after all the hot, wet pussy I'd put on him last night, he'd still managed to bust camp right after daybreak so he could come ram another girl. I had practically thrown cum back his way, but nothing had worked. Now I saw why. It was official: I'd become common.

It was painfully obvious I was in deep with him, but from the wild, reckless way he was handling my heart, I was just one among many hoes' names on his roster. After I had given up the chance to earn a bachelor's degree so that I could help him racketeer, he damn well had better start taking our relationship more seriously. This getting used shit was starting to get played out. It was time to rattle his life up some and let some secrets loose. It was about time he got reunited with some pain.

Infuriated, I started the car, then revved the engine. Fuck watching my investment; it was time to protect it. First, I pulled up close enough to ole girl's car to read the license plate, and then I burned rubber down the street in order to get out of sight. I did not even think twice about slowing down after almost running down a dust bucket–looking nigga in my getaway. "Get the fuck out of my way, old head," I yelled out loud, swerving to prevent catching a case. He barely noticed almost becoming roadkill as he nodded in the middle of the street, in his pajamas.

Chapter Twelve

Murk

I'd be lying if I said I was shocked about how Artavia had cut up this morning, especially after I had rocked her guts loose with this monster. She'd been in love with me since we were teenagers, and me not making our relationship official years ago had her heated. I wasn't fronting like I wasn't leading her on. I knew shorty was starting to develop feelings that were way too deep for the messiness that I was on. But I wasn't used to catering to no chick's feelings, especially since I was technically traumatized from the issue with Marilyn.

I had always thought the teachers and counselors at school weren't doing nothing but trying to fuck with Grams and put me in the slow learners' class when I was in elementary school, cutting up—but that was because they had seen the red flags early. I had acted out to get attention. Then had acted out when I didn't get it. I probably would've gotten caught up in the jets on some dumb shit if Tay hadn't started coming around and keeping me distracted. Her feisty ass had been a valuable player in my life, but I really didn't know how to handle her—or accept the *love* she was giving. Having my cake and eating it to would be Tay playing her role until I smoothed out all the kinks in my life. Thankfully, she'd printed all the checks for Tom to run through the banks this afternoon *before* her explosion, so our pockets would be laced for the li'l hood festivity later. But I also needed her to keep making money moves like she'd been doing, so there would be no hiccup in the game plan.

After picking up my cell, I went to call her so I could smooth things over and make sure we were still on the same page as far as our hustle was concerned. But I was sidetracked by Bird's sexy text messages. This girl was wild as hell, and I was loving it. She was sending pic after pic of her li'l tight coochie, and in an instant, I was ready to beat it up. She was one of the freakiest short-ies I'd ever gotten down with. It was downhill from there as far as Tay was concerned, at least for now. Bird had my undivided attention. She was something new, fresh, young, and dumb to get down with. I liked the thrill and rush she brought to the table; plus, I wasn't tied down in a relationship to worry out repercussions. With her, there weren't any strings or attachments, and she didn't know anything about my past that she could try manipu-lating me with. It was also a major bonus that she had a li'l boyfriend. Wasn't shit about what we were doing but pure freaky fun.

I propped up my pillow, then leaned back on it and flipped through the pictures she had sent and stroked my meat till it was ready to explode. Then hit her back with a photo of my own. My text message said only, Come through, and I knew without a doubt she'd be here in less than five minutes. I couldn't wait to bend her over and do her dirty—after I choked her out. Bird's head game was better than that of some of the older women I'd popped off. I ain't even gonna lie and say my toes ain't curled at her tongue action on more than a few occasions.

After she messaged she was on her way, I hopped up and washed up with a soapy rag real quick so I'd be fresh and clean to taste. Then I put my cell on "do not disturb" mode, grabbed my video recorder out of the closet, and discreetly propped it up facing my bed so it could capture my raw dogging Bird. I had all kinda footage of me and her having sex that she didn't know about—and I had some of the other girls I had got down with. My bootleg porn collection was massive. Sometimes I'd watch them and stroke my ego, and if the video was of a pass-around girl that me and the fellas had a bet on, of course I'd share the flick like a trophy. But they were mainly for fun and just some shit to have. I guessed you could say I had a fetish for it.

The only person I didn't tape was Tay. She was chasing a title, but she had something far more important—an ounce of my respect. I didn't care nothing about the chicks I was sexing in the streets. I had trust issues, communication problems, and ain't give a fuck about making a chick's life unbearable. I stayed giving hell. And after hearing the bombs Marilyn had dropped last night, my insecurities had only got worse. Which meant I was bound to ruin a lot more lives.

Bird

After turning the doorknob quietly, calling myself creeping in, I tiptoed inside the house and tripped over Murk's size 13 Timberland boots and oversized sweat suit lying in the middle of the floor. Oh, this nigga must've gotten into some pill-popping partying without me, I thought. Hearing sports highlights playing over his surround system in the bedroom, I hurriedly walked up the hallway, ready to see my boo.

I stepped inside his bedroom without knocking. His Bulgari cologne lingered heavily in the air, heightening my arousal even more. Murk was already underneath the covers and was sitting up against the cherrywood headboard, intrigued by something on his phone. *That nigga probably watching me masturbate for him. I hope he's ready to put it on me and make me cum, since Jayson was on that birth-control bullshit*, I told myself silently. Murk's lower body was covered only by a sheet, and I could see him jacking his meat to full attention. *Yeah, he's gotta be watching me get off.* My body started to tingle again, as I was getting turned on. I was a cum chaser for sure, ready to pick back up right where I'd left off.

"Hey, baby, you ready for me?" I said, coming up out of my clothes. I wanted Murk to know my age did not mean I couldn't handle him.

"Hell yeah. Hit the RECORD button on that camera and bring that fat cat over here!" he exclaimed. I loved when Murk got rough and controlling. I knew this was just the start to a freaky morning wake-up the right way.

"You do not have enough footage for you collection yet?"

"Naw, I can never get enough of looking at that sexy-ass body," Murk said, all the words my young ears wanted to hear.

"Good, because you've got some making up to do," I replied, letting him know I was salty about being played last night. I knew he hadn't spent the whole night alone. Murk loved licking, sticking, and doubling back on pussy. Somebody had got the attention—it just hadn't been me.

Shaking his head, still beating his meat, he continued to mean mug me, licking his lips at the same time. "Come on now, B. You know the rules. You first."

"I'm sorry. Let me get in line." Purring, I walked over toward him, feeling the need to model the body he'd been slow working for weeks. My cleavage was exposed, and my plump titties were screaming for his kisses. "Let me show you what you missed last night by not answering my calls."

"Well, go on and get to work. When you're done, I'll slam your pussy back real quick," he said, pulling the sheet back, tapping on the spot reserved for me. I did not care if a chick had been cuddled up there right before me; I was jumping in headfirst. His razor-fresh hairline, big black-ass chest, and the way he licked his lips had me lost in the attraction. My clit was thumping at the sight of him.

"Start with some knob slob. Slide you pretty little head underneath these covers," he spat rudely, jacking harder but still smiling.

I did not care, though, 'cause he was my boo. I liked the way he controlled me in the bedroom. It turned me on more than any teenager I'd let bang my walls had.

"Let me teach you some new tricks," he commented, with a smirk on his face. He seemed so ready, so eager, and judging by the pulse in my body, so was I. Following his directions, I finished undressing and joined him, ready and willing to cum.

"I'm ready, Daddy. Make it happen."

"Open up," he commanded, rubbing his thick manhood.

I obliged and allowed him to stick his precum-dripping tool in my mouth. As he forced himself down my throat, I gagged on his manhood as tears gathered in the corners of my eyes. His hands wandered down my back, cupped my cheeks, then tapped lightly on my clit. My hips began to buck, and I sucked hard to make him feel good.

"Yeah, just like that. Keep it up, girl." He viciously grabbed the back of my head. He was so demanding when getting head that it turned me on.

I did not care about the girl who'd just slobbed him down. I was bobbing for head title 'cause I wanted him to be my full-time man once I graduated. There'd be no reason for him not to be. He held the sides of my face still as he forced himself deeper down my throat.

Slobber fell from my mouth and ran down his dick, then dripped onto his balls.

"That is what I'm talking about. I love your mouth, Bird," he screamed, pumping harder. "Give it to me good for the camera, girl!"

He started his rhythm again, and I got in tune as his fingers reintroduced themselves to my young coochie. I'd forgotten about the camera being on, but by now it was too late. I'd given them a show thus far, and from the work he was putting on me, I'd be his sex slave on this tape for minutes more to come. My inner thighs were sticky, and I couldn't control myself as I deep throated him. I wanted to please him so bad. Hell, I wanted him to please me.

"Um, yeah, play with my balls," he commanded, moving his thickness in and out of his favorite place.

Saliva was slipping from the corners of my mouth. The wetter I got, the more excited he became. Following orders, I fondled his nut sack, suckling and slobbering on his knob. He flipped me on my side. The more I gagged, the harder he fucked my mouth. Head tilted back, eyes closed, Murk was giving me the business.

"Put those nuts in your mouth, baby girl. You know how I like it."

I did more than I was told and began to rub my tongue up and down his shaft while sucking. I wanted to be better than any girl he'd had and any girl plotting to have him. I was a pro at sucking dick; I'd been doing it since my toddler years. I could tell he was nearing the finale. I sucked tighter and pulled harder.

"Yeah, I know you want this nut, girl. Feel how hard this dick's getting," he said, slowing his pace, then pulling out all together. When he shot a fat nut onto my face, I couldn't believe he'd taken it there. "Look at the camera and lick ya' lips."

He shook a little, rubbing on his manhood, making sure each drop landed on my face. "Naw, I'm not finished. Lay back and spread those legs," he commanded, pinching my nipples.

I did as I was told.

"Good girl. Now you can get what you've been begging for all night."

After going down, he began sucking on my inner thighs. My body quivered, but I had no control as he held my ankles tightly. My secret place began to throb and lust for his touch as he ran his tongue up and down my stomach and breasts. I could feel my nipples harden as his fingers started to explore the insides of my body. The tingling sensations were amazing, and my moans got louder and I begged for more. I was glad Shayla was gone, 'cause I knew she'd hear me getting it for sure today.

"Aah!" I yelled, my body tingling, and as I couldn't hold my cum back any longer. My legs flopped down, as he'd just released what Jayson hadn't.

As I lay there, almost limp from coming hard, he plunged into my mouth until he released his thick, warm semen down my throat. I choked but swallowed each and every drop of his bitterness. This whole session had turned out to be a dick-sucking event.

"Go on and get cleaned up, so you can get back down the street to your li'l boyfriend," he said, putting his pleasure piece back in his underwear and crawling back underneath the covers.

"I've been over that little boy. I'm more interested in a grown man," I replied sweetly, lying back on the bed, out of energy.

"Since when? I saw his run-down hooptie pulled into your driveway when I got back to the hood. You ain't gotta lie to kick it. I'm gonna fuck with yo' young ass anyway." Him being brutally honest with me was turning me on.

"Well, you can trust I'm about to make him old news. After that sex session you put down, there's no need to go backward. I'm here to stay."

"Do not go ruining your life for me, baby girl. Trouble is my middle name."

"You've got a lot to learn about young B." I disappeared back underneath the covers to show him how much of a bad-girl level I was on.

Chapter Thirteen

Yoshi

"Wow. No wonder you hit me up, being so persistent about coming over here. If you were trying to make up for the baby shower, you have and more. You came stunting, passing out gifts like Santa Claus." I was in awe of the gifts she'd come through the door with for me and Yani. There were sleepers, three-piece outfits, booties, and even packs of diapers. I couldn't hide my happiness or surprise.

"Girl bye." She playfully rolled her eyes, with an innocent grin on her face, like she was finally happy she could pass out something for a change. "You can quit capping, 'cause you know good and damn well I do not even know how to stunt."

"Hmm. Well, from the looks of it, you better start learning how to flex on them, friend. I see you're also dressed fly from head to toe, and those gym shoes do not even got a crease in 'em yet. Bird ain't coming up off nothing she hasn't worn a million times, so what job you got? Are they hiring? Or did you come up off that coochie and got a sponsor?" I'd gone from admiring Shayla's outfit and sneakers to asking a million and one questions.

"A dude checking for me? Please! That would never happen. Tom-Tom came through with these clothes, kicks, and the money for me to finally buy my goddaughter some stuff."

"Damn! And what did he do? Hit the lottery?" I'd never known Tom-Tom to get a good-paying job where he could afford the name-brand wear Shayla was rocking. Not having a GED qualified him only for bag boy jobs at the grocery store, working at the car wash, or quite possibly running the lottery machine at the liquor store, if he was lucky. And I wasn't judging. I knew the struggle all too well, because I had been applying for jobs left and right but hadn't landed any callbacks because the application was lacking major in the education department. Not even the fashion stores or the food court at the mall was trying to hire a high school dropout. Those jobs were reserved for students transitioning to college or working their way through. I did not want to believe the constant digs from my mother that I would be a single mother and would survive off welfare for the rest of my life—just another statistic—but I *was* starting to lose hope.

By the time I came out of my thoughts, Shayla was finishing her sentence, but I hadn't heard one thing she'd said.

"Thank you! Tom-Tom got me together a little bit." She smiled, always happy when her brother came through for her. Shayla and him did not have the normal back-and-forth, bickering sibling relationship. In fact, the two were so close, they were often mistaken by new folk to the neighborhood for boyfriend and girlfriend. The new folk did not know Tom-Tom was the hero in a saga that was called her life. I'd seen him go days without eating to make sure her necessities were taken care of. She was lucky to have him—they were lucky to have each other's loyalty. As much as I knew Shayla wished her mom had been the one to raise her, from the outside looking in, she had it made. People were around me, but who was really in my corner? I never let these words slip from my mouth when I was talking to Shayla, even though I was sure she knew that I wished Karen had ridden out in that same cab with Rose.

"A'ight, girl, enough small talk and introductions. Roll up!" I said. I couldn't wait to get high. It was the only way I was able to keep my mind off my pitiful life. Me and Bird might've known each other longer, but it was Shayla whom I confided in the most.

"Where's Yani?" she asked as she sat down at the black Ikea table, pulled out a fat back of Kush, dumped the contents out onto a magazine, then began breaking the buds down. "Did you put a towel up to the bottom of the door, so she won't catch a contact? I ain't trying to get no baby high!"

"I got this, girl. Of course I did. Plus, I left the window cracked. She'll be straight even if she does get high. Maybe the smell of it will calm her nerves and keep her asleep for longer than an hour at a time." I helped the process speed along by breaking the swisher sweet down. I hadn't blown any good weed since I was about six months pregnant. The doctor had forced me to quit, claiming Yani wasn't gaining enough weight, so today would be my reintroduction to being a marijuana fiend. Many nights I had been restless 'cause I ain't had my good-good.

"You're crazy as hell, Yoshi Crawford! You must get it from ya' mama!"

"Speaking of that bitch . . ." As I went deep into the details of what had unfolded after she and Bird pulled off, then what had transpired with Duncan earlier this morning, Shayla sat listening with an attentive ear and getting spaceship high with me. "I'm just fed up and frustrated," I said when I had finished my story.

"Why did you tell him Yani wasn't his? How are you gonna financially make it without his help? You know your moms is dead serious about teaching you a lesson."

As she said the obvious, Shayla made me realize I needed a plan. Luckily, I had one. "All I can do is hope and pray them teachers do not be on nothing petty, so I can graduate. I filled out a couple applications for jobs that will get me enough money to afford my own place, but I need that piece of paper before they'll even give me an interview." Blowing a thick cloud of smoke out into the air, I felt my stress start to melt away. This was the first time I'd told anyone of my plan, and it sounded good rolling off my tongue.

"Then it sounds like you need to quit procrastinating on doing that makeup work. I can feel you, though, on wanting to move. Me and Tom-Tom have talked about it a few times, but we can barely afford to live free where we're at."

"Have you thought about getting a job after graduation? I mean, what are you gonna do?" Shayla was the quiet one between me, her, and Bird. It was easy for her to fade into the background, because she did not speak up much. I guessed I did not worry too much about her having a major issue, besides how she felt about Rose, since Tom-Tom kept a close eye on every move she made. I think he was worse than an overprotective father.

"I do not know yet. I was planning on talking to a counselor at school about getting a few applications in for college, so come January I could at least get a refund check. But Tom-Tom hooked up with Murk yesterday, so we'll see how that works out." She kicked some more new gossip onto the table, and I was wide eyed to hear what Tom was about to get in on.

"Quit playing! Hundred grand? Are you serious? I know that nigga Tom about to go crazy for you in these malls! You and him are about to come up *for real* for real." I was happy for my girl. She'd been down so long, living in the shadows of me and Bird; this would certainly be a good look. Still, I felt a slight tinge of jealousy that everything for my girl was starting to look up. I just wished the sun would start shining brightly on me again.

"I knew Murk got hella props, but you, Bird, and Tom act like that nigga is king."

"Girl bye, if you haven't figured it out by now, you will once it's all over. Murk is the motherfucking man."

After me and Shayla blew through a few blunts, I flat-ironed her hair until it flowed down her back, then talked her into letting me cut a few layers into it as well. Half of me was being sincere, while the other half of me was using Shayla to hurt Bird's feelings. The more Shayla glowed, the sicker I knew Bird would be.

"You might as well be fly from head to toe, literally." I spun her around in front of the mirror to give her a quick glimpse of how pretty her hair was.

"And you might as well get some flyers and start doing hair," she said, complimenting my work and skills.

"I might actually do that, if I can ever move out of here," I mused, getting her right for the picnic so she'd low key be my model.

She couldn't be caught dead out here dressed fly but looking like she had a rag on the head. Since me and Bird were beefed all the way out, it looked like Shayla was my only comrade now. I was about to use the whole situation to my advantage. Shayla was weak minded and easily manipulated. She was my girl and all, but desperate times called for desperate measures. I needed to get out of the dark cloud I was living under, and staying connected to her could do just that. If Tom-Tom was getting down with Murk on any level of work, Shayla was no doubt going to get kickbacks. If I could find a man even half as good as her brother, me and Yani's struggle would be nonexistent. He took care of his family. That was something I admired, desired, and was envious of.

I couldn't wait for the picnic to start. The young girl across the street had agreed to babysit Yani on the promise that I would pay her next week. I was grateful for li'l mama looking out and was already planning on using her services again if today went smoothly. To keep her pacified about the payment, I had loaded her up with snacks and microwavable meals using my Bridge Card. I did not care that Yani was an infant and technically too young to stay with a thirteen-year-old. I needed the break badly. Besides, I'd be able to check on them from time to time. I was willing to pull off whatever stunt-double move I needed to. Today's event was going to be the breakthrough I needed to get back on the map. For the past few years, I'd spent so much time loving up and chasing behind Duncan that the fellas in the streets were no longer whispering my name or checking for me. They were respecting boundaries and my relationship with Duncan. It was time to change that. I was single and ready to get my life back.

Chapter Fourteen

Artavia

"Mama Murk," I yelled into the old, abandoned house after I opened the front door. "I have a surprise for you."

I hurried to the back bedroom and unlocked all the dead bolts Murk had installed. I had a spare key for every key on his ring. Once when I'd taken his truck to go grab some ink from OfficeMax, I'd swung by the local hardware store to duplicate his keys and thus ensure I'd never be locked out of his life. Call it crazy, but I bet you follow suit from here on out. I entered the bedroom.

"Hey, baby," his mother said in a weak voice. "I'm so glad you're here." She was scratching and shaking, and I knew her body was kicking its own ass, desperate to get the crack rock it desired.

A few times over the past month or so, I'd come over here behind Murk's back. It was something I did not want to do, but I couldn't stop myself. As long as I fed Marilyn a few burgers, chips, a pop, and her dope once a week, our visitations would stay a secret.

I had stumbled upon her by mistake. A few months ago, when Murk's location points on the GPS kept being this address, I felt for sure it had to be some bitch . . . until I pulled up to this boarded-up dump. For sure, I thought my GPS application had to be misleading me, so I followed him for a few days, until he led me here himself. When I saw him go in and stay for longer than thirty minutes, I couldn't sleep until I knew what was inside that house. After a few weeks of him constantly coming and going here, and me watching the scene to make sure no one else frequented the place, I broke in. I did not expect to find Marilyn handcuffed by her ankles to a rail bed and lying on a dirty mattress. The first time I saw her, it was like seeing a ghost.

"Ain't no time for small talk," I said now. "Hurry up and put these on." I went over and picked the lock to her handcuffs, freeing her ankles. I'd picked up a pair of underwear, a bra, leggings, and a T-shirt from the Family Dollar store before coming here. She could use a hot bath in bleach, but since this place did not have running water, that pressing need would have to wait.

"Oh my God, Tay baby. You're a saint." She tried hugging me, but I jumped back, not willing to allow that.

"Come on now, Mama Murk. You know ya' ass is foul," I said as I patted her on the shoulder, meaning my words in more than one way. She knew the real, so there was no reason to sugarcoat it. "Just hurry up so I can get you out of here. Your son doesn't know."

"Oh, I see you're still keeping secrets." She smiled widely, exposing a mouth of half-rotten teeth and gums.

Chapter Fifteen

Tom-Tom

"What up, man? I'm on the porch, dressed and waiting." I'd been calling Murk since I got up, but this was the first time he'd answered. I was eager to get the workday started. Today was payday Friday for many folks, and like he'd explained to me yesterday, I'd be among many true check cashers at the bank, which would make me seem less obvious. I'd dressed in wheat-colored slacks, a salmon-colored polo shirt, and new brown Cole Haan loafers, since I knew I'd be cashing some better checks today.

"Damn, bro, that is what I'm talking about. You're a quick learner, I see. Give me a minute to wrap things up with shorty, and I'll be right out," Murk said.

I hung up the phone, but I did not know which girl he was referring to. Shayla was already gone and was not answering her phone, so I did not know if she was already cliqued up with Bird or not. I guessed I'd see in a few short minutes.

The neighborhood had a different look to it this Friday morning. Usually there were fiends out in high numbers, chasing a rock; half-dressed girls chasing dick, and the li'l crew I rode with chasing the next nickel-and-dime scam. But at this hour, the streets were pretty empty. I figured people were still chasing winks of sleep in preparation for the picnic coming up tonight. People from all sides of the D were expected to come out, so those who were backing this event financially were out making sure things were being set up. The picnic was scheduled to start at 3:00 p.m., and it would go till the birds woke up tomorrow.

The ladies from around here who knew how to burn in a good way on the grill were already up getting their meat started. I couldn't wait to get more than a few plates to stock my fridge for one of my weed-induced munchies attack. The aroma kicking off from the mixture of all the seasonings had my stomach twisting up in knots. Ice-cream trucks dedicated to robbing our pockets blind with upcharged frostbitten Popsicles were starting to pull up in doubles to line the strip around the park. And minutes after that, the inflatable bounce houses were being set up for the kids, along with rented tables and chairs. The block club, which was sponsored by a few of the money-making dough boys from this hood, presented this event as their way of giving back. Donations were taken from all around, which was why no one came to the picnic with drama. People had a tendency to act more civilized when their own money was involved.

Suddenly Bird literally fell out of Murk's front door, and my focus shifted from the picnic to her.

"Ugh. Had I known he was rushing me for you, I would've kept his dick in my mouth longer." Bird rolled her eyes, laughing.

I guessed Shayla wasn't with her. "Shut up, with your trifling ass. I ain't even trying to have you ruin my mood this morning." I couldn't stand Bird. I hated her bony-built ass with a passion, as a matter of fact.

"Boy bye, you can quit perping like you do not want to wake up to this every morning. Do not kid yourself. You miss me." Bird was talking loud enough for more than just me to hear. What tip was she on?

"Lower your fucking voice!" I growled, ready to leap across the porch and strangle her.

Not long ago, we'd both agreed to keep what went down when she was a kid a secret. One time, when she and Shayla were about twelve, Bird came over to keep Shayla company and slept over at our house. In the middle of the night, she snuck into my room, acting like a grown-ass woman. Bird's dad had fucked her over in the worst way, 'cause baby girl was turned all the way out at the age of twelve. She did things to my sixteen-year-old body I'd only imagined during a wet dream. So I knew Murk was getting totally broke off with her now that she was grown and fully experienced.

"And if I do not, Thomas Harris?" She was still the same spoiled brat from when she used to spend the night.

"I'm gonna slap the shit out of you! What? Are you high or something?"

"As a matter of fact, I am. Murk has got some super good work. I can see if he'll let you get a line of it." She started giggling uncontrollably. The cat was out of the bag: Bird was high off Molly.

"Naw, I'm straight on that tip. Why don't you go on and get down the street so me and my manz can get to business?" I did not know how much she knew about me and Murk connecting on the scam he had going, but I wasn't about to be the one to send her high, babbling ass off to spread the word. I had to watch what I said, but, more importantly, I had to get Shayla to cut her ties with Bird. No sister of mine was about to get caught up with the new, mind-altering street drug that was about to take Bird on another spiraling roller coaster.

"Yeah, whatever. I'll get out y'all way. See you at the picnic later." As I watched Bird walk away, I knew she really high off that shit. She had the same way of swaying and leaning to the side that Ricardo had inherited when he first started dabbling on the dark side with drugs.

Murk stepped out of the house just then. "Damn, chief, you do clean up well," he declared, looking me up and down, admiring my transformation.

I put aside all thoughts about Bird's downfall, ready to play my position to get this money. "Thanks. There ain't shit out here money can't make shine."

We hit about ten banks that morning, with checks all over two grand, some as much as five. We did everything from cashing payroll checks to taking early advances on 401(k) savings. If Murk had a template for a check, he'd have a replica for it too. The whole operation ran smoothly, as each teller foolishly traded me thousands of dollars for a fake piece of paper. Murk had it well planned out, and once again, I followed each rule and order to the tee. The more hits we drove out of the parking lot with, the more confident I became. I had told that nigga the first moment we talked through my plan on feeding me and Shayla that I was no quitter, so he knew I wasn't letting up till I was all the way on like him.

After a day's work, we did the same thing we'd done yesterday: we splurged at the mall till it closed, loading up on frivolous items. My deep pockets were now stuffed with nothing but big bills. I made sure to buy Shayla the best handbags, outfits, and gym shoes, and the trendiest pieces. I caught Murk scoping out the young groupies he was dating, including Bird. I wanted my sister to outshine that snake bitch so bad that it hurt. After tearing the mall down, I walked out with five bags in each hand. Now I was ready to step my game up in another way.

After Murk got behind the wheel and I climbed into the front passenger seat of his Infiniti, I turned the radio down. "So what type of shit a nigga gotta do to get a whip like this?" I asked. We'd gotten cooler since we started hanging together, so I started to move more like his homeboy than his protégé.

"It's gonna take a lot of fraudulent check cashing to get you on this level." He patted me on the back. "But start stacking yo' money. I can see about putting you on to a whip more in your price range. I've got a dude that works down at a car lot who might be able to put you down for the right price."

"Bet! That is what's up. I'm on that shit starting next Monday fa sho. It's about that time, you know, for me to boss my game all the way up and give these clowns something major to talk about. I've been hearing them whispering, but it's time to make the block hot!"

Cats around the way were starting to hate 'cause my gear game was starting to go through the roof. I wasn't the young, scruffy nigga no more, the one rocking bootleg kicks from the gas station till the soles fell off. In just ten days of grinding with Murk, not only was I changing my shoes just for the fuck of it, but I was also walking like my nuts were swollen. Them niggas knew what was up—ole son of a crackhead Tom-Tom done hit a lick.

"Be easy on giving them li'l niggas something to bark at, Tom. Shit ain't like how it used to be. Loyalty ain't nothing but a word in the dictionary now. Back in my day, cats were all about the conglomerate. Now it's all about self-preservation, every man for himself. *Every* means do you, but do not lie with snakes and not expect them to bite you."

Weaving in and out of traffic, Murk kept spitting knowledge to me, and I couldn't help but absorb every word of it. What he was saying about my dogs around the way not wanting to see me eat after seeing me starve for so long was nothing but the truth. In a way, I think I was looking for a father figure, because father had cracked out many years ago. Murk was picking up the slack, putting money in my pocket, and making a way for me not only to provide for me and Shayla but also to do it in a helluva way.

"I've got some business on the other side of town to tend to. You with riding out?" he said after he finished his lesson for the day.

"Fa sho. I ain't got nothing else to do." Reclining in the seat and unbuttoning my polo shirt, I got comfortable, knowing our licks were done for the day. I did not know where we were off to, but with Murk, I felt all right.

Soon the sounds were banging inside the Infiniti, the Kush smoke was clouding up the small space, and Murk was bending corners through the east side of Detroit. These parts looked more abandoned than the streets we came from—and damn near destitute—as the few fiends nodding on the corners waved at the truck as we rode by. Murk never stopped, but he nodded his head, acknowledging each gesture.

At one point, Murk turned the sounds down, though he did not have to, because he already had my attention. "Listen up. We're into some heavy shit with this check business, bro, but I can promise you double, if not triple, a day on this new li'l hookup I've been casing."

"Say word? You already know my position out here, man. How can I turn down whatever proposition you're putting on the table, G?"

"Cool. That is what I wanna hear. Most cats out here are worried about the feds swooping in on 'em, but you're out here reckless with it. That is gonna get us to the top real fast."

"I sure hope so," I told him. "I've played being at the bottom all the way out. Whatever your game plan is, you can count me in fa sho."

Murk did not say two words the rest of the ride, but his facial expressions seemed tense, and you could tell he was in deep thought. He did not give any details about what he was planning or what my involvement would be in it. All I knew was that when the time came, I'd show my loyalty. That was the only way I knew to ensure my place in his camp. The only thing I did not suspect was that the time to prove myself would arrive so soon.

Murk

I loved having a li'l nigga I could mold. That shit was like music to a gangster's ears. I couldn't wait to pull Tom-Tom all the way in on me and Tay's hustle, especially since he was a new face. He had come to me broke down and hungry; that was how I knew his thirst was real. Many cats around here would've touched the type of bread Tom-Tom put his hands on, then immediately turned to set me up. He was proving to be one of the more loyal players in the game, and that was why I had taken a liking to him. Either way, business was business. It was time to get to it.

I'd been calling and texting Artavia since me and Tom got out here in the streets, grinding, but she hadn't picked up or responded to one text message. She had always stayed at my beck and call, so she must've been trying to prove a point. It did not take a rocket scientist to figure out she was still probably caught up in her emotions from earlier, but it was time to move on. This was why I never should've mixed business with pleasure.

Tom sat in the passenger seat, getting blown back, as I swerved through the streets, impatient with the traffic. My first thought was to go check on my moms, but this detour was more pressing. I had to make sure everything was straight with Tay—and, more importantly, with 5-Star. I couldn't wait until I could get out of Detroit and start a new life.

Chapter Sixteen

Bird

"So, have you figured out what your plans are going to be after you graduate from school? Your grandmother and I would love to see you spread your wings and get out of Detroit," my mother said, trying to spark up a conversation with me as she stood in my bedroom doorway.

"Well, hmm. Let's see," I mused dramatically, putting my fingertip to my temple. "Maybe I can relocate to New York City and study acting, or maybe I'll try my luck in Los Angeles, since that is the land of stars. I mean, I have been playing a damn good role and lying to people for years about your vile-ass character. I've put on such a good act that nobody would ever believe you'd set me up to get raped by that no-good nigga and then put the gun in my hand to kill him."

"Wow, Bird. Don't you think it's about time you let the past go? It's 'bout time to forgive me and try moving on, so we can have some type of relationship. Haven't I done enough to prove to you that I'm sorry for the part I played in all your pain? I've worked my ass off to keep you on a pedestal, buy you whatever you ask for, and I have taken all the jabs you've sent to my gut over and over again. That has gotta count for something."

"Bitch, please," I shot back at her with attitude, rolling my eyes. "Am I supposed to bow down or thank you for tag teaming with ole pedophile-raising-ass Clara in buying me guilt gifts so y'all could sleep better? Nah, y'all can get the fuck on with all that. I'm riding the hate game out till both of y'all are six feet under and I can collect on the insurance policies. You can quit wasting your time trying to get me to forgive you, lady, because that is never going to happen. Letting your daughter get fondled by a nigga, just so you can get stroked by that same sick-dick nigga, makes you unforgivable."

My mother slammed the door, and then she probably ran to her room to cry. She was weak. Everything I wasn't. And that was how my father had gained so much control over the household and my innocence. I broke her down every chance I could, but I guessed the foolish hope she had for us couldn't stop her from coming back for more punishment. She was gonna die catching hell from me because that was what she deserved. Instead of handing me a gun, she should've shot the son of bitch herself. She'd lost her daughter a long time ago.

Through my open bedroom window, I could hear the hired DJ spinning beats and doing sound checks at the park to make sure he was on point. Today was about to be hella epic. My bedroom was a mess. I'd tossed clothes, shoes, and accessories everywhere as I tried to find the perfect outfit to strut around the park in. I knew after the morning me and Murk had just had, he would not be able to keep his eyes off me. Finally pulling out the perfect booty shorts and crop top, I knew he would not be able to keep his hands off me either.

Now that I had decided on an outfit, I picked up my cell and dialed Shayla.

"Hey, you still with Yo-Yo?" I asked her as soon as she picked up.

"Naw. She's busy with Mommy duties with Yani. Hopefully, she finds a sitter so she can join us later. Are you done with ole boy? 'Cause the park is starting to fill up. I'm trying to find a good spot."

"I feel you. I'm about to throw my clothes on, and I'll meet you at your house in about twenty minutes. Mom Dukes's pathetic ass was just in here, slowing me down," I huffed, grabbing my clothes and rushing into the bathroom. "Calm down, though, boo. Everybody ain't about to be kissing your ass over no Maxes or no Foot Locker fit. No shade, but you're too hype!" I'd seen Shayla trying to floss earlier, but that overexposed mall gear wasn't nothing to me.

"Damn. You've got a funny way of not throwing shade. I thought you, of all people, would be happy for me."

"I am. I am. Let me take a chill pill and get ready. I see you're still over there on some emotional shit." I laughed, then hung the phone up. I really had to work on getting me some new friends.

Chapter Seventeen

Artavia

After climbing out of the shower, I grabbed my towel and wrapped it around my cold body. I had been in the shower, trying to calm down and relieve my stress, for so long that I'd used all the hot water. I knew better than to take a shower that was over thirty minutes long, but I couldn't help it. My nerves had been wrecked ever since I snuck Mama Murk out of that nasty-ass house and to a hotel across town. I was scared that I'd made a reckless mistake by using her to try to mend my broken heart and that she was going to end up leaving the hotel.

With some of the money Murk had left on my dresser earlier, I'd bought Mama Murk some essentials, like soap, a toothbrush and paste, and a comb and brush, plus some grease, lotion, and a few T-shirts and leggings. She was skinny as a twig, so she did not require much. She did not even require as much drugs as I'd brought with me to get her high with. As monstrous as Murk was, I felt like I could control Mama Murk—which meant staying in the hotel room and following my instructions—if I gave her a supply of her favorite drug as well as livable accommodations. I made sure that the hotel room was plush and that she had everything she had requested from the store, plus food. I also made sure Mama Murk had my direct cell, in case she needed anything.

I was praying my plan would not backfire. I did not know what I planned on doing with Marilyn exactly, but I knew Murk would come panting back to me, worried and needing my help, once he found out Marilyn was missing. The first thing I was planning on suggesting we did was dip out of the state and start over, especially since we had been planning on dipping from Detroit anyway. Whoever that bitch was I'd seen earlier, she could count her last dick strokes.

After drying off, I took a few sips from the glass of wine I'd brought into the bathroom with me. I was chasing a buzz that would totally relax my mind, but I wasn't trying to take a nosedive to get it. Although the pill bottle said not to drink and take antidepressants, I popped the cap to my Zoloft prescription and threw the blue pill down my throat. The only thing I was slightly worried about was the side effects, because I had taken one pill this morning and had just doubled up on the daily dosage. My life was on an emotional roller coaster, and it seemed impossible to get off it. Maybe if I had not stopped taking my medicine regularly, I would not be off balance. I hadn't felt this aggressive, dangerous, and impulsive in a very long time.

Sliding on my robe, I walked into the kitchen and poured myself a glass of Kool-Aid, then warmed up some leftover soul food I'd gotten a couple of days ago. I was about to smoke the rest of the blunt I'd started before I got in the shower, smash, then get some work done. Then I decided to head straight to work. The second part of my plan on healing my bitter heart was to fuck with Murk's money.

Checking my phone, I saw Murk had called a few times, but I'd set his contact on DND. I knew he was pissed that he was sweating me and I was ignoring every single one of his calls, but it was about time he got a taste of his own medicine. This morning was a wake-up call that I'd been giving Murk too much room to toy with my emotions and give attention to other women, who weren't as deserving as I was. I was in the mud with Murk. In the trenches. He could never say I wasn't in the gym, shooting with his ass, because I was the chick who had bought him the basketball. Murk's gun was loaded with bullets out of my purse. That was the type of ride-or-die bitch I'd been for him, so I felt betrayed and like he needed to feel some helluva repercussions for not showing me the same loyalty. I'd been starving for attention, but now I was pressed to serve his ass up with some consequences he couldn't sleep behind.

5-Star Consulting might've been his idea ultimately, but it was my baby. It was I who had taken an idea he saw on social media and had turned into a thriving scam, one that was making it possible for us to live like we were pushing bricks of dope or were CEOs of thriving corporations. It was I who nursed 5-Star twenty-four hours a day. It was at my house where the whole illegal operation was set up. I was the one who had put in countless hours coming up with bogus mission statements and marketing techniques to drum up applicants that we'd never hire, and I was the one who burned my eyes out staring at computer screens as I forged documents. This business would not have a life if it weren't for me.

I picked up my plate of leftovers and a fork and went into my second bedroom, which served as an office, and I sat down at my computer, eager to get to work. *Since he loves me for business, I'm gonna show his ass the business*, I thought as I set my plate and fork down on the desk. The craftiness in me had come out. Murk had a tendency to forget we were from the same projects. I might've stayed clinging to books instead running with the crowd, but that did not mean my heart couldn't pump ice cold on a scorching hot summer day.

After pulling up our company's email, I hit SELECT ALL, then forwarded the twenty emails I had just received to an anonymous email account I'd created. Instead of me and him sharing the wealth, my plan was to start my own subsidiary and stack money on the side. He would be led to think the hits on the site had plummeted, while I continued to thrive from the scheme. Me being a team player and wanting to see him win was out the window since he wasn't being loyal to me. Maybe if Murk's money started to dry up, he'd invest a little bit more time catering to my needs. Whatever he chose to do, my money game was about to be up, so I could get out of Detroit with or without him. And it wasn't about to be off the measly percentage he rationed.

My front door slammed, and my nerves went into overdrive again. "Hey, yo, Tay! It better be a good reason you're not answering my calls!"

Hearing Murk screaming at the top of his lungs, I jumped up, not knowing if the cat was out of the bag about his mom already or if he was angry over being ignored. I started moving as quickly as I could, deleting the evidence of what I'd done. Although Murk wasn't tech savvy, I couldn't rely on nobody's stupidity. Especially when they had access to money. If he found out I was going against the grain and getting ready to basically take money out of his pocket, he'd kill me for sure. He was another type of crazy, according to Marilyn, and I thought I was the only one keeping secrets between us two.

Luckily, I cleared the screen just as Murk pushed through the office door. I damn near used the bathroom on myself when I saw how disgruntled he looked, and I did not even have to pee. He'd never put his hands on me before, but I thought for sure he was about to open-hand slap me across the room.

I thought quickly and braced myself. "What are you here for? It's not business hours," I said, playing it off like I was not answering him because I still was in my feelings from earlier.

"Didn't I tell yo' stupid ass to have your act together by the time I got back? That emotional shit is a turnoff on the real. You ain't been right since I left, because I been blowing you up and you haven't answered."

I picked up my fork and started eating. I was flat out ignoring him. By now, the coast was clear on the computer, so I was determined to be in rare form and to be the bitch he deserved this morning but ran out on. Especially since he'd come here on good bullshit and about the fact that Marilyn was missing.

"I'll knock that plate on the floor and that food out your mouth, Tay. You better quit fucking playing with me," he threatened.

I swallowed what was in my mouth, then went to take another bite, but Murk grabbed my arm.

"Oh, so you think I'm playing about breaking this muthafucka off?" He yanked me up by my arm and extended it while applying pressure.

"Get yo' hands off me, Murk." I tried yanking my arm back, but his grip was too tight, and my efforts only made the pain worse.

"Oh, so you can talk?" he smirked. "Do not have me flex on you again to get an answer out of you, Tay. Now, again I ask, why weren't you picking up your phone? You know how we rock, and it could have been an emergency."

"Well, to be honest, at first, I was ignoring you because I was in my feelings over how things went down between us this morning. And as pissed as you might wanna be because I was in my emotions, I have them. But the last few times you called, I did not even see them, because the ringer is silenced. The emails were jumping, so I was trying to focus and get a printout down," I halfway lied, but I was making a real attempt at getting him to let me go.

"I ain't even gonna keep tripping on that emotional shit, though. I ain't got the energy for it," he said. "But you can't let that get in the way of us making these moves and keeping the money flowing. You gotta play the game a li'l bit more with your head and not your heart. That is how we'll end back on some poor shit." He let my arm go completely, then reached behind him and grabbed a gang of shopping bags, which I hadn't seen before that point. "Here. I copped your spoiled ass some fly shit while I was out today. You're gonna have to deal with whatever do not fit since you wasn't answering for me to confirm the size." He handed me the bags.

Smacking my lips, I played like I wasn't geeked to see he'd gone shopping for me. I was hoping it wasn't written all over my face and I wasn't blushing. I was still very much in my feelings over Murk messing around with that girl, but I was also starving for his love, his attention.

"Do not just stand there with an attitude. Open that shit, before I take it back," he ordered. He was getting an attitude.

"No you will not," I said and started opening the bags. He'd gotten me clothes, sneakers to match, and a purse that was actually cute as hell. He never bought me sexy clothes, always hip-hop homegirl clothes. Now that I knew he was creeping with the young trick, I was starting to read into everything Murk did. I questioned our entire dynamic. I was insecure as hell, but I forced myself to push it down.

"Well, I'll take these as 'I'm sorry' gifts since I know your stubborn behind won't use those two words. Thank you for them." I wrapped my arms around his neck and pulled him in for a hug, and as I did so, I noticed the welt on my arm from his grip. We for damn sure had a toxic love, because I was still eager for his love, affection, and attention. And I was still wildly attracted to his sexy ass. I'd always been like putty in his hands. Graveyard love was what you called it.

"That is more like it. You're welcome." He flipped the script, then took us straight to our comfortable spot—sex.

Like a savage, he let his hands start roaming my body hungrily. He leaned over and kissed my neck, then licked on my earlobe, which had my thighs shaking. It was crazy how crazy this man made me. "Your thick ass feels and smells so good," he told me as he gripped my cheeks roughly.

"Show me how good you feel," I replied, pulling him closer, hot and ready to give him some coochie. Even with everything that had gone down between us, I was still attracted to him and wild for him. Plus, makeup sex was the best sex. Every bad thought and negative emotion—about Marilyn especially—left my mind as I had the one person I desperately wanted. I was about to throw this juicy fruit on him and make it hard for him to ever let me go.

"We've got company out front, so mush your face into the couch cushion so he doesn't hear me beating up your guts," he instructed. He led me to the couch and bent me over, not giving me time to question him about the company. Murk was private when it came to where he laid his head and who had access to him, which meant whoever it was held some sort of value to him. I did not have time to think on it at the moment, though. . . .

With the quickness, he flipped my robe up and pulled my G-string to the side, then slipped into my wet box with ease. The anticipation had me wet. Him filling me up had the floodgates completely open.

Tom-Tom

"Hey, yo, Tay! I've got company, so make sure yo' ass is straight," Murk yelled through the front door. Then he opened the door, walked inside the apartment, and waved for me to follow him. "Have a seat and make yourself comfortable. I'll be right back." He then moved through the well-decorated project apartment like a madman, then disappeared down the hallway to what I supposed was the back bedroom.

I took a quick glance around the crib, then ducked into the kitchen for a glass of water. All the back-to-back blunt I'd been blowing on had me feeling dehydrated. Unlike all the other subsidized units I'd seen and been in, this apartment was decked out like Murk's crib was: it had leather furniture, a cinema-looking flat-screen television, and a bunch of expensive-looking black art on the wall.

No sooner had I gulped down the coolish tap water, than I started hearing screaming coming from the back room. At first, it was a woman's voice that was bouncing off the walls, but then it was Murk's voice that was rocking the baseboards. They were arguing over something personal, so I let them niggas have their personal space. After sitting my cup in the sink, I went into the living room, found the remote to the TV, and fell back on the couch to chill until they finished up their beef.

After tuning in to episode one of the very first season of *Power*, I leaned back and took in ole girl's apartment, with the thought of getting my own spot. The only thing about the government-subsidized unit was that it was small, but every amenity and feature had been completely upgraded. She wasn't living subpar like the rest of the residents in this high-rise. Truth be told, her crib might've been better than Murk's. The flooring, marble countertops, and the custom paint job, which matched the custom blinds, were all symbols of the money she was touching. Taking a closer look at the photographs that sat on her side and coffee tables, I realized that her and Murk had a history that was obviously still part of his present, which was hidden.

"Artavia, this is Tom. Tom, this is my business partner, Tay. She's the woman behind the master plan." I was so busy staring at the pictures of him and Tay that I hadn't heard them come out of the back room. They both were standing there like they hadn't just been arguing.

I snapped out of it and stood up to shake her hand to be respectful. "Nice meeting you," I said as I extended my hand. That was the least I could do, since I was in her spot, on her couch, and using her electricity.

I couldn't help but get caught up by her natural beauty. Baby girl did not have any makeup on, but she was sexy as hell. Even though she was rocking a pair of Victoria's Secret Pink jogging pants and a white T-shirt, I could tell her curves would have me cumming for days. If Murk wasn't hitting her off, I probably would've tried my hand at getting on. I had to catch myself before either of them realized my instant attraction.

"The pleasure is all mine. I've been waiting to meet you. You've been doing the damn thang moving those checks through the system. Welcome to the team." She winked, then sat down across from me. There was something about her body language that was screaming she was feeling me, but I wasn't sure if my mind was playing tricks on me, because I was crushing on her fineness.

Murk turned off the TV, then took a bottle of Patrón off Artavia's wet bar, and poured us all a shot. "A'ight, Tom.

You've mastered hitting the banks, so now it's time to introduce you to the next level of the game," he said as he passed out the shots.

After taking the shot and downing it, I saluted him and Artavia both. "I'm most definitely ready for the next play."

"Oh, you're ambitious. I like that," Artavia said, then downed her shot with her eyes locked on mine.

Again, I did not know what was up with the vibes she was giving me, so I repositioned myself on the couch to give off a more closed-off vibe. I wasn't trying to fuck with my homeboy's girl.

"Now that we've toasted to a partnership, let's get to the particulars." Murk took his shot back, then leaned back like a don and started telling me the next level to the game.

In less than forty-five minutes, him and Artavia had blown my mind. I now understood how their homes were decked out and lavish. I thought Murk's money had come from cashing checks, like I was doing, but it was apparent the bulk of his money and assets had come from this next level of the hustle. They both were living like kings off fake identities and people that had excellent credit. Their come-up was someone else's misfortune, but it did not matter, because the money they were stealing was insured. At least that was the speech Artavia gave me. Murk wasn't lying when he said she was the brainchild of the scam they were running. She made the hustle seem legit and damn near dummy proof—as long as I kept up with the path they'd set.

The little check cashing I was doing was merely pennies compared to what they said I could bring in. Artavia searched the dark web for credit card numbers, used social engineering and phishing to get information about people to dig deeper into their credit profiles, and hacked into servers that held personal information. Her whole role in the scheme was uber technical, and it would make my head hurt if I had to do it, because it was too intense and time consuming.

After gathering all the information, they'd get credit cards, lines of credit, tradelines, and then they'd burn them out. On any given day, Murk said he could have ten different people's credit card information to burn a hole through. The plan would be for me to form my own check-cashing subsidiary, with my own gang of trusted check cashers, and then I would get a piece of their cut. Me and Murk would become more like business partners than me being his little lackey. Even though I wasn't fucking with Jabari as heavily as I had been before I linked up with Murk, he would be the first friend I'd kick it with about making some money. Hopefully, he'd be ready to put on the crown and get down.

Murk

Just as I had expected, Tom wanted in on the hustle, even though he'd heard how deep in the game we were, and that was exactly what me and Artavia needed to hear. The money was about to start flowing in really fast in a short amount of time after we took this trip to Ohio I had planned. Tay was going to make a bunch of fake IDs with Tom's pictures on them but different names, and then I was going to drive him to the bank and have him open accounts to do rush check-cashing jobs. Tay had come across a stream of numbers for dirt cheap, and we had to move fast to capitalize in a major way. Scared money did not make money, and I was trying to stack as much as I could before the well ran dry.

On our road trip to Ohio, Tom would be the one setting up the accounts we needed to do a rush job of checks.

We'd use the identities stolen off the internet to create fake ID cards and checks for the people me and him gathered for our subsidiary team. By the time the banks got onto 5-Star, Artavia would've pulled the plug on our site and ads. We had only a week to burn Ohio out. I hoped Tom was truly ready for the dedication to the grind that it was about to take. I was counting on him to sell the fake business, bogus checks, and con artist game that me and Tay had been schooling him in to help our racketeering businesses grow. His naïve ass had no idea he was getting ready to be hella used.

As I sat back, sipping on my celebratory beer, I watched Tom drool over Artavia. I wasn't jealous or mad but relieved. Maybe if she had some fresh meat to fuck, she would not be so mad over me not wifing her. Hell, a nigga was still young and balling hard, out of control. I wasn't looking to be a husband; I was looking for a ho. And the willing participant I had in Bird had my nose wide open. The freak fest I had going on with her wasn't about to let up no time soon.

Chapter Eighteen

Shayla

As expected, the annual picnic was off the chain. People were out in masses for all the free food, music, drinks and, of course, drugs floating around. This event was known to be the biggest party of the summer, so anyone who wanted to be known, who had the title of boss, or just simply wanted their hand out for a freebie flooded into the park. Once a year, no matter what, beefs were put to the side so everyone could have a chance to enjoy the fruits of their hard street-hustling labor. Women and men alike respected the golden rule, which was to never leave behind a tragedy, surrounded by yellow caution tape, during the annual picnic.

Barbecue grills were sending smoke signals into the air about some well-seasoned ribs, coolers were open for people to help themselves, and card tables had been set up for people to have places to eat, play, or just chill. Damn near every household had put up a few dollars of their food stamps for snacks for the kids, as well, so even they had juice, candy, and chips galore.

I was feeling myself no doubt, especially since Yo-Yo had flat-ironed my hair, and it was flowing down my back. My hair complemented my brand-new outfit, with the kicks to match, and my ego was on a million. I even had my feed on the Gram rocking with nothing but selfie pics, and they were getting major likes. I hated to admit it, but I now realized how easy it was for Bird to be the bitch she was. But today, though, I was ten steps ahead of her instead of ten paces behind, in some of her throwaways. I'd even outdressed her.

"Let's slide over to the courts real quick so I can holla at Jayson and get it out the way before he be checking for me," Bird said to me as we sat at one of the card tables.

"Oh, okay. I'd be keeping tabs on his fine ass too. These groupies around here are looking dehydrated thirsty today."

"Girl bye, the only reason I'm trying to get at him is to break up with him. Trust when I say that I'm over that young nigga. Murk got this cat purring his name." She nonchalantly pulled a compact mirror and lip gloss from her purse and touched up her makeup before waving to Jayson, so he would acknowledge her presence. "See, girl, his dumb ass do not even realize his time with me is about to expire." She hopped up.

"You say that now. But when one of those groupies waiting thirstily by the sidelines get their mouths on him, you gonna be pissed."

"That'll just be one less female I've gotta worry about trying to get at Murk." Bird seemed more than determined, so there was no reason to keep wasting my energy trying to talk her out of it. She sashayed over to the courts, breaking through a gang of groupies, and finally met Jayson, who was holding a basketball. All eyes were on her, as she was the most hated-on young female from around here. I had to give my girl props whether I supported her decision or not. Many chicks wanted to get at Bird for her uppity attitude, but her psycho personality had most of her nemeses in check from afar.

Bird

"I do not think we're working out," I whispered into Jayson's ear as he hugged my small frame.

"Bitch, what? Are you serious?" I could tell I'd struck a nerve, but nursing his feelings wasn't my problem anymore. I wasn't trying to raise a man.

"Come on now. Do not act like you did not think there weren't gonna be consequences to blowing up on me earlier. You already know I'm not about that life." Tapping my foot while folding my arms, I wanted to make sure I wasn't about to give this breakup a second thought. "And, by the way, I'm not gonna be too many more of your bitches."

"Yeah, I got you, B. Go on and do you." He started bouncing the basketball nonchalantly. After hawking up a glob of saliva onto the pavement, he looked me coldly in the eye before throwing the ball directly at me. "I'm out."

"You ole pussy-ass nigga." I was able to step back, but not fast enough to evade the ball, which hit me in the stomach. I grabbed my middle but stopped myself from doubling over in pain, as I did not want to let him see me sweat. The whole scene had turned embarrassing for me. Even the trick-ass groupies watching had the nerve to laugh.

"Yeah, okay, Bird. Then your whore ass must love pussy-ass niggas. You were slobbing on this monster last night." Jayson grabbed his nuts, then proceeded to pull his basketball shorts down. He was going all out for the crowd.

"Yup, you're right. What girl do not suck her man's dick? The real question is, how many men out here lick up another man's cum?" By now, my stomach wasn't hurting anymore. I was now in rare form, ready to pass out a few verbal thrashings. "You should be raising your hand instead of pulling out that li'l thang you call a monster. I had you tongue kissing Murk's left-behind cum." Laughing and grinning, I ran my hand across my coochie, then tapped on it lightly. "So I guess that means we both love the dick."

"I'm gonna kill your trick ass." He lunged in my direction but was snatched back by the group of guys he was just balling with. "Fuck that ho! Let me go," he screamed, alerting the whole park that we were definitely over.

"You can let him go. He ain't gonna do shit," I muttered. I did not know that for sure, but if he wanted to run up, he could. If I could shot my own daddy, taking a random nigga down in the street was nothing.

"Do not try me, bitch!" I heard Jayson's words loud and clear as the guys dragged him away.

I knew we'd meet again but I really did not care.

Tom-Tom

The picnic had already gotten started. On the way back from Artavia's, we'd stopped and loaded up on liquor and juice for the entire park. I ain't gonna lie; I was feeling on top of the world to be linked up with people who could guarantee me money. It was time to unwind, act a fool, and celebrate.

Murk swerved as he pulled his truck across the grass, then parked nearest the courts. No one spoke out about his rebellious act, since his subwoofers were banging out Detroit hits. Big Sean had the city rocking with his mixtape. After we unloaded cases of wine, boxes of beer, and bottles of Rémy 1738 for our own sipping pleasure, Murk tossed me a fat bag of Kush so I'd roll up a few blunts. I had packs of cigarillos for days, so this whole sandwich bag of loud was about to broken down and blazed. It had been a long day of hustling, grinding, and getting down on clowns. I was ready to unwind.

"Hey, chief," I called out to Murk, who was already flirting with another girl. "I'm about to run these bags back to my crib, roll up a few, then meet you back over here in a few. I ain't trying to fuck up my work threads either."

"Cool. I'll be over here seeing what it's working with."

The girl he was eye fucking up and down started giggling and blushing. That bitch was all smiles only 'cause Bird hadn't seen them yet. Murk was playing with fire. Beatrice might've been young, but a lightweight she was not. Me and her had enough of our own crazy history that we could write a book. That girl had more than a few screws missing in her head. I dipped off, leaving that explosion to go off on its own. I did not want no parts of Murk's hot boy dating life.

"Hey, Tom-Tom," Shayla's friend Yoshi sang out to me as she strolled up the street with her daughter.

"What up, girl? Should you be out already? Didn't you just have your li'l one?" I looked her up and down. It did not even look like she'd ever been pregnant. Her snap-back body had a nigga wondering what it looked like without clothes on.

"Yeah, almost a month ago. But I'm all good. I needed some air. Plus, you already know this picnic is about to slam. I'm just waiting on my sitter to get back from the store."

"No doubt. I feel you on that note. Murk got a spread by him. Plus, I'm about to roll up this sack. We all about to be hella straight." I couldn't front. It felt good to be the one holding green weight in my pocket that I could roll, distribute, and brag on. Even though this wasn't my baggie, I could easily pay for more grams.

"Damn. You're cute and modest," she laughed. "Shayla told me you and Murk were hanging, and I see you're rocking the hell out of those new Cole Haans. So I know Murk did not lay the spread out all on his own." Snickering, she ran her hand down my polo shirt, and I couldn't help but blush at her blatant flirting.

"Oh really? Well, what else do you know?" I was suddenly interested in Yo-Yo.

Yoshi

I guessed the rumors around the hood were true; Thomas Harris was on the rise. As I looked him up and down in his salmon polo, his khaki slacks, and his two-hundred-dollar loafers, a dozen shopping bags in his hands, I couldn't believe just a few weeks ago he had been rocking the buy one, get one free Champions from Payless shoe store. You couldn't have paid me to give Shayla's brother a second. He was the type of nigga who looked dirty—until now. And even though I had never told Shayla, because she was my friend, everyone that stepped foot in that house came out smelling funky. Too bad it wasn't in that good Kush kind of way. They didn't even have a dog, but it smelled like one was there as soon as you hit the door. Even though I hated to do this, 'cause me and Yani were bound to come out reeking of death, I couldn't let this opportunity pass.

"Can I use y'all bathroom right quick? I don't think I'ma be able to hold it long enough to make it around the corner, and I really don't want to use one of those filthy porta-potties." That was just a play off. I did not have to pee, and the urinal was probably in better shape than Shayla and Tom's toilet. But desperate times called for desperate measures, and I needed a slick way to get more of Tom's time.

"That ain't a problem. Come on."

As I followed behind Tom, it wasn't hard to notice that even his walk was different now. This nigga must've been getting major money for real. I knew Murk's reputation wasn't to be slept on, but I hadn't known he'd put young Tom down like he'd obviously done. My gold-digger radar was ringing louder than Yani when she cried for a bottle. Since I really didn't have to use the bathroom, I used that time to freshen my kitty cat and make sure my face was still put together. Shayla had some smell-good body wash and spray, which I helped myself to before leaving out. Girls were about to be flocking to Tom, since he was on the money team. So if I wanted to become the first lady, right now was my time to strike.

"Where y'all at, Tom-Tom?" I called as I stood in the hallway.

"In my bedroom. Come in here."

Once I got to the bedroom doorway, I saw him holding her while he was hanging up his clothes.

"Aw, my bad, Tom-Tom. Did Yani give you a hard time?"

"Oh, naw, li'l mama was perfect. I just did not want to leave her cooped up in that stroller downstairs, and we both needed to come up here." After handing her over, he moved back to his closet and continued to hang up his clothes.

Just like I expected, he was doing big thangs. Not only did he have True Religion, Joe's, and red bottom shoes for both himself and Shayla, he even had bags set to the side for her with MAC makeup falling out of them. Not being able to help myself, I couldn't catch myself from getting jealous. "Damn, you're setting your girlfriend up straight." I picked up one of the MAC bags and dangled it. I wanted to swipe a few glosses and eye shadows for myself.

"Quit trying to play me, Yoshi. You know bitches ain't been checkin' for the broke nigga. And I fa damn sure ain't about to be catching no gold-digging broad to waste my money on. Those are for Shayla. Maybe you can help her out with a few makeup tips for prom." Tom had just ruined my hopes of bum-rushing him. Apparently, he wasn't as dumb as he used to be broke.

"Oh, no doubt. I put my homegirl together today. Have you seen her since she left my house?"

"Naw, but I'm sure you did. I ain't never seen you have a bad day. Even when you were pregnant," Tom said, paying me a compliment, which had me blushing. "Speaking of my sis, let's get over to the park, so I can check in on her. If she ain't with you, she must be clicked up with that Bird's hot ass. I swear to G, I wish she'd leave that bad news bitch alone." Tom was now moving with some pep in his step, and the look on his face was one of pure disgust. The attention being focused on me had gone faster than it had come.

"Okay, well, it looks like I've got another reason to hate that trick. Let's go. I'm right behind you," I said, holding Yani, as we headed downstairs. I wasn't trying to sound deflated about him ending the impromptu quality time I'd lied my way into having with him, but I was saltier than ever.

Tom came to a sudden halt at the bottom of the stairs. "Wow, wait. Since when did the triple-threat trio become a dynamic duo, with my sister playing the middle?" Tom had figured out with ease the new way our relationship was set up.

"Yesterday is when it all blew up. I'm so over Bird and her drama." Biting my lip and tapping my foot, I was starting to get pissed all over again.

"Calm down, shorty. I see you're really worked up over whatever popped off. But this might work out in our favor. If we're both against Bird, then we might convince Shayla to leave her on the outs too. Stay strong for the fight. I'm counting on you to work with me."

"You've got a point, and you better believe I will. You've got a deal." I really did not give a fuck about Shayla and Bird's friendship, but I had to manipulate Shayla to get what I truly wanted—Tom.

Chapter Nineteen

Shayla

I'd seen Murk and Tom pull up. It was hard not to with all the attention they had brought to themselves by jumping the curb. When Bird hopped up, I knew our little girl's session had ended.

"C'mon, let's go sit by Murk and his fellas," Bird said, then pulled me toward where he and a few other guys were posted up, throwing a card game around. She'd recovered well from the confusion with Jayson.

"Do not go over there tripping, B. You know how them niggas get down once they get that liquor flowing into their system. It do not be nothing nice!"

"I'm not about to go over there tripping. I'm about to make it known I'm the chosen one. Let me show you how it's done."

Against my better judgment, I followed her over to where the drama would unfold, shaking my head the entire time. I did not know what shenanigans Bird had up her sleeve, but from experience, I knew her turn up was real.

"What up, li'l baby? You came over here for some attention?" Murk called her out as soon as she stepped up. He was the freshest out of the crew, dressed in nothing but name brands.

He glanced at me for two seconds before returning his attention to Bird, and I felt utterly dismissed once again. "You want some more of this good dick?" he asked her. Rubbing between her legs, he let his eyes roamed around and jump from each one of his boys, making even me feel uneasy. All at once they laughed out loud, like some type of inside joke was going on. I knew for sure Bird was in way over her head with Murk.

"You already know it," she said, giggling, like she wasn't used to attention.

I fell back into the shadows, something I often did when Bird got to flirting.

"I was kind of hoping you had something else for me too," she added.

"Check you out! That is my girl. You already know Papa is gonna take care of you the right way. Just be patient." The way Murk's words rolled from his tongue, I sensed nothing but trouble.

"So, you like your fit, Shayla?" he asked, catching me off guard. I wasn't expecting him to acknowledge me. "My manz Tom was persistent about getting you straight for the 'nic."

"Yeah, I was hella geeked. But he's always looking out for me. I guess that is what big brothers are for." I gave Murk a condescending wink, not knowing how else to respond. Even though I was happy to get a few moments of solo attention, he did not have to put me on blast. Yeah, I wanted to be seen but not put on front street. I was slightly embarrassed.

"Shit, girl, I must be a fool. 'Cause that was what I thought having a man was for," he said, then laughed at my expense, giving his homeboy a high five. He shifted his attention back to Bird, and I saw that even she was laughing at the joke, which I did not find funny.

What the fuck is with this non-funny-ass nigga trying to clown me? I do not even get down with foolery. I knew it was a bad choice to come over here. I should've followed my first mind, I thought, seething.

"I think that is my cue. I'm about to go find a spot to chill at. Holla at me when you're done with this little cake bake session, Bird," I said with attitude, then turned, about to walk off. Murk did not know me like that, and I did not care to know him. Bullying and putting me on blast just wasn't acceptable, and to be quite clear, I wasn't in the mood. Bird could get down with her little publicity freak show stunt on her own.

"Have it your way." She shooed me away, as if I was an afterthought.

Truth was, the more involved with Murk she got, the more our friendship frayed. *Fuck it, though. It's nothing*, I thought.

I took a seat on a lawn chair nearest the basketball court and watched the wannabe hoop stars throwing up a game of street ball. With friendly wagers on the table, cats were checking, dunking, and scoring left and right, all trying to show off their individual skills. Even Duncan was on the court, getting a few "and ones" called in his favor, in addition to putting up mad points. A few of the opponents from the other team tried checking him with heavy defense, but he was too skilled for these street-level ballers. He was manhandling the ball the same way he had manhandled Yoshi yesterday. The more I watched him in his element, the more I understood why Yo-Yo was riding his coattails so hard. His winning layups and jump shots were gonna take him on one helluva ride from this gutter-ass neighborhood to the NBA for sure. After Duncan scored thirteen of his team's twenty-one points, making his team triumphant, he pocketed his winnings, then took a seat on the sidelines, waiting for a few opponents to rest up for a rematch.

Yoshi strolled up just then. She seemed to have a glow about her and to be moving with a little pep in her step. I chalked it up to her being happy to have a break from Yani. "Hey, Shayla boo!" she called.

"Aw shit. Look who found a babysitter," I replied. "I'm glad you did, because Bird done dissed me for ole black-ass Murk over there." I looked in their direction, giving them the evil eye. Yoshi followed my eyes to check out the scene before taking a seat on the lawn chair next to mine.

"Girl bye, do not let that ruin your mood. You already know how Bird is over some dick. Let that shit roll off your back so we can have a good time. I fa damn sure ain't worried about her bony ass!" She scanned the court to see if Duncan, I assumed, was on deck.

"You're right. I'm too cute today to be sweating that nonsense. She can do her all day." I looked Yoshi up and down. She was cute, but too naked for Duncan's taste. "On another note, are you sure it's cool to be out here dressed like that with your boo just about twenty feet away?"

"Let him tell it, we're done. So I'm out here to find Yani a stepdaddy," she laughed, leaning over and pulling the romper from her booty crack. "And please believe I'm onto one."

"Yeah, okay, that is on you. But just so you have a heads-up, I won't be trying to get his big behind up off you if he comes over here with a problem. I've seen him fight girls. I'm straight on y'all drama."

"We already know you ain't busting no grapes. You showed me how you rolled yesterday," she said jokingly and nudged me. "But it's cool. I do not think he'll be coming anywhere near me after our argument earlier. So I do not think you have anything to worry about."

Not too long after Yoshi joined me, men started gathering around us. Bird was the hot girl, Yo-Yo was the sexy tomboy, and I just tried fitting in where I could. The guys were happy she seemed to be among the available again. And even though Duncan was sitting across the court, ready to explode as he watched her giggle, hug, and flirt with so many guys, she kept tempting her admirers and paying him no never mind. Some of them were even giving me a little attention for a change, so I followed Yoshi's lead on how to take it in.

Me and Yoshi were having a ball. Tom-Tom bought us a few bottles of coolers and even a bag of Kush to go with all the other free blunts floating around. Between the little session we had going on by ourselves and the dudes who spread their generosity with their turn-up supplies, we were A-1 good. If this was any indication of how my life was about to be, I was ready for the adventure.

"Ugh, look at your nasty-ass friend." In the middle of blowing out a stream of smoke, Yoshi started choking and pointing across the park, toward Bird.

"Oh, hell naw. That bitch is straight tripping." I did not know how to react or what I should do.

Bird looked more than comfortable and willing as she bounced up and down on Murk's dick in front of his whole crew. This was way too much. Some freaky-type shit had gone down in the hood before, but this took the cake. Her too-short shorts were no longer covering her booty but were halfway off as Murk's hands gripped both cheeks, making her dance on top of his meat. From the sounds of her moans and the hungry look in his eyes, you could tell he was hitting it hard and was almost ready to explode. It was like watching a porno going down in public. I couldn't believe it.

"Damn, I might not be speaking to Bird right now, but it would be fucked up if we did not go over there to at least try to stop her from making a fool of herself. It's just always something with her," Yoshi said, turning to me. Her eyes pleaded with me to back her up, but I couldn't move from the lawn chair I was sitting in.

I couldn't believe Yoshi was actually considering going over there to look out for the very girl who'd deliberately pulled off on her getting beat down yesterday. I knew our clique usually wasn't into holding grudges, but even I would've acted sideways after hearing all of what went down with Yo-Yo after Bird started the entire fiasco. And I was the neediest of the crew. Yo-Yo was on some true loyal girl–type shit.

"I'm not going back over there. That nigga Murk came at me from the left earlier, so me and him need fifty feet between us at all times," I announced, keeping it real. As engrossed as I was in the sexual scene going down with one of my best friends and a nigga I now hated, I wasn't going no closer for my sexual needs or to prevent Bird from later regretting what she was doing.

"Well, dang. I guess this is how it feels to have the shoe on the other foot. I guess the unspoken rule in our friendship is, 'Every girl for herself.'" Yoshi was putting on a front like she was just getting hip, but she'd already peeped their so-called three-girl-clique was starting to dismantle.

"I can't call it," I replied. "What I do know is that I'm tired of getting caught up in her twisted-ass drama."

We might've shared moments in each other's lives and been there to blow some weed in an effort to deal with the bullshit we'd had to experience. But by no means could any of us truly count on the other two to be there no matter what. We were thick like thieves but loose like change. I guessed this was a glimpse into the future.

Bird

My eyes danced across clouds as Murk took control of my willing body. I was completely submissive to him and loving every moment of the attention. I was his, and he was mine. Everyone knew it now. There wasn't a chick around the way who could lie and say he hadn't been tagged. This wasn't embarrassing for me. I was living in the moment.

My adrenaline was feeding off his, but it wasn't a match. He was grilling into my guts, drinking Moët, and claiming king into the camera.

The harder Murk stroked me in front of all his boys, the louder I screamed, begging for more. Me and his small-time posse had been partying hard, playing cards, horseshoes, and shooting the shit. It felt good being the main chick, the one he gave all his attention to, so I was living in the celebration big-time. We'd been downing one cup after another of the liquor Murk had brought, in addition to smoking a few laced blunts. Anything could've gone down with me tonight, including a train, and I probably would not have contested it. With Jayson no longer a factor in my life, there were no limitations to what I could do, so I wasn't worried about consequences or repercussions. All I wanted to do was cum. Murk was just the type of nigga I needed to match my wild side with. This rush I was riding on felt amazing.

"Tell the world whose pussy this is," he ordered, turning my face to the camera and smacking my cheeks to the command. The stinging sensation from his hand had me moaning loudly from the intensity of pleasure and pain.

"He's murdering this shit. It's his," I panted into the bright light, dizzy off the strokes and feeling all the liquor we'd been guzzling over the past few hours start to bubble up.

Murk

This was the exact reason why I was in love with turning Bird out. My boys all had devious grins on their faces as they held their camera phones up, filming me and her getting down. They'd formed a circle around us when I proposed the drunk and high dare to Bird and she accepted. The group wasn't big, but if Bird continued to scream, we'd for sure gain a lot more attention. I was trying to break Bird's back with my thrusts to her gut. And each time she called herself throwing it back, I gripped her hips tighter and controlled the rhythm. Wasn't no way my fellas were about to catch me on tape nuttin' quick. As I took a big guzzle of champagne, I decided it was time to see just how ratchet Bird was willing to go. She sure as hell was dripping wet.

I lifted her up off my still stiff manhood, turned her around, and rammed my meat back up in her dripping wet vagina. "Damn you feel good," I told her.

I held up the bottle of Moët as I fucked her good on film, and then I poured it out and watched it splash on her ass. It was wobbling, bouncing, and looking oh so tasty and delicious. A nigga couldn't hold back no longer. "Oh, shit, I'm about to bust a fat one."

Tom

This summer was gonna be a hot one for sure. And with me getting money, I was going to make sure it was lit. Instead of staying turned up with Murk, his crew, and Bird, I kept a safe distance away and monitored Shayla. My baby sister did not have high self-esteem, but she was far more beautiful that any of the girls all throughout the neighborhood. Once she started believing in herself and her beauty, I was going to have open beefs and murder cases. I had vowed when I was thirteen always to protect li'l sis. The thought of purchasing a gun was high on my list now that she was glowing. I'd peeped her getting double takes and glances from the fools around here. The same fools who had never paid her any attention when they'd considered her dusty. It was the same look I was catching from females who had once refused to take a compliment from me because I wasn't a cool kid rocking fly kicks.

I wondered about Yoshi, though. She seemed different; and from the bits and pieces I knew about her, *a hard-knock life* was putting it lovingly when it came to describing how she was living. The same reasons I was curious, though, were the same reasons I knew I needed to move with caution. When you spent your life struggling, you started grasping for straws—which I knew all too well. I'd been a wishful watcher too. When you did not have much, you watched niggas who did, wishing it was you. Yoshi could be looking for a quick escape hatch from her situation. As I watched Shayla, I noticed Yoshi never left her side. Either she was being loyal or Shayla had told her I was touching money with Murk. As far as I was concerned, everybody's motives were questionable, since I'd never truly had a real person in my corner. And since it was clear I was high and my thinking was all over the place, I stopped thinking and got even more fucked up. I ain't never had a pocket full of money, so it was most definitely time for a celebration.

Chapter Twenty

Artavia

The small room I'd isolated myself in all day was starting to spin. While Murk had been out getting gritty, I'd been in here printing checks and getting documents ready for our team to make its next move. Since Tom seemed eager to execute the plan me and Murk had sat before him, I did not want to come up short on my end. 'Cause, most importantly, I had an ulterior motive that needed to play out like magic.

Unlike with other work sessions, I made sure now to devote more than half of the time manipulating the business we shared to work in my favor. Murk had set the rules. This was just the best move I could make in the game. He might've come in here with some bullshit-ass apology gifts, but that was just to pacify me and to cover up what was really going on. He was just making sure I stayed loyal to the team. But, oops, the joke was on him. I hadn't been fooled.

I pulled hard on the blunt I was smoking while twiddling my prescription pill in my fingers. I did not feel like popping it, calming down, or having it put me in a sleeplike trance. This was one temper tantrum I wasn't trying to have Zoloft or my psychiatrist help me deal with. As I played back the sex video, a fifteen-second clip, his boy had just posted on Instagram, I felt the need for vengeance grow inside me. Murk had ignited a fire within my soul I was pretty sure he could put out. For the next week, I was gonna play cool so we could get this money, but after that, I'd be onto some new-level shit. Too bad for him I wasn't the type of bitch you wanted to make an enemy out of.

Tom-Tom

I woke up to the sound of Ricardo slamming the front door and whistling up the block, and I wondered what he'd stolen to get some credit or cash for a hit. Whatever it was, if I cared, I'd buy it back for double later. Nothing changed about the game with Ricardo but the date, time, and year. After sleeping on the proposition, I knew without a doubt that shooting this mini road trip would be worth my while. With Shayla's graduation and our birthdays right around the corner, I needed my count game high so I could make some much-needed moves.

Scrolling through my new phone and scratching my balls through my boxers, I tried to see what female I was gonna check for tonight. They could smell money like hound dogs, but I wasn't paying to upgrade none of these rats around here. If they'd shut me down in the past, I wasn't giving them gym-shoe money or even a few bucks for a head job to get my dick wet now. I did not give a fuck how it sounded. I was into holding grudges. They weren't getting a title up off me, now that I was knee-deep in the game. The only person I planned on saving from this gritty-ass hood was Shayla.

The Kush blunt I was blowing on was getting me high, while the leftover Rémy VSOP I was sipping from last night was keeping me faded. I was ready to get into round two of recklessness, but for some reason, the only chick who kept crossing my mind was Yoshi. For some reason, I really wanted to see what that girl was working with.

The sound of my phone's ringtone ended my day-dreaming. It was Murk, so I picked up.

"What up, my nigga? You up or still tapped out from last night?" Murk asked, and then he laughed into the phone loudly, just as crunk as he'd been last night.

"Naw, I'm up, trying to recap all that went down, actually. You and ole girl got mad crazy, yo! That shit is all over the internet."

"You're lying. That is some bad news I did not want to start this morning off with. Damn. Cheesy-ass niggas can't be discreet about shit nowadays." He had the nerve to sound surprised someone had uploaded the footage, but I wasn't. Everybody and their mama wanted their number game up when it came to likes, comments, or hits, so this video of them having sex publicly had taken no time to go viral.

"Hell, naw, bro. Y'all out here with hashtags like hashtag-detroitfuckfest, hashtag-onlyinthed, and hash-tag-levelstothisshit. I'ma just be real when I tell you this. It ain't like you and Bird were trying to be inconspicuous. A nigga like me thought it was some type of amateur porn competition going down." Murk was straight fooling. He had performed for the camera last night, but today he was acting like folk were wrong for filming it.

"Real talk, I must've popped too many bottles. I've gotta give that shit time to blow over. I can't blow the spot up with so much on the line, ya dig? So if you need me, I'll be laying low, getting everything in order so we can be out on time come Monday."

"A'ight, playa. I'll be around here getting Shayla together for graduation in the meantime. Do not forget I'm gonna need the hookup on that crib and car."

"No doubt. Once we touch back down, I got you for sure."

Chapter Twenty-one

Tom

For a week straight, me, Murk, and Artavia had been getting down in the check game in a major way. I had even got the chance to live it up in Ohio, getting several accounts opened and even more fraudulent checks cashed. Everything was working out in our favor, and my swag couldn't have been better. I did not know how Murk was balancing Bird and Tay, but somehow he was coming out king. I wasn't worried about him, though. I had enough on my plate with Shayla needing me to look out in a major way for her senior activities. Besides, I was trying to be only his right-hand man, not his keeper.

Before heading back to the D, we had one more bank to hit. I was trying to have my cash load on swollen for all the future spending I was getting ready to do. By the time we pulled up to the bank, Murk was on the phone, checking in with Artavia, and I was gearing my ego up to play the game. I was feeling too cocky to fail, so this would probably be the point when I fucked myself in the game as well. Once Murk ended his call, I climbed out of the car and headed inside the bank. There was no line, so I went straight to a teller's window.

"Good morning, ma'am," I said as I slid the checks Tay had printed out through the slot, as usual. "Here's my ID, and nope, I do not have an account here." Moving too fast, answering questions she hadn't asked, that was my first mistake.

"Oh, okay, Mr. Harris. Well, with checks for these amounts, we require a twenty-four- to forty-eight-hour hold. So in order to cash them, you must have an account."

"Are you sure? I've cashed my checks before without them being held up." I was giving her the side eye, and she was returning the same.

"Yes, sir, I'm sure." She rushed to give me an explanation we both knew wasn't true. "Maybe that was before the policies changed," she said. "But I am more than happy to help you open an account if you like." She was smiling like she was being friendly, but nothing about this white woman said she trusted me, even though I'd cleaned up well.

"No, I'm good. I have to get back to work. I'll come back when my shift is over." I'd made up what I thought would be a good enough excuse for her to hand the checks back and let me go on about my day. Instead, she made matters worse.

"Well, I would not want to cause you the inconvenience of having to come back. Let me see what I can do. Um, Amy!" When she waved to a whiter, brunette woman, I instantly panicked.

"No, I d-do not have time. Can I have my checks back?" I stuttered as Amy headed over.

"Amy, Mr. Harris here doesn't have an account with us but has two payroll checks over the limit he wants to cash. Can we expeditiously open him an account or do an override?"

I watched the tall, lanky brunette woman look over the checks before responding. "Thank you for calling me over here, Kathie. You're certainly right that our first need to meet is that of the customers." Amy turned toward me. "Mr. Harris, this will just take a few minutes. I'll take care of this transaction personally." Her wide smile seemed genuine, but you could never tell what white people were thinking from their shifting, beady eyes.

"Thank you, Amy. I appreciate that. And you, too, Kathie, for going the extra mile." I was hoping the con-artist game I was trying to run over on them was working.

"Not a problem. I'll be right back."

What Amy the manager meant by taking care of the transaction was to photocopy the checks and my identification card while having Kathie type some long memo into the computer. I'd never seen this procedure done, but I was too far in to undo it all. Instead of causing a scene and giving the bank manager reason to suspect I was up to shady business, I tried to be inconspicuous as I kept staring out the window. I'd show these cracker jacks a real nigga getaway if any cops pulled up or the security guard started to act suspicious. I was nervous as hell. Something just wasn't sitting right with me.

"Kathie, please disburse $3219.42 and make a note on the account. Mr. Harris, can I have your thumbprint on each of these sheets?" Amy had returned, and I was happy to have the ball back rolling. She wasn't acting like there was a problem.

I moved quickly, not caring if it seemed suspicious or not. Within seconds, I had put my thumbprint on four different sheets and was getting the bills counted down to me.

"Here you go, Mr. Harris." Amy finally handed my ID back. "Have a nice day."

"Thanks. You do the same." My feet couldn't move fast enough. It was time to get back to the D, to my comfort zone. This shit right here might've been way over my head.

Shayla

The last week of high school was unlike every other week of my educational experience since ninth grade. I'd been the last person on everyone's radar before, but now with Tom-Tom raising my stock, I'd become the popular girl, and people were checking for me. Every boy that had looked the other way at the small-time crush I might've had was now all up in my grill. Their small-time money wasn't on the level my brother and Murk were getting money on, though, so I was no longer looking their way. Not only had Tom-Tom funded everything for my senior activities, but he was throwing me a party too. I couldn't lie. My ego was growing, and it felt good to have everyone making me the center of attention.

Bird had started to throw mad shade my way since I wasn't her fix me up project anymore. But she could miss me with all that hating. I had come from the bottom and wasn't ever going back to being her lackey or charity case. I was popping tags on a daily, Yoshi was doing my hair on a regular, and she'd even shouted me out on Instagram so my number of followers could jump. At first, I'd been hesitant about Tom doing business with the man who was turning my friend out, but now I encouraged it. She was getting kickbacks her way, and I was getting mine. My meager lifestyle had been upgraded like a mother-fucka!

"Shayla Harris," my counselor called out as she stood in the doorway to her office.

I rushed over, and she ushered me into her office. Then she handed me my cap, gown, and graduation tickets.

"Tomorrow this time, you'll be a graduate in the class of twenty-thirteen," she said solemnly. "Have you made a commitment to a college yet?"

"I'm planning on taking a few classes at the community college to get a feel for what I might want to do there. This whole high school career of mine was more tormenting than enlightening," I revealed. There was no need to put up a wall for my counselor. On more than a few occasions, I'd been in here over family or social problems.

"The only advice I can offer you, my dear, is not to get lost in this gritty world. If you're not careful, it will chew you up and spit you out. Please make sure you maximize all your potential. I'm proud of how far you have come, and you should be to."

"Thanks, Ms. Jones. That means a lot coming from you. I'll see you tomorrow."

She was right; I had come a long way. And now with money cleaning me up, I was bound to go even further.

Yoshi

The testing center was jam packed with people of all ages. Despite it to being so early in the morning, everyone seemed to be bright-eyed and bushy-tailed, ready to conquer this GED exam. I, however, was feeling my stomach do flips. This shit wasn't about to be an easy feat. But I had to try to conquer it anyway. If I did not at least get this piece of paper saying I knew the basic skills of reading, writing, and arithmetic, me and Yani would not have a chance.

After sitting down at a desk, I took a sip of my Pepsi, trying to calm down, but I kept tapping my number two pencil erratically. My mind was straight gone, I was completely zoned out, and the blunt I'd smoked on the way over here probably wasn't the best idea. I hadn't gotten a wink of sleep last night between trying to cram for this test and staying up with Yani. She must've missed her daddy, 'cause she would not sleep for longer than thirty minutes at a time. Then I had walked out the door to a process server waving a motion in my face that indicated Duncan's mother had filed papers against me to confirm the paternity of Yani. I had cried the whole bus ride over here because attached to the motion was a list of all the accusations they were making against me that made me unfit to be Yani's primary custodial parent. They claimed that I was mentally unstable, that I lacked an education comparable to what Duncan had attained, and that they could offer her better schooling, housing, and emotional support. The shit was threaded up with so much legal jargon, I couldn't even make sense of it all. I hoped I didn't smear anything important with my tears, because I couldn't stop crying. I needed to see a witch doctor or some shit, 'cause it felt like a curse was on my back.

"Okay, group, please put all your electronic devices away and clear the desk of all items except for a number two pencil. The exam will start in five minutes promptly. If you have to use the restroom, I suggest you do so now. No one will be permitted to re-enter the testing room once they leave." The instructor ticked off the rules as I damn near threw up in my mouth from nerves.

Come on now, Yoshi. Get your nerves together. You can do this. Naw, scratch that. You've gotta do this. Yani's counting on you, I told myself silently. I needed to knock this test out of the park so I could use it as evidence in the court case. I slid the court paperwork into my backpack and said a small prayer. If I could show the judge I was much more than the high school dropout his conniving mom had painted me as, there might be a chance of me keeping Yani. But as of now, my character looked wrecked.

The instructor went on. "When you are done, please turn your test in to me and enjoy the rest of your day. The results will be mailed to you within one week. Take your time, read each question thoroughly, and get through those you know first. It is not a race. How you do on this test will determine your steps for the future. Good luck to each one of you."

Bird

The last week of school irked me more than every day of the past four years. It was like the shit would never end. All week long I'd been taking finals and turning in extra-credit assignments and missing papers that I had slacked on throughout the year. My teachers were gracious enough to allow me this privilege since they did not want to put up with my displeasing attitude for another year.

Ecstatic, Shayla ran over toward me with her cap and gown in her hand. "Hey, Bird! We're finally about to be out this bitch. You coming to my party tomorrow, right? I ain't heard from you all week." Ever since her dirty-ass brother had joined up with Murk and upgraded her from a F grade to a C- grade, she'd thought her swag matched mine. I'd straight beefed out with Yo-Yo, and I had a feeling Shayla was about to be next.

"Yeah, I'll probably come by for a second. I kinda already planned something a little special for my dude, since he's been on the road so much, but you know I'll show my face for my girl." Giving Shayla a fake smile, I did not care if my rude disposition was obvious. She was excited about getting money. This shit wasn't new to me.

"Oh, okay, cool. Well, I was going to ask you for a ride back to the crib, but I'd hate to be an inconvenience," she commented smartly, then rolled her eyes. "I'll see you later, B." She walked off, heading toward the bus stop, and I walked off to talk to my counselor about my fate. Hopefully I'd done enough makeup work to graduate with my class.

"Well, Ms. Beatrice Normandy, I see you've been working very diligently this past week to make up almost every heavily weighted assignment for this past semester." As Mr. Cartwright flipped through my work, he did not seem impressed.

"Yes, sir. I'm trying to walk with my class." Shifting in my seat, I was starting to feel uneasy as he slid his chair around the desk.

"I'm not going to sugarcoat this for you, Beatrice. Your overall grade point average is low, these made-up assignments are subpar, and you have no extracurricular activities or gleaming recommendations to help push you over the edge. I'm not sure you'll be a candidate for a diploma tomorrow." Mr. Cartwright totally killed my dreams as he handed me the summer enrollment form.

"Naw, man, what the fuck! I busted my ass all week on those papers. This is unbelievable!" Jumping up out of my seat, I was ready to knock my counselor down to the floor. His bald-headed Uncle Tom ass had had it out for me since ninth grade, when he'd caught me slob knobbing Jayson in the boys' locker room.

"I'm going to have to ask you to calm down and lower your voice, Ms. Normandy. From searching on the World Wide Web, I know you have some other talents that might get you a glowing recommendation from me." He waved his phone in front of my face, showing me the clip of me and Murk getting freaky at the park.

I looked up at my counselor and recognized the look in his eyes immediately. My dad's eyes had danced with the devil when he wanted some of my juiciness back in the day.

"I want my cap and gown when we're done," I insisted.

He unzipped his pants; then I dropped to my knees. I knew the routine. If you'd met one dirty old man, you'd met them all.

After swerving into the driveway, I hopped out of my Malibu almost faster than I shut the engine off. My mother's car was in the driveway, so I rushed into the house to tell her the good news. *Thank God she's running late*, I told myself.

"Ma! Ma, where you at!" As I ran through the house, I was screaming out for my mother. I still had cum crust around my mouth, but it did not matter. By now she should be used to me being a ho. "Ma!" Clutching my cap, gown, and graduation tickets, I wanted to thank her for allowing my dad to train me up. Had it not been for him creeping into my room on her clock, I might've been sweating in summer school next week.

I reached my mother's bedroom and peeked inside. She was still in bed. "Why are you still cooped up in that room and not at work?" I said from the doorway.

She didn't answer or even move a muscle.

"Ma?"

She did not budge or turn over or say a word. I screamed her name from the doorway, then finally went over to the bed and shook her to wake her up. Her shoulder felt cool to the touch.

"Oh fuck! Ma, wake up!" I screamed, sure I could be heard for miles from here. Then I noticed in her hand a prescription medicine bottle. When I took a close look, I saw the name Sandra Meriwether printed on the label. My mother was a home health aide, and Sandra was her patient and suffered from lupus. From the looks of it, my mother had taken Sandra's pills and overdosed. "What in the fuck did you do, Ma!"

I left her body lying limp on the bed and ran to call 911.

Chapter Twenty-two

Marilyn

At first, I'd thought Artavia was my saving grace when she found me, starved, dehydrated, and damn near dead, in that abandoned house, where my "sick in the head" son had been holding me hostage like a dog. I'd lost count of how many days had passed after the first week, because it was hard to keep track of time without brain power. And I didn't have brain power, because he had barely fed me. I guessed it was a good thing I'd been abused by men all my life, because all the training had prepped me for Marvin's punishment. And I expected karma to be swift for me.

I knew his anger toward me, his hate, and even his death wishes went back a long way; they'd developed long before I popped into his life unexpectedly. I didn't blame him for harboring those feelings against me, because I deserved them. No child deserved to live with the weight of abandonment simply from being born. I ain't even fault my mom for telling him part of the truth. I *was*, however, shocked she had kept my whereabouts a secret from him. It might've taken years for me to get started, and it for damn sure wasn't much, but I had sent my mom cards containing cash for him every month, and I'd doubled the amount on Marvin's birthday. She'd even got pictures of her other two grandkids. I had done everything but put my address on the envelope.

Rolling around in the bed, I was trying to fight off the demons that were heavy on my back. For years I'd been doing a good job of pushing them down and functioning, but being locked away with my thoughts, and forced to go back and forth through withdrawals, had my body still going through weird shit. No matter how high I got, I couldn't chase the depression away.

Instead of my high sedating me, it had my mind playing tricks on me. The more dope I snorted courtesy of Artavia's pockets, the more paranoid I became and the more vivid the hallucinations were. At times, I was sure I saw Ruth Mae standing over my feeble body, shaking her head. I knew she was probably rolling over in her grave at the disgraceful mess I'd become. I wanted to beg for her mercy and even ask her to talk to God about possibly forgiving me, but I had no hope. I hadn't even forgiven myself for the decision I'd made.

When I met my ex-husband, he immediately swept me off my feet, and we immediately started a family. He was kind, hardworking, and dependable—different than any of the men from the projects I grew up in. Spiderman offered me the world. I was a well-kept wife who did not have to work or worry. And when I compared my life to the struggle Ruth Mae had had with me while I was growing up in the projects, I decided not to risk Marvin's well-being by bringing along with me and allowing him to be the stepchild from hell. Him and Ruth Mae were just a drive across town, but I let my firstborn son grow up thinking his mother didn't love him. And since I was being honest now, it wasn't that hard to start a new life with a husband and two kids. For thirteen years, I successfully outsmarted karma, but that bitch always had a way of finding you.

Weeks ago, Marvin found me drunk, high, and beaten half to death in an alleyway on the east side of Detroit.

When I woke up, I discovered my ankles were handcuffed to a bed, but I did not panic, 'cause I knew my time would come either way. I wasn't gonna live forever, and I sure wasn't cherishing life to give a fuck if it was gone.

Whatever Artavia's plan was, it wasn't gonna work. I couldn't hide from Ruth Mae. When I closed my eyes, I saw her. In the music in my headphones, I heard her voice. And even though I was alone in this hotel room, I felt her presence.

"Poor chile of mine. You've ruined your life. And I didn't raise you to do your children like that. Your boys needed you to show them how to treat women, and your daughter needed you to show her how to loved, respected, and valued."

"I'm sorry. I'm so sorry, Ma," I said aloud. Rocking back and forth, I continued to hear my mother's voice.

"You've ruined those kids' lives. I did not raise you to be this weak."

"I know, but I'm too far gone to get better, Ma. This shit has got me bad." Either the hallucinations had control over me or God had sent his angel down to speak to me. I kept blinking, trying to wake up from a dream that was truly my reality. Ruth Mae seemed so real, like she was here with me in the flesh. Her hair was tightly pulled up into a bun, while her creamy skin glowed.

"All your life you've been a runner. Try something different, Marilyn Rose." Her image disappeared.

Seconds later, I was running down the hotel hallway to the lobby, then sprinting out the front door. I was heading toward the nearest bus stop. It was time for me to find my way home.

Chapter Twenty-three

Tom

Rocking my red and white Detroit Versus Everybody tee, my black denim True jeans, with my shirt tucked into my pants to floss my Louie V belt, I stood back from the mirror in my bedroom, admiring my swag. I'd stepped my game up to a million, following in Murk's footsteps like only a real protégé could. Sliding on my bloodred Giuseppe Zanotti high-top sneakers, I couldn't wait to step out on these lames tonight. Fuck scuff-marked shoes, run-down soles, and worn denim jeans. I'd burned my old wardrobe the first day our bank licks popped off. This might've been Shayla's night, but I was about to shine right along with her.

Tonight was going to be epic. I'd set Shayla up like a queen for this graduation–eighteenth birthday celebration she'd begged me to finance. But it felt good to finally be able to make good on the word I had promised her nine years ago. With the money me and the crew had turned over in Ohio, I was planning on securing us an apartment and paying the rent for at least one year. That was the biggest gift I had for my baby sister; but for now, I was settling for another shopping bag of gifts.

I bumped into Ricardo as soon as I came out of my bedroom. "Damn! You stay lurking," I muttered. "Do not get no bright ideas, and if you have any now, I suggest you lose them. This room better be just how I left it when I get back," I warned, daring him to come at me, like he'd done a few weeks ago. My trigger finger was itching to test its aim.

"Anything under this roof is mine, li'l nigga," Ricardo whispered under his breath, knowing I would still hear him.

"Try that theory out and ya best cop a black suit from the thrift shop for the county to bury you in. You've been warned, old man."

If I did not quickly get Ricardo out of my sight, the entire night would be ruined. He wasn't worth that type of sacrifice. I wasn't trying to ruin Shayla's night by taking our father's head off. My word was my bond. So I told myself, *Get ya' game face on*, as I sped down the hallway, tapped twice on Shayla's door, then walked straight in, hoping she was all good. Not saying a word, I tossed the Louboutin shoebox onto her bed and waited to see her reaction.

"Dang, you could've knocked first," she whined, throwing me attitude, which I'd been getting a lot of from her lately. "I almost messed up my makeup."

"Damn me for creating a monster," I mumbled as I leaned back against the wall and watched her in the mirror. I couldn't believe she was all grown up. I wasn't looking at my sister in that incest type of way, but her curves had filled out, her hips were spreading, and the innocent look she had had at nine was just a fading memory. She looked more like Rose than she probably could account for. Her long hair, caramel complexion, and the curve of her lips when she smiled all reminded me of our mother.

"Since you barged in on me, can you make yourself useful by taking my dry cleaning out of the plastic? I'm wearing the Fine-Ass Girls crop-top jogging suit."

Bossing me around like a true woman, I thought. If it wasn't totally her day, I'd be putting Shayla in her place. I was getting fed up with the bratty-girl attitude.

"Yeah, you've got it, sis." I gritted the words through my teeth. My ego obviously wasn't the only one swollen in this house. Money had made us totally different people.

"I can't believe you, Tom-Tom! More gifts?" Astonished, she snatched the top off the shoebox, tossed it on the floor, then held up a bright red pair of Lou Spikes to match the Draya-inspired fit she was wearing. "Oh my God! These kicks are mad cold, bro. You're shopping in a whole new tax bracket. Keep this up and I won't ever be leaving home." Shayla apparently had no idea about the final surprise I'd be giving her tonight.

"We've been down for so long, I gotta make sure we stunt hard when we're up. We've got more coming up to do. Besides all that, I'm proud of you for not getting twisted up with all the craziness Rose left us in. I know it's been hard growing up without Mom. You could be fucked-up crazy like Bird or already on baby number one with a jerk like Yo-Yo, but you're out here doin' the damn thang. You did as right as you could with so much wrong going on around you."

"Thanks, bro, but do not be getting all mushy on me. I can't go tearing up. I've worked too hard on this makeup. Fuck Rose, since that is how she made it. I've got one helluva big brother holding me down." Since she ended the discussion before it could get started, I could tell the fact that we had been abandoned still ate at her, but she was playing the tough girl role.

Not trying to ruin the vibe, I let the topic go, lit a congratulatory blunt, and waited on her to finish getting ready. It had always been me and Shayla against the world. Tonight would be no different. This would be her first big party since Rose had left us.

Murk

Me and Tay had been counting up money for the past week, but nothing seemed to make her forget about the video with Bird. As fucked up as it may have been, 'cause I was banging her too, she'd known from jumpstreet the type of man I was and that I did not like to be kept.

"The site has slowed up some, probably because the ad is old. Instead of making a new one, I think it's time to crap out," she announced. "I'm gonna make this last print down, then start packing shit up. I think we've got enough to pull all the ads from 5-Star and start fresh somewhere else."

"Damn! Slow down, Ma. Why are you in such a rush? We haven't even dug deep enough into Ohio yet. I'm liking how this setup is going for now."

"Nigga, what! We were supposed to be hitting a quick lick and moving on. Do not tell me you've got all emotionally tied up with that bitch when you told me you wasn't trying to be kept. Or did you find your new best friend? Sounds like you're on some real sucker shit right now!" She was screaming her head off all in my face, acting like she had grown-man balls. I could smell the Kush and liquor on her breath; then she made a drastic decision to put her finger to my forehead and push it back.

Before I knew it, I lost my mind and went crazy on Tay. "Bitch, you better find some common sense. Do not put your fuckin' hands on me!" I slapped the spit from her mouth two times, then yoked her up, losing myself for a minute. I was getting ready to put her head through the wall, but I came to my senses.

"Get up off me, Murk! Are you crazy, nigga!" She was still going hard, even though I had the upper hand.

"You gonna fuck around and have me catch a case." I let her fall on the floor, and then I snapped up my duffel bag full of cash and darted to her door. "I ain't got time for this basic shit, Tay. Holla at me when you get your mind right!"

"Naw. How about you come for me when I send for you!" she shouted.

I rushed out the door, and she slammed it after me.

I flew down the stairwell to get the hell out of Dodge. Artavia had a point. Tom had become my homie, and I was going to support him while he did it big for his sister. I respected him for holding his family down, so I wasn't getting ready to tolerate the shit Tay was serving.

Chapter Twenty-four

Shayla

Thanks in part to the DJ and the personality Tom-Tom had paid to be on the mic, my graduation-birthday party was turning out to be better than I could've ever imagined it would be. Never, ever had I thought I'd actually be the center of attention at a party, and it felt damn good. All the birthday parties I used to cry over not having had been made up for on this one day—and the party wasn't even over yet.

The social club was packed with people from my school, plus all the people me and Tom-Tom were cool with around the hood. There was an open bar for everyone that was of age, but the food got smashed almost an hour into the party because people had come in like savages. Tom had paid for pans of chicken and waffles, spaghetti, a taco bar, and some fruit, and now there wasn't a crumb left. The same dudes that had clowned my brother his whole life were now eating off him, and it felt good seeing him live within his celebration.

"Yo, sis, slide over here and take some pictures with yo' bro," Tom called, waving me over to where he stood with the cameraman.

Do not get me wrong, females were dressed in their finest threads, but none of them were getting even close to my level. Smiling hard and posing, I made sure each time the hired photographer snapped an image of me, it was fabulous. I guessed you could say I was living within my celebration as well. And could you blame me?

I'd never been a drinker, but tonight was much different. I was getting lit! Everyone was giving me shots like I was the legal drinking age, but it was nothing, 'cause in my hood rules did not apply. I was hella fresh, loving the attention and, most of all, addicted to the limelight. With all eyes on me, the attention I was getting fed felt wonderful. I'd been starved for attention for far too long.

As I swayed from side to side, feeling the shots, I heard the crowd making a fuss. I turned to see Jayson walk through the door with a girl on his arm. *You've gotta be kidding me!* I said to myself. I did not think he'd really come to my party. I'd given everyone an invite, but I just knew he wasn't trying to have a run-in with Bird. Dressed fresh to death in some True Religion cargo shorts and Timberland shoes, he was mixing a New York swag with his *D* fitted cap. Even the girl he had draped on his arm was a dime piece. I knew once Bird showed up, this whole party was gonna get turned up quick. Her and Jayson might've broken up, but her ego couldn't take being replaced so quickly.

Once I locked my eyes on him, for some reason, I couldn't get them to move away. I'd never been attracted to Jayson or ever looked at him in that way. And up until last week, I had never even given him a reason to give me a double take. The Moët must've had me feeling extra tipsy, 'cause I was feeling slightly out of my element and out of control.

Everything about him was turning me on. His strong jawline, muscular build, and deep dimples had me ready to cash in my V card, even with my brother only a few feet away. And that was when it hit me. My pussy started tingling too. I started thinking back on all the stories

Bird had told about his sex game—some shit about him fucking like a thug. For a few seconds, I caught myself wondering how he could work my virginity out. My young little body had never been worked over, but seeing him touch and grab his mysterious date and command so much attention from her had me ready to see for myself what the hype was all about.

Just then Yoshi ran up and hugged me from behind, a bottle of Moët in her hand. She was obviously enjoying the party. "This party is slapping, baby girl. Congrats!" she exclaimed. "Now, let's getting it popping, 'cause twenty-one or not, you have done the damn thang. Around these parts, a high school diploma makes you grown, my little graduate." After pulling on my tassel, she put the rim of the Moët bottle to my lips, and I tilted my head back and guzzled down the remainder of the champagne. By the time I finished, she already had a replacement bottle in her other hand.

"All right, chick. Let's turn up until the sun comes up," I said. I dipped onto the dance floor, with Yoshi close behind, and enjoyed the verses of Future as we danced. We looked hella cute, she in a flowing summer dress, to conceal the leftover baby blubber, and I in my Draya-inspired dress. With all the moves she was throwing on the dance floor, you could tell she was a certified baby maker. Hearing her words repeat in my head about being grown now, I threw my reservations to the side, bent over, then imitated Yoshi twerking.

"Do it, boo. Check your hot ass out, Shayla. You better work it." Yo-Yo started waving people up from their seats onto the dance floor. At first, I slowed down my moves, but once the crowd circled around me, hyping me up by screaming my name, it was on fa sure, and there was no turning back. Dropping it low and touching all over my body, I got lost in my zone. The dress bent each curve of my body as guys pushed up on me, trying to get a feel. I popped back on the few that were cute but threw shade toward the ugmos. I had some nerve, since I'd just been upgraded from the ugly duckling click.

That was when I saw Jayson staring at me. He was fixated on the way my virgin body could keep up with the best of 'em. I wondered if he could tell I was putting on a front. Either way, I now viewed my dancing as a means to keep his attention. It was crazy, but I did not care that he was Bird's leftovers. I was worried only about myself and this eye-fuck marathon we had going on. When he tilted the brim of his fitted cap in my direction, I knew without a doubt I was doing something right.

Yoshi caught his gesture, stopped dancing, and took me by the arm. "Um, excuse me. I know you're grown and all, but you can't be serious. Are you trying to have beef with Bird too?" she said, calling me out but not making me back down.

"Bird is the furthest thing from my mind right now. You see how his eyes are fixated on me?"

"Whoa. Yeah, this is a whole new Shayla. I think I like her!"

Bird

"Well, I do not," I snapped, chiming in on the secret conversation that was going on. I wanted to make my presence known. I'd come here only to let them know they were fake as hell for not checking to see what was up after seeing an ambulance at my house.

Yoshi turned around, totally caught by surprise. "Oh, wow, Bird. I did not know you were here."

"Yeah, well, surprise, surprise. And from the looks of it, I'm right on time." As I gazed back and forth between

Jayson and Shayla, I felt my pressure start to rise, knowing that somewhere down the line I had started getting
played. Shayla was obviously too drunk in love with my
ex-dude to see she was in for one helluva fight. "So what's
up with the dynamic duo?" Rolling my eyes and snapping
my neck, I was putting both of my supposed homegirls
on the spot.

"Nothing much, Bird baby. We just out here getting
white girl wasted turning up," Shayla responded, giving
me the side eye. I picked up on her vibe that it was nothing but fakeness going on. I couldn't expect much more,
since me and her hadn't gotten back to the bestie level
after the spat in front of her house. So, from this point on,
it could be whatever.

"So, it's like that? Do I look blind or dumb? Y'all ain't
been dangling off my leash for that long not to remember
I bust grapes in my sleep. Keep trying me, Shayla!"

"Girl bye. I ain't trying. It's already done. And I'm done
dangling or being walked." Shayla had really grown a
pair.

"Oh really? So I turn my back for one minute and you
go checking for leftovers? All this time your snake ass
been fronting like you were sweet, but you're really a
snake. Can't give po' folk shit!" Looking down at her and
shaking my head, I knew it was a low blow, but I really
did not care. I'd made Shayla, so no doubt I'd break her
too.

"I'm the wrong one to be throwing shade at, B. You ain't
so special if Jayson came here with another girl on his
arm. So go pop off thataway."

Yoshi giggled at Shayla standing up to me. I was sure
she was pleasantly amused, but I was about to show
every onlooker that I wasn't.

"Oh, I got your pop off," I seethed. Before I had a
chance to think about the consequences of what was

about to go down, I had my hands around Shayla's throat and was slow-walking her back into the wall. I couldn't help but lose my mind. If she thought I was blind to her eye fucking Jayson, she was hella wrong. This bitch had broken the friend code, so I was ready to break her neck.

Yoshi

This wasn't my beef, but I'd been waiting on an opportunity to get back at Bird. Were it not for her, that whole explosion with Duncan never would've happened. I was about to beat the brakes off this boogie bitch. Grabbing a half-empty bottle of Moët from one of the reserved tables, I gripped the neck of it, thankful I finally had my chance to get it cracking.

Crack! I smashed the bottle over Beatrice's head, then wrapped my hands around her mangy weave. "Back up off my girl!" I yelled. As I attempted to pull her down to the floor, she put up one helluva attempt not to let go of Shayla's throat.

"Get your hands off me, Yo-Yo!" Bird stumbled back, then caught two quick punches to the face.

As Shayla grabbed at Bird's wrists and pried her fingers from her throat, I took the opportunity to sneak punch my former best friend a few more times. "Never that. Square up, trick."

Shayla did not have to fight to breathe any longer, because Bird had finally let go on her own and had turned to attacking me. I was ready for her, though. This became a one-on-one fight we both had obviously been spending our lives waiting for.

"Hey yo! What the fuck! Clear the club, whoever want it over my sis," I heard Tom yelling as he ran through the crowd, tossing dudes left and right.

I did not know how the fight broke up. All I knew was I beat the brakes off Bird until Tom pulled me off of her.

"Yeah, looks like Duncan got me fighting like a 'trained to go' killer!" I told Shayla.

Chapter Twenty-five

Shayla

"Oh my God. This pain is so intense," I moaned. I slipped my pillow out from underneath my head and covered my face with it. "And please close the blinds. The sun is making it worse." I probably would have cried were I not scared I would make the throbbing in my head more intense. It felt like I was still getting hit in my shit.

"Dang, friend. You look miserable as hell." Yoshi closed the blinds as I had requested, then went in her purse and cracked open a big prescription bottle. She took out a horse-sized pain pill, lifted the bottle of flat soda pop that was standing on my nightstand, and held them out in front of her. "Here. Take this and just chill until it kicks in."

I took what she was offering, and I was quick to pop the pill, without even asking what it was. All I cared about was the pain going away; plus, I knew that whatever Yoshi had was probably some real deal, since she'd just had a baby.

"I know you feel like crap, but please believe Bird is over there nursing a few knots too," Yoshi assured me. "I was letting off on that bitch like a tornado, until your brother pulled me off her." Yoshi was happy but even more satisfied that she'd gotten her chance to knuckle back up with Bird after getting jumped. It was crazy how our clique had blown up.

"Last night was mad crazy, Yo-Yo. I thought I was dreaming or some shit. But thanks for having my back." I would've been complaining over more than a migraine had Yoshi not jumped in. Without a doubt, Bird would've dragged me all over that hall had we been left to scrap it out one-on-one.

Yoshi shrugged nonchalantly. "It ain't no thang. Say less. First of all, you already know she had it coming for all the shade she has been throwing my way, acting all fake and shit. And then two, she was super wrong for attacking you when she knows you do not know how to fight. That was a bully move she was trying to boss up on. I'm glad the hood got to see me put her on her ass. That ass whupping was for everybody."

I cracked a smile, then went to laugh and grabbed my head. "Oh shoot! Do not make me laugh. I swear, it feels like my brain is about to drain from my ears, it's throbbing so bad." I was still kinda chuckling. Despite all the pain I was in, knowing Bird's pride had been knocked down a few levels was soothing. Yoshi was absolutely right. She'd been nothing but a bitch to us lately.

"My bad," she laughed. "But that pill should be kicking in, in a minute."

"I surely hope so." I sipped some more pop, in an attempt to help the pain pill dissolve in my bloodstream faster.

"Do not worry. It will. And once you're higher than a kite, I'm going to raid your closet. You've been holding out. There's nothing but brand-new outfits in there, and they've got the nerve to be fresh. Since when did you get some taste?"

"Uh-uh. Do not come for me," I said and giggled lightly. "But you do not have to wait until I'm off that pill to help yourself to whatever is in there. Not even counting last night, how many times have you looked out for me?

What's mine is yours." I still couldn't believe Tom-Tom was touching enough money to flip our lives upside down. Both our closets and our dresser drawers were stuffed to the max, especially his. He'd grown into a sneaker head overnight. I still had to find out what scam Murk had Tom-Tom involved in, but I did not even care at this point. I was just happy to be off scraps and able to flex for a change. Humbly, of course.

"To keep it a buck, Shay . . . you've looked out for me just as much as I've looked out for you on li'l materialistic shit. And materialistic stuff can't compare to loyalty. You deserve all that is about to come your way, 'cause you've been starving long enough."

"You too, sis. You and Yani. Now, quit getting mushy and pick something out to wear for the concert." Tom-Tom had surprised me with tickets to the Get Hype concert as one of my gifts last night.

"I can't believe your brother got tickets. It's been sold out for weeks. Downtown is about to be bananas tonight." She excitedly started pulling pieces off the hangers and putting them up to herself in the mirror. "I am so glad my baby fat has started falling off."

"You look good with or without it," I told her just as Tom-Tom barged into the room and passed out compliments, catching us both off guard. I wasn't used to him coming in my room without knocking, or passing my friend compliments, but Yoshi was eating it up.

It was like I wasn't even in the room as they silently caked for a few seconds. It made me wonder how long they'd been flirting, because it was quite obvious, judging by Yoshi's flushed cheeks, that this wasn't the first time. I couldn't wait until we were alone again, so I could begin my line of questioning about this secret squirrel-ass crush she had on my brother.

"What's good, sis? Do you need to go to urgent care or something? Bird was boxing you down last night." He'd gone from flirting with Yoshi to trying to be funny.

"Whatever!" I threw my slobber-filled pillow at him as he plopped down on the bed. "Why are you in here? What do you want?" I grunted playfully.

"Well, li'l slugger," he said, continuing with his jokes, "I only wanted to check on you, because I am about to head out for a few hours. I should be back before you leave for the concert, but if I'm not, here's something for your pocket." He peeled off a few fifty-dollar bills and put them in my hand before turning to Yoshi. "And here's something for your pocket too, Yo-Yo. It was a good look that you had Shayla's back last night. I appreciate that."

"Like I told Shayla, it's nothing. I'll bang that bitch out again if she runs up," she said and shrugged. "I've been tired of her acting like a fake-ass friend anyway."

"Well, you better stay ready. I would not be surprised if she was on the front porch, waiting on y'all to come out. But I'll clear the premises this time." He started laughing as he headed out of my room.

I wanted to ask him so badly where he was going, but I didn't want to put Yoshi in the middle of whatever business he was trying to keep secret. Instead, I pushed the questions I had to the very back of my mind and started thinking about what I was going to wear to the concert. I'd only ever been to, like, maybe two concerts in my whole life—and, of course, that had been on Bird's dime—and I had dressed like a Salvation Army model. Today was about to be even better than the block party and probably even my graduation-birthday party, because I would get to stunt for the entire city.

"Your brother is busting bank!" Yoshi excitedly fanned herself with the money he'd just given her. "We're about to floss so hard today, I can't fucking wait. I'm about to go make sure Yani is straight for her daddy, well, her ugly-ass grandma, then link back up with you."

"Okay, sounds like a plan. I'm about to get up and wash my funky ass." I caught a whiff of my underarm funk, and my head started thumping even harder.

"Uh, yeah, whatever. You're probably about to start sending messages to Jayson when I walk out this door. At least you need to." She winked, then left the room and closed the door as I threw my pillow across the room. I was sick of her clowning me about Jayson. I *was* crushing hard as hell on him, though.

I ended up going back to sleep for two more hours after Yoshi left, and that was just what my body needed to recuperate. I woke up feeling way better, but I had to hurry up. I rushed into the bathroom to keep from peeing on myself. I'd guzzled two full glasses of water before I went back to sleep to help with my cotton mouth, and it was a good thing I hadn't peed on myself in my sleep. When I was done, I jumped in the shower and got my hygiene together, then decided on cleaning the house from top to bottom. I'd already cleaned my room and put smell-good plug-ins in the wall to keep the air smelling springtime fresh, but the rest of the house was in desperate need of attention. The dollar-store supplies we'd been using weren't strong enough to break down the buildup of germs and funk, especially with Ricardo dragging his funky ass up in here every day with trap house residue all over his clothes and skin. It was a blessing he used only the half bathroom that was off his bedroom.

I threw on a T-shirt and some pajama pants and grabbed a few dollars from the stash of graduation cash I had got at the party last night. Then I slid my flip-flops on and walked to the store for some name-brand cleaning supplies, sponges, and smell-goods that could fight the funk afterward. Then I rushed back to the crib and cleaned it till I was funky all over again. I even made a list of household things we needed, such as groceries, and tackled some overdue bills. As nice as it was getting spoiled by my big bro, I was trying to remember our responsibilities before whatever this hustle was ran its course.

Yoshi ended up convincing me to ask Tom-Tom to get us a rental car for the concert, and he actually agreed. I wasn't supposed to be driving it, though. That didn't mean Yoshi didn't let me whip the wheel once we got out the hood. The only reason I didn't drive it all night was that I didn't want someone from the hood seeing me and running back with their big mouth. I didn't have my license yet, but Bird had taught me how to drive. She was good for letting us drive her home if she was too lit and scared she was going to tear her car up.

Anyway, the night was warm, and it was perfect weather for hanging out downtown. As turned up as the hood got, downtown Detroit had a chill artsy type of vibe. I'd caught the bus down here a few times and chilled by the water with my thoughts a few times.

I was feeling good and looking cute, which had become a common theme for me lately. Yoshi had my hair slicked back in a genie ponytail, and my makeup was still popping from last night. Trifling as it might sound, I had skipped washing my face and had only got the crud out my eyes. I had tried calling ole girl for an appointment, but she had been booked solid because everyone wanted to get their makeup laid for the event. And as cold with it as Yoshi was with hair, she wasn't about to color all over my face. Makeup wasn't her thang.

We had the radio blasting in traffic, as did everybody else, while we waited to get close enough to the venue to park. Besides the concert, there was a festival going on at Hart Plaza and a comedy show at the Fox. We wanted to sip on a li'l wine and smoke on some tree before the concert, but we couldn't chance it with all the police packed down here. I though they patrolled the hood, but I'd never seen so many badged-up cops in my life. They were strolling on foot and riding around in cruisers. I knew we'd be able to sneak in a few puffs once we got inside the venue, though. And I most definitely knew we'd pull some drinks from some dudes who were old enough to get carded. It was crazy how much my confidence had grown.

"Will Jayson and them be down here, Shay?"

"Probably. They didn't get tickets, but he said him and Duncan were coming down here to hang out." I hoped the mention of her baby daddy didn't spoil her mood, but she skipped right past.

"Awww shit! You better throw it back as hard as you can tonight. It's the perfect opportunity. And with the cash Tom gave you this morning, you can even get y'all a room."

"Girl bye. If he wants some of this coochie, he's gonna have to at least get the room."

"Girl bye, yourself. You sound crazy as hell. You better invest now so you can reap the benefits later. That boy ain't got no hotel room money, but he's gonna have a contract sooner than later. You better think out. Just make him wear a condom."

I thought about what she had said, and it did make sense. And it wasn't like I punched the clock for the money I was going to spend on the room. The way Tom was putting money in my hand, plus all the monetary gifts I'd gotten at my graduation party, the money wouldn't be *that* missed. And I couldn't front and say I wasn't ready to get cuddled up on by Jayson. We'd been texting all day, and even we'd talked right before I started getting dressed.

"I'll think about it, but for now, I'm just trying to see my boo Future."

Almost forever later, we'd finally gotten to our seats in the venue. Tom had us sitting pretty. We were on the floor, four rows back from the stage. I just knew I was going to pass out once my favorite rapper hit the stage. We were so close, I was going to feel his sweat falling off his face.

On the roster for tonight were four of the hottest rappers, plus a few local opening acts that were trying to make it big out the city. Me and Yoshi weren't really impressed with the local music scene, so we used that time to take pictures and grab some large slushies from the concession stand. We decided they would taste good with some liquor, but first we had to find someone to buy us a shot. And that wasn't hard to do, since Yoshi had her ass and titties out. Whereas I was dressed in a teal and white Adidas tennis skirt, a crop top, and fresh white shell toes, she had settled for the ten-dollar special at the Korean beauty supply store and was rocking a two-piece spandex set that barely held up the ass and titties Yani had blessed her with. And that was what her goal was. She was trying to attract as much attention as possible, which was why the outfit was the loudest shade of neon yellow I'd ever seen. It was like they jumped some glow-in-the-dark paint in the batch of coloring when they made that outfit. Her ass was looking like a yellow highlighter, but I didn't want to spoil her mood by critiquing her style. It had been forever since she'd popped out of the house without a belly or a baby.

Right on time, this dude stopped us in mid-step, but he talked to Yoshi. "Ay, yo, shorty. You here with you nigga or naw?"

"Naw," she quickly responded, scanning him from head to toe, with a smirk on her face. I already knew what time she was on.

"Come here and let me kick it with you, then, sexy. You lookin' finer than a muthafucka right now." He grabbed her arm and pulled her out of the crowd, and I was right on her heels. We followed the code "No friend left behind." And it didn't matter how trustworthy or handsome the dude was. If one went, we both went.

"Thank you." Yoshi was blushing. "And you are too. I see you flexing with ya' Cartier." She got him grinning too.

They sparked up some small talk, and I busied myself with my phone. Just because I wasn't breaking girl code didn't mean I was about to be all up in their conversation. And I wasn't about to be all thirsty and in his boys' faces either. One, I didn't have the confidence for that. But mainly it was because they weren't hitting on nothing but ugly. Jayson had all them beat in the looks department, even the cutie that had my homegirl's undivided attention. Yoshi's advice was running through my mind, making me want to text him to see if he was interested in a hotel after-party. I didn't know how that would work, though—especially since I overheard Yoshi making plans with ole boy.

"Okay, we'll check for you after this is over," Yoshi announced.

"Where y'all sitting at anyway? My squad got a suite if you wanna fucks with it," he said. He was really talking to Yoshi, but of course, he invited me out of default.

"Aw, shit. A suite? I'm down!" She turned to me. "You wanna roll?" Yoshi jumped on the offer, but I quickly shut it down.

"Naw, I'm good. The only way I'm moving is if it's farther *down* from where I'm sitting at. You know I wanna touch my fav's shoes," I said. I didn't care if it seemed like hating. I wasn't about to go to the rafters. I'd been sitting in the rafters all my life. I wasn't about to give up a floor seat for nobody—not today.

"Oh yeah," Yoshi giggled. "I forgot your infatuation with Future. Back to the original plan of us getting at you after the show. We came together, and we are staying together."

He nodded. "Fa sho, shorty. I respect that. But you better use my number." He licked his lips, and I had to hear all the way to our seats how that gesture had her panties moist.

"Um, TMI. Too much information," I said in a low voice as we headed toward our row. I wasn't trying to hear all that.

"My bad, but I've gotta get my bounce back somewhere."

"Call me crazy, but I kinda thought you and my brother were trying to catch a vibe earlier."

"To be honest, since you brought it up, I will admit that we've been flirting since the day of the party, but nothing serious," she revealed. "It's odd, since we practically grew up together, but I do like the attention, and he has been looking cute lately."

I made a barfing gesture, like I was going to throw up. "Ugh. Again TMI. I really don't want to hear about how you're attracted to my brother, but the flirting y'all have been doing hasn't been low key. I peeped that shit instantly. You bet not play my brother."

"If it even went that far, I wouldn't, out of my respect for you and our friendship first, but I can't tell if he's serious or not. Besides, now that he's dusted himself off and has been fresh as hell, I'm not the only girl checking for him. He's been turning heads. In between me partying and beating Bird's ass last night, I saw Patrina all in his grill."

Patrina was this thot from the block, and if she was checking for my brother, I was about to start marketing Yoshi to him. I would've been cool with Yoshi being my sis for real. The only problem was her crazy-ass baby daddy. I didn't want Tom wrapped up in any of their drama or trying to play Captain Save a Ho for Yoshi when Duncan started going upside her head. I knew my brother, and I knew he didn't go for men putting their hands on females. So, if he knew she was a victim of domestic abuse, he'd probably choke the life out of Duncan and, ultimately, his future career as a basketball star.

Finally, all the local acts were done performing, and the MC came onstage and announced that the main event was about start. The crowd started going wild. All the seats had filled up until at least intermission. The DJ had the venue hype like we were at a club, as he was playing all the top mixes. Me and Yoshi were dancing and singing all the songs as loud as we could. I wasn't even feeling froggish with my offbeat dance moves in front of the people we were sitting by. I was in my zone, especially once the MC announced my self-titled boo was about to hit the stage. I started drooling on instant and wanted to run up there for a solo song to be sung to me. I was happy as hell and on cloud nine for the entire concert. Every artist showed up and out for Detroit. It was going to take forever and a day for me to thank Tom for this gift.

The next morning was like déjà vu from the morning before, but this time me and Yoshi weren't talking about the graduation-birthday party. We were reliving the concert. It was like I was living someone else's life. We went through all the pictures, videos, and blow-by-blows of everything that had gone down over some Coney Island breakfast combo meals that Tom-Tom had brought us; and even he sat down and kicked it with us. Even though I still had a million questions about how he was getting bank, I couldn't front and say I wasn't happy for him. His confidence spoke volumes. He no longer dropped his head when he entered a room. He now commanded respect. It felt good seeing him that way, 'cause I'd witnessed enough of him suffering and getting clowned. He was my big brother, my protector and provider, so it was like my hero finally had the shield and superpowers he had always deserved. I chose to keep my worries to myself—not wanting to pop the bubble we all were in—though I did confide in Ricardo. It was easy to tell he wasn't happy about Tom's change.

Tom-Tom might've been putting better clothes on our backs and sprucing up our wrecked rooms, but he wasn't doing shit for Ricardo but walking past him with shopping bags. He wouldn't even get Pops a haircut. And when he came through the door with food, he didn't bother giving him any, not even the leftover trash. I didn't tell Tom he was wrong for doing that, even though I felt a little bad for Ricardo, 'cause I understood why Tom was making him struggle. But that didn't mean Ricardo wasn't twisting his face up. And I was sure his dope-fiend friends were ragging on him because his son wouldn't give him a few dollars. The hood was small, and word traveled fast. So everyone knew Tom wasn't scraping his knuckles anymore. Even more so after he threw me that all-star graduation party.

"I feel like my stomach is about to burst," Yoshi declared, then leaned back, rubbing her stomach. "I haven't
been this stuffed since Yani was up in here."

"Me too. I damn near ate a package of bacon," I said. I
had got greedy and had ordered double bacon with my
meal. Going years without having much made it easy to
overdo it now that I had access to a few dollars.

"Well, I hope y'all ain't too full. I got a surprise for you,
sis. And, Yo-Yo, you can ride too, if you still got some
time out the house," Tom-Tom announced.

Yoshi nodded. "Even if I didn't, I'm not trying to go
back there, so hell yeah, I'm down to ride."

"Oh my God, bro! I swear, you are spoiling me. What
more can you surprise me with?" I was secretly hoping
we were about to ride to the dealership to get me a new
car, but I didn't want to shout that out and not have that
be it. I had felt *too* good whipping that rental around
yesterday.

"There's nothing too much I can do for you as long as
we've struggled. I already told you that. Now go on and
get dressed. We're gonna run that rental back before
noon, then hop in the truck with Murk."

My eyes jumped at him when he mentioned Murk, but
again, I kept my mouth closed and got dressed, like
he had requested. I was too busy worrying about what
Tom had up his sleeve for me next.

Forty-five minutes later, the four of us were in Murk's
truck on the expressway, and the rental car was back at
Enterprise. I finally understood why Bird was crushing
on Murk and my brother had developed an attachment to
him. Murk gave off boss vibes. I had to stop myself from

staring at him, especially when he caught my glares in the rearview mirror twice—and they were back-to-back. The last thing I needed in my life was for Murk, Bird, and, most importantly, Tom-Tom to think I was checking for Murk. I was only trying to pick up on his vibes. Right or wrong, my heart was feenin' for Jayson. I was bold enough to admit it. Especially since it was crystal clear to me that his and Bird's friendship had been severed. I wanted to explore the feelings I had been pressing down.

Yoshi nudged me. "What are you over there thinking about? Or should I say who?"

Busted, I blushed. "I know you do not think I'd be wrong for pursuing something with Jayson because of Bird, but do you think I'm wasting my time with him, since he's about to go away for college?"

"Nope, I do not. As a matter of fact, I think that is even more of a reason you should try to see what could pop off between y'all. You never know. I might end up visiting you on a college campus, instead of it being the other way around, like we thought."

It was crazy how much our lives had changed in a few short weeks.

After all the drama last night, I should've been running as far from Jayson as I could, but the attraction felt too strong. Yoshi nudged me a more few times, but I was in too deep of a trance to care.

"I did not know this was going to be a road trip," Yoshi complained half an hour later, rolling her eyes up into the air and then glancing out the window. "We sure aren't in Kansas anymore."

"Naw, not at all. And if Duncan was any type of a real nigga, he'd take you across city boundaries for a change," Tom-Tom replied. He shifted in his seat and laughed along with Murk. They obviously had an inside joke going on.

"Whoa. What's with the low blow? I thought we were better than that," I groused, looking surprised that Tom had put her on blast. I had to admit I was a little shocked too. Bird was usually the friend he reserved his jabs for.

"This ain't a low blow, baby girl. It's me schooling you. Sit back and chill so I can show you what real bosses do." He turned around and glanced at Yoshi. He was looking at her the same way he'd checked for a few of the low-budget skeezers I'd seen turn him down.

"I'm all ears, baby," Yoshi replied before sitting back. "I'm an excellent learner."

I was too busy watching Murk's eyes peer at me through the rearview mirror to give two fucks about the weird flirting going on between Yoshi and Tom-Tom. *Why the fuck is he grilling me? Had Bird put him up to something?* I wondered.

Over the next fifteen minutes or so, Murk continued driving farther and farther from the city. At first, I thought we were hitting the outlet shopping mall, but I was thrown off when his truck turned into a luxury apartment complex. The scenery was breathtaking, much different than the concrete jungle all of us were living in. There were lawns of green grass, small ponds with ducks swimming around in them, and perennial flowers blossoming everywhere.

My knees started trembling when I thought that I'd figured Tom's surprise out. "Is this what I think it is? Tell me it is! Tom-Tom, are we moving here?" Unable to contain my excitement, I was jumping up and down on the seat, eager to spring from the truck and race into the leasing office. "Please tell me this is our new home."

"Yeah, baby sister, we're movin' on up, like the Jeffersons. My manz Murk got connects, so he's putting me down with one of them units today. We're about to be gravy."

Ricardo

"It was good seeing you. After all these years, I always said if I got the chance to talk to you or whatever, I'd apologize. If it wasn't for me, you would not be fighting this demon."

"Just let me see Shayla or Thomas, Jr., Spider. I do not want to rehash the past with you. Where are they at?"

"Fancy you coming back after all these years, after your son is finally getting money out here in these streets. What? You want a piece of the pie? You think that stingy nigga coming up out of something for you? Is that what this is all about? Well, let me spare you the trouble. If it's been 'Fuck me," and I'm the parent that stayed around, you can definitely rest assured it's gonna be 'Fuck you," with a 'Go to hell' behind it." I laughed in her face as she sat in the same living room she had walked out of nine years ago.

"I just need to right my wrongs, Spider. What's their numbers?"

"Here's the forwarding address they left for me to give the mailman. You're welcome to come back here and stay once they turn your junkie ass away. You look terrible." It might've been wrong, but it was right. Being light skinned with long hair had been a calling card back in the day, but now it was a headlight to her craters, track marks, and imperfections.

"Go to hell," she spat, walking toward the front door.

"Been there, done that," I muttered as she walked out. I slammed the door behind, intent on continuing to get high, but then I was disturbed by two hard knocks against the door.

I laughed out loud, figuring it was Rose coming back.

"What, Marilyn Rose? Did you come back to escort me to hell?" I swung the door open, with my crack pipe in hand.

"Yes, sir, Detroit Police. We're looking for Thomas Harris, Jr. And from the looks of the paraphernalia on your person, we'll be needing to speak with you as well," said one of the officers at my door.

Epilogue

Shayla

"Oh, wow, so it wasn't a dream," I whispered. I slowly opened my eyes, hoping my surroundings did not suddenly change once my eyes were all the way open. I'd been too used to living unlucky to be comfortable when good stuff started happening. Sitting straight up on the air mattress I was using temporarily as a bed, I did not even care that it had half deflated overnight and I was damn near on the carpeted floor. I was on a brand-new carpeted floor, in a condo nicer than any house I'd ever been in. The "luxury" in the condo development's name wasn't false advertising at all.

I stood up, made my bed as best I could, and then looked around my new bedroom at all the brown boxes and garbage bags of clothes on the floor. My high school diploma already hung on the wall. Just a few weeks ago I had barely had enough clothes to make it through the month, but now I was popping tags on new outfits daily. Life was finally looking up for me.

I grabbed my cell phone off the floor. I saw that it was a little after ten in the morning, which meant I'd slept for eight hours straight without any interruption from gun shots, arguments, or my father getting high to Sam Cooke.

The condo had a formal living room and a dining-room space, three bedrooms, two baths, plus a den and a loft area. Plus, it had fabulous amenities, like a dishwasher, central air, and a pool on the grounds, not too far from our unit. It was a far cry from the lead-infested house I'd called home my entire life—and the cruddy hood. The only noises I heard on the regular were birds and crickets chirping. There weren't any speakers blasting music out the windows; kids running up and down the block, bouncing basketballs; or hustlers posted up in the parking lot, pushing product. It was actually *too* quiet, if that made sense. But I wasn't complaining. I'd slept eight hours straight without hearing Sam Cooke playing on repeat or my father stumbling through the house, too high to function, and those were sounds I could go on living without for the rest of my life.

I slid on my shorts and gazed out my bedroom window.

That was where Yoshi found me when she came into my new bedroom, singing some song. She had the widest smile across her face. "Hey, sis."

"Damn, straight up? That is how y'all got down, huh? I see the liquor and weed did not stop last night, after I tapped out."

"Girl, we've got a whole lot to talk about when I get back. Tom is about to run me to the hood to get my mail. If I passed that GED test, we're about to go all the way in tonight," she informed me.

"Then let me get my ass in the shower and get ready. I'm sure you knocked it out of the park."

Tom and Yoshi headed out toward the hood. I wasn't shocked them two had hooked up—they'd been flirting enough. I did not know if Yoshi was hooking up with him for a rebound or for some quick cash for herself and Yani, but I couldn't worry about none of that. I'd sex texted Jayson last night.

Just as I was about to step in the shower, someone knocked hard on the front door.

"Use your key damn," I yelled out, wrapping a towel around myself.

Whoever it was did not respond and kept knocking. I stepped out of the bathroom and rushed to the door, then swung it open, annoyed that Tom was being so lazy. "Do not make no habit—"

"Hi, Shayla."

I must've been seeing a ghost. It was Rose.

A little while later . . .

Yoshi

"They're gonna have to get that janky-ass elevator fixed," I muttered as I grabbed onto the handrail and caught by breath after trucking up four flights of stairs. My legs felt like spaghetti. In shape I was, but after the long night of hustling I'd just put in, I felt like I was about to tumble back down each one of them muthafuckas. I hated having to live in this slumlord-owned piece of property, but it was the best of my options for now.

Barely having enough energy to turn the key to unlock the door, I somehow managed to open the door. I walked into my one-bedroom apartment and dropped my ho bag on the floor. The thuds of my boots hitting the wood floors were surely going to get me fussed at by my crabby downstairs neighbor, but I'd deal with her nagging in the morning. Tonight I was tired as hell. Every limb, joint, and bone ached. Hell, even my skin felt stretched to the max from working the stage, the pole, and the room all night.

I'd been chasing money since the lunch shift, which had started at noon, and it was now past four in the morning. Although the set technically closed at two in the morning, the dancers who made big bank during stage dances or group dances stayed around for their splits. On a good day, we'd walk out of the club and into the sun. Unfortunately, but fortunately, tonight did not end like that. As badly as I needed the cash, I hadn't been in the mood to pop for paper after midnight, because it was Yani's birthday. But I'd had no choice. I'd much rather have cuddled up with her and watched a Disney movie, decorated for a birthday party, or even simply watched her sleep and dream. Anything over shaking my booty cheeks on a bunch of strangers.

I was about to hit a blunt super hard, then hit the bed even harder. I was in my feelings super hard and just wanted to sleep the rest of the day away. I couldn't wait to cuddle up in my bed for a double shift of sleep. I wasn't planning on leaving the house until Monday, actually. As much sinning as I'd been doing, I'd also made Sundays my day of cleansing and relaxation.

Undressing while I walked from the front door to my bedroom, I added to the mess that had been growing for the past week, and dismissed it. One more day of living like a slob wasn't going to hurt. I'd been chasing a check and hustling all week so I could get Tommy's attorney the final balance he needed to file the motion we all were praying would free him.

Yeah, that was right. Tom-Tom was in jail and had been for the past three years. He had got caught up in some fraud shit: he'd been cashing checks as part of a scheme Murk and some broad named Artavia were running. I tried not to speak about Murk in a negative way to Tom, because that was his brother and all, but it was more than obvious that mysterious nigga had made it convenient for Tom to be the fall guy in case anything went down. The bank did not have Murk or ole girl on camera, but Tom-Tom's face was all over the camera, and a teller gave a video testimony about how he had manipulated and conned her into cashing fake payroll checks almost every Friday for consecutive months.

The judge went hard on Tom, and it tore me to the core when I found out the only man that was good to me, loved me, and respected me was going away for three to five years. The news sent me spiraling into an even deeper depression than the one I was in when Duncan first started beating my ass. Tom had swooped into my life and had made all the messes seem inconsequential. He had given me the strength to deal with them head-on, as well as the ability to walk away from them without fear. In spite of my and Karen's dysfunctional relationship, I had been scared to venture off into the world by myself, because I hadn't had legs to stand on. Thomas had given me that. I couldn't wait for him to finish walking down the final two years left on his bid.

After going through a bitter breakup with Duncan, which ended up with us in court, fighting for custody, I had relied on Thomas to hold me up. Duncan, his mother, and my mother—whom I'd since cut completely off— took turns bagging my parenting skills to the judge. The few people I had on my side giving character testimonies weren't weighted as heavy as those on Duncan's side, and the attorney Duncan's mother had hired was a beast that stayed sucking my soul from my jugular. A diamond couldn't cut a spade in a card game, and I was that diamond. I ended up losing custody of Yani. Life was cutting me off, shoving me down, and applying pressure to my neck for me to stay low. I'd been starving for love, attention, and acceptance my entire life, so I guessed that was why I'd been *happy* when I found out I was pregnant with Yani. Unconditional love—that was what I knew a baby could provide. When I lost custody, my heart broke into a million pieces. I couldn't kiss her chunky cheeks every day and shower her with love.

In most custody cases, the court aimed to keep children with their mothers unless the mother was unfit, and I wasn't neglectful of or abusive to Yani. Hell, I was the one who had suffered both emotional and physical abuse. Yet sadly, the judge stayed stone-faced and emotionless as I relived one occasion after another of how Duncan couldn't keep his hands off me, recounted how his aggression had intensified with his secret steroid usage, and even told how he had tried to kick Yani out of me when I was pregnant. I'd at least expected the judge to sympathize or maybe even empathize with me as a woman, but naw, not even that moved her to show me an ounce of mercy. And the more I fought, the more money Duncan's mother threw at the case, and I was sure the judge got broke off swell.

The judge did not care that I was a young mother doing the best I could, giving Yani love and affection 24/7, with little to no support. She still snatched my baby away and awarded custody to Duncan, scarring me to the core. I damn near died when I heard her judgment call. The judge had to threaten me with an overnight lockup to get me out of the courtroom, and even then it took the bailiff to drag me off the floor. I was devastated. Defeat was starting to feel way too fucking common in my life.

Duncan and his family had custody over Yani, and they were all living up in Lansing, not giving two shits that they'd separated a mother and daughter. Although I got visitations with Yani every other weekend, it wasn't enough to fill the huge void in my heart. I might've said a few million times that the responsibility of being a mom was overwhelming and hard as hell, but that did not mean I wanted to give Yani up. I was supposed to be in Lansing this weekend, having my court-ordered visitation with my baby girl, but as always, Duncan's mom had flipped the script and taken Yani on the road to see him play ball.

If and when I got my money up, I was going to lock in a consultation with a family attorney I'd been recommended to see, if he'd take my case. I needed a shark to match the sharks I was up against. Even though the court had granted me visitations with Yani every other weekend, Duncan and his mother always came up with excuses as to why my time slot interfered with their schedule. The only upside in all this tragedy was that I did manage to get my GED and a job, all because the bitch had taken Yani from me and I had a lot of free time.

But lately I'd been feeling so down about the loss of my child. Thomas did the best he could do from behind bars to keep me from losing my mind, but I'd slipped up and started popping pills to cope. This chick that I danced with kept a bunch of different pills, coke, and marijuana in her ho bag, but I'd mustered up enough courage only to try the pills. I popped at least two Xanax tablets a day to keep the drowning feeling away.

No sooner had I made it to the bed and slid underneath my comforter than my cell phone rang. As I curled up to my pillow and became one with my sheets, it felt so good to be in bed, and even better to know I was about to cake with my bae for the next thirty minutes.

It was Thomas calling. He always called me in the mornings to make sure I'd made it in from work. He hated that I was dancing in the strip club, but he understood I had to hustle. My GED qualified me only for fast-food jobs, and a bitch couldn't get off her knuckles and keep money on his books making seven bucks an hour.

"You have a call from the State of Ohio Federal Peniten-
tiary," the recorded voice announced as soon as I picked
up. Then I heard Thomas's voice a second later.

"Hey, baby. You good?"

"Yeah, I just got home from work. It was a slow night,
but I still managed to walk out the door with five hundred
dollars," I told him. It seemed like I was making less and
less, but I was still bringing home more money than all
the bitches I knew who were punching a clock from nine
to five. Five hundred wasn't nothing to shit on, but the
seven hundred I made before having to tip out the bar,
the DJ, the owner, and the house mother would've been
a lot better.

"I can't wait until I'm out and can take care of you. I'm
going to sit you down, pamper and spoil you, and make
up for these years I've had to be away." Thomas always
made promises that I was sure he'd keep. He hadn't met
me on a "looking for love with an inmate" type of website.

"I know you've got me, bae. And that is why I do not
blink when it comes to holding you down. Say less on
that." I did not want to waste any more time talking
about it—especially since it was time that I'd paid for.

"I got you. So what do you want to talk about? Tell me
something good. Tell me something bad. Just kick it with
me, like we would if I were there."

"Well, I was supposed to be seeing Yani this weekend,
but they took her to Duncan's game," I said. I was deep
in my feelings.

"Where's the game at?"

"Indiana."

"Okay, your license is straight. Them hating-ass mutha-
suckas can't stop you from seeing Yani at the game."

"Dang, that might be a good idea," I mused. I sat up to
start looking up the game's information on his website.
"He might have a reserved section, though."

"And so? Call 'em up and tell them you're there. De-
mand to see Yani. You might not be able to cash out
and fight them in court, but there's no rules saying you
can't fight to enforce your parenting time and start doc-
umenting when they refuse to let you see her. You're the
most chill baby mama I know." He laughed.

"Shut up." I laughed, too, taking note of everything that
he'd said, because it was the bible. Thomas was giving me
great advice and was lifting my chin through the phone.
He stayed keeping my head up. That was why I was in
love with him.

We stayed on the phone, kicking it, coming up with a
plan on how I was going to shake the ground for Yani.

Yoshi

"Have you talked to my brother today?" Shayla asked
in between bites of the chicken and grits she was forking
into her mouth like she hadn't eaten all day. You would
have sworn she was carrying twins.

"Um, yeah. He calls every day, by eight in the morning.
He said he sent you a message the other day, but you
hadn't responded yet." I gave her the side eye, because
even though I wasn't picking sides between her and
Thomas, I was wondering why she hadn't been keeping
in touch with him as much. I mean, I understood it was
hard having a relationship with a nigga in jail, but that
shit did not apply to her and Thomas. I knew my baby
was hurt behind Shayla not hitting him back.

Thomas

As soon as I'd gone up . . . life crashed down on me super hard. This shit I was in was worse than karma or hard

luck. Having my freedom snatched from me was worse than having Rose abandon me, worse than Ricardo being addicted to drugs, and far worse than being broke on my knuckles. I couldn't take a piss or wash my balls in privacy, and what got me jumped on the first few days in here was me crying. Yup, I broke all the way down and then got broke down even more and spent a week in the infirmary.

Every day in this hellhole got worse than the last, even after three years. I wasn't built for this shit. When I walked into that bank Murk put me up on with that first check, I knew I was hitting a lick. I knew that was fraud, basically robbing a bank. But I also knew it was quick, fast, and easy. That rush . . . was a hard lesson as I sat still every day, going over ole girl's testimony. It was wild thinking back on the last few times I fraudulently cashed a check there, and she was in on the setup, as the detectives were watching me from the background. They had me on camera and had been building a case against me for weeks, while I was out blowing cash and living like I was untouchable. If only I could've moved smarter, stopped quicker, got in and out of the game, instead of letting myself become a fall guy . . . if only. I'd been over the what-ifs over a million fucking times.

What really got my head messed up, though, was how Murk had set me up all along to be the fall guy, even though he was my whole brother. Rose had more skeletons buried than a cemetery. I blamed her more than Murk 'cause that nigga was acting out the same hurt, pain, animosity, and grief she had put him through by abandoning him. Though I did not deserve to take the full rap for all the fraudulent checks the police had linked back to Murk and Artavia's business, at least from the time they had me walking into that first bank, I'd understood he was not willing to sit in a cell either. I'd known the risks. I'd simply been willing to take them.

Bowing my head, I prayed that Shayla was straight. I'd been waiting to get a message from her, but she'd been ghosting me for the past week. She hadn't been taking Yoshi's calls either. I did not know what tip she was on, considering she knew all I had was her and Yo-Yo to hold me down, but I was gonna end up smacking the shit out of her at our next visit. I'd been too easy on Shayla, and a nigga being in jail had shown me that. She was more than likely somewhere caught up with Jayson, securing the bag that I needed her to, but still . . .

I was anxious as hell to walk down these last few months of jail. It had been three long years, and whereas I had thought growing up with Ricardo was a struggle, I had learned living in confinement was far worse. The first twelve months of being the government's property were the hardest months of my life, but I was now a grown man with a mature mind. I was one of the few inmates that took advantage of the GED program, obtained my degree, and then picked up plumbing and electrical as trades.

Shayla

I was screaming, "Fuck family," because family hadn't been doing nothing but fucking me over for years. And yeah, I was even putting Tom-Tom in that category, 'cause his dumb ass should've never tried hustling checks through a bank. That type of scam was a white man's scam, a federal crime, and charges no state-issued attorney would be able to wiggle their client out of. He was lucky they had tapped into only five years of his life. I was distraught when he was arrested and then depressed when they sentenced him. I'd gotten so used to having my brother as my confidant, savior, and best friend that it felt like half my soul died when the judge's gavel sounded off. Jayson had to pick me up off the floor from me passing out over the verdict. I wasn't being dramatic; I was beyond devastated. Especially since I knew all Tom-Tom wanted to do was take care of me. My lazy ass should've tried harder to get a job. That was a burden I still carried on my back—and it was what had created a wedge between me and Yoshi.

For her to know how messy my brother was moving with Murk and to keep it a secret from me was foul and selfish on several levels. And I didn't care if Tom had asked her to keep it on the low. Yoshi knew how dangerous fuckin' with a federal crime could be. But she hadn't cared about none of that and had probably motivated him to do it daily. In my eyes, her trifling ass had been sacrificing my brother for her stability. He was her way out of her mama's house and the way she was putting a roof over Yani's head.

Everything that was good for Yoshi had been snatched away, and I kinda felt like that was her karma for not trying to speak sense into Thomas. The Feds had been trailing him for a minute, with pictures of his scamming and statements of witnesses going back for months and months. Her and Yani were even in the background of a few of them. I was so angry at Yoshi that I had called Duncan's mother and had told her all about Tom's case and how Yoshi had helped him scheme. I had even fabricated lies and said she was helping them make documents and checks. I needed her to hurt as bad as I was hurting over not having my brother, and not having Yani cut her to the core.

I didn't even bother going to see the little girl whenever Jayson and Duncan linked up, because I wasn't trying to see her face. I still *loved* Yoshi, but I just hated her and didn't have it in my heart to forgive her. And maybe that would change once my brother got out. But we had two more years to see about that. Until then, I was going to keep trying to make Jayson happy—which was making Bird miserable.

Bird

"Bird baby, can you please get me a glass of water so I can take my medicine? I feel like the room is spinning." My mother's voice was a whisper.

She'd gotten so sick that she was too weak to take care of herself, so of course, I was stuck with the burden. But this was all her fault for taking her patient's pills. She called herself trying to commit to suicide, but she was about thirty milligrams shy. Were there an easy way for me to just finish the job and get on with my life, I might've done it. But she couldn't use her arms and had to be fed her medicine, so any overdose would've been a flat-out murder. Crazy, I was. But not enough to get my mother's blood on my hands.

I wasn't even as angry with her about her botched suicide job as I still was for the hand she'd had in my father's sexual abuse of me. That was why I felt like her suffering needed to be done alone. That was why some days I didn't feed her, bathe her, or even turn the television on so she'd have noise in the room I made sure she stayed cooped up alone in. It wasn't torture. I, too, used to stay cooped up in that same room, crying for her to save me, and it hadn't been torture in her eyes. I had learned how to care for her from being cared for by her.

"You can't swallow them muthafuckas with some spit?" I was annoyed, so I turned up the television, so I didn't have to hear her answer or her complaints. All she did was whine and cry about being sick. I hated having to be responsible for her. The only good thing that came out of it was the checks I got for being her caregiver.

I never ended up going to summer school, because my pride was broken down to shreds after all that shit blew up in my face with Murk, Jayson, and my so-called friends. I hated Yoshi and Shayla so much that I wished them dead on a daily. I'd popped a bottle of champagne when I found out Duncan's people had got custody of Yani. That was what that heifer deserved for flipping on me. I'd even gone down to her li'l stripper job and taunted her and tipped her with a stack of ripped-up dollar bills. She'd thought Tom-Tom's ole dumb ass was going to be her saving grace out of the hood, but that had just shown how much of a dick rider she really was. We stayed clowning Tom, so it was a shocker that she was all in love with him all of a sudden. But then it made perfect sense once it came out how Tom was making money. The whole hood was shocked when they found out how he had afforded to move them out of the hood. But even more so when Rose had reappeared. She was even back living in the house with Ricardo.

After swirling some of my spit around in my mother's water, I took her the cup and medicine and made sure she popped all the pills and swallowed each drop. Then I ran through my house to locate my ringing phone.

"Hello," I answered, out of breath.

"Nothing if you're not alone. Don't even say my name." The familiar voice knocked even more wind out of my lungs.

"I'm alone," I quickly responded so he wouldn't hang up.

"Good. I need you to do me a solid, baby girl. Are you at your crib right now?"

"Yeah." I started peeking out the blinds.

"Bet. Meet me around the corner to get the key to my house. I want you to run in and grab some money for me."

"Okay. Give me a minute." I wanted to go freshen up real quick. I hadn't seen him in forever and wanted to look my best when I saw him. I was happy as hell I'd just gotten li'l Ella to braid me up with some box braids the other day, so my hair was crisp.

"Naw, B. I ain't got a minute. You know I'm hot. I just need you to do this solid for me, please." I heard the desperation in his voice, and I had never heard Murk sound like that. He was always in control. Him actually *needing me* made me want to give in to whatever request he made.

I slid on my sneakers, then rushed out of the house, the whole time still on the phone so he could direct me to where he was low-key posted at. I damn near buckled at my knees and fell when I saw him, even though he had the brim of his hat so far down I could barely see his face. I couldn't help but rush over to him and hug him, and though he let me hold him for a second, he was quick to push me off him and hand me the key.

"Don't hang up. I need you to follow every single direction to this bag of cash so I can make it out of this city. I'ma go to jail if you don't do this solid for me."

"You ain't gotta worry, baby. I got you."

I didn't care about anything ill that had happened to us in the past. I was going to have Murk's back. I loved him. And if he trusted me enough to look out for him with this, then I knew he'd reach back for me once shit had cooled down. I didn't even think they were still checking for him, because the hood hadn't even been hot, but I knew this wasn't the time to have a conversation or rationalize with him. He was shaking so bad that his nerves were rattling mine.

I headed to his house, my phone plastered to my ear, and used his key to gain entrance. I listened to him closely as he gave me the directions through his house and to the safe, which held a duffel bag filled with more cash than I'd ever seen in my life. After hoisting the bag over my shoulder, I hurried out of the house and locked the front door so I could rush back to him. He kept telling me to pay attention to my surroundings, but I thought he was being paranoid—until an unmarked police car pulled up on me when I was walking into the apartment building where Murk said to meet up.

"Freeze!" one of the cops shouted as he opened his car door. Then he ordered me to get on the ground.

I started panicking.

Starving for love had me caught with the bag, but Murk was nowhere to be found. . . .